Books by
Historical W

Series

MacLarens of Fire Mountain

Tougher than the Rest, Book One
Faster than the Rest, Book Two
Harder than the Rest, Book Three
Stronger than the Rest, Book Four
Deadlier than the Rest, Book Five
Wilder than the Rest, Book Six

Redemption Mountain

Redemption's Edge, Book One
Wildfire Creek, Book Two
Sunrise Ridge, Book Three
Dixie Moon, Book Four
Survivor Pass, Book Five
Promise Trail, Book Six
Deep River, Book Seven
Courage Canyon, Book Eight
Forsaken Falls, Book Nine
Solitude Gorge, Book Ten
Rogue Rapids, Book Eleven, Coming next in the series!

MacLarens of Boundary Mountain

Colin's Quest, Book One,
Brodie's Gamble, Book Two

Contemporary Romance Series

MacLarens of Fire Mountain

Peregrine Bay

Burnt River

Aqua's Achilles, Book Three by Kate Cambridge
Ashley's Hope, Book Four by Amelia Adams
Harpur's Secret, Book Five by Kay P. Dawson
Mason's Rescue, Book Six by Peggy L. Henderson
Del's Choice, Book Seven by Shirleen Davies
Ivy's Search, Book Eight by Kate Cambridge
Phoebe's Fate, Book Nine by Amelia Adams
Brody's Shelter, Book Ten by Kay P. Dawson
Boone's Surrender, Book Eleven by Shirleen Davies
Watch for more books in the series!

The best way to stay in touch is to subscribe to my newsletter. Go to www.shirleendavies.com and subscribe in the box at the top of the right column that asks for your email. You'll be notified of new books before they are released, have chances to win great prizes, and receive other subscriber-only specials.

Fletcher's Pride

MacLarens of Boundary Mountain

Historical Western Romance Series

SHIRLEEN DAVIES

Book Eight in the MacLarens of Boundary Mountain

Historical Western Romance Series

For permission requests, contact the publisher.

Avalanche Ranch Press, LLC
PO Box 12618
Prescott, AZ 86304

Fletcher's Pride is a work of fiction. Names, characters, places, and incidents are either products of the author's imagination or used fictitiously. Any resemblance to actual events, locales, or persons, living or dead, is wholly coincidental.

Book design and conversions by Joseph Murray at 3rdplanetpublishing.com

Cover design by Kim Killion, The Killion Group

ISBN: 978-1-941786-82-6

I care about quality, so if you find something in error, please contact me via email at shirleen@shirleendavies.com

Description

He'd do anything for a second chance.
Could her secrets and haunted past allow him back in?

Fletcher's Pride, Book Eight, MacLarens of Boundary Mountain Historical Western Romance Series

Fletcher MacLaren lives a charmed life. He works hard and plays even harder. Handsome with an easy smile, he hasn't considered settling down. Not until his gaze lands on the loveliest woman he's ever seen. Creamy skin, golden blonde hair, and blue eyes so deep and clear, they sparkle. The first time he saw her, slowly descending the stairs of the saloon, she captured every man's attention.

Madeleine Colbert shouldn't want the tall, ridiculously attractive rancher whose heated gaze burns right through her. A haunted past and inability to stay in one place for long doesn't bode well for any kind of relationship. And her job in the saloon isn't what a respectable cowboy would consider suitable for anything other than a few fiery moments.

He can't get her out of his mind. Fletch spends his days thinking of Maddy and his nights visiting the intriguing woman, until he needs her more than his next breath. But one short discussion with his father changes everything.

The note he sends cuts clean through, causing her heart to crack. Knowing he'll never return, and with ruthless outlaws tracking her, Maddy makes the only decision possible. She runs.

Returning after several months, Fletcher's first thought is of Maddy. The time away has been miserable. All he wants is to make amends and continue with what they had before he left.

For the first time in his life, he learns what it's like to not get what he wants.

Hardship continues to plague Maddy. When the outlaws discover her new location, she finds herself on the run again, returning to Conviction. But not to the man she loves.

She may have outrun the people chasing her, but it doesn't mean she's escaped the one man who offers nothing except another broken heart. And now, Maddy is hiding her biggest secret of all.

Fletcher's Pride, book eight in the MacLarens of Boundary Mountain Historical Western Romance Series, is a stand-alone, full-length novel with an HEA and no cliffhanger.

Book 5: Heather's Choice
Book 6: Nate's Destiny
Book 7: Blaine's Wager
Book 8: Fletcher's Pride

Visit my website for a list of characters for each series.
http://www.shirleendavies.com/character-list.html

Acknowledgements

Many thanks to the wonderful members of my Reader Groups. Your support, insights, and suggestions are greatly appreciated. And as always, a huge thank you to my husband who is my greatest fan.

As always, many thanks to my editor, Kim Young, proofreader, Alicia Carmical, Joseph Murray, who is superb at formatting my books for print and electronic versions, and my cover designer, Kim Killion.

Fletcher's Pride

Prologue

San Francisco
June 1866

Maddy huddled behind a barrel, holding a soaked cloak over her head as shivers shot through her slim body. Heart racing, she crouched lower at the sound of male voices and pounding footfalls. They were close. Too close.

She needed to find a better hiding place or risk being discovered by the same group of men who'd been following her for well over a year. Brutal, lawless, and unforgiving, the type of men anyone with sense stayed away from to survive.

Their leader, a man hardened through years of fierce fighting for the Union Army, ruled with a firm fist and little patience. Maddy knew this firsthand, had experienced the type of justice he doled out to those who defied him.

"I saw her run down this alley."

She recognized the gruff voice, wincing at the memory of the last time she'd seen him perform his leader's bidding. It had been bloody, painful, and almost deadly. Maddy remembered it well. The beating had been directed at her.

"She couldn't have gone far. Not in this storm."

Her stomach clenched at the familiar sound of their leader's voice...a voice that haunted her every night and most days. Scooting until she'd taken up all the spare space behind the barrel, Maddy bit her lower lip, wincing at the coppery taste. The pain was necessary to keep her teeth from chattering, a noise she felt certain would give her away.

"Maybe she slipped into one of the stores, Colonel."

"Check each until we find the faithless chit. We're too close to let her get away again." The severe determination in his voice left no doubt he'd continue the search all night if that was what it took to find her.

They'd chased Maddy since her escape from them in Kansas, continuing to follow her trail through Colorado, Utah, and Nevada before losing her when she'd crossed the boundary into California. For a brief period of time, she'd found freedom in Conviction, a growing town on the Feather River.

And she'd found love. At least it had been for her.

Then she'd received a terse note from him, delivered by his cousin and accompanied with enough money to provide her a choice. Stay in Conviction, praying he'd change his mind and return for her, or run.

The decision had been taken from her the same night. Amid the raucous sounds from the saloon, the unmistakable harsh voices of the men who tracked her somehow wafted upstairs. The same voices she heard a few feet away from her hiding place in the dank alley tonight.

"She's not getting away from us again. Not this time."

Maddy recognized the colonel's most trusted man, another shiver of fear wracking her already trembling body.

"Please, please..." Her whispered plea was muffled by the hand she clamped over her mouth. The suffocating weight in her chest caused bile to build in her throat. She needed this night to be over, needed to get out of San Francisco and return to the one place in her short life where she'd felt safe.

Hearing heavy boots move away, voices fading, she took a deep breath, peering out from her hiding place. Maddy's heart stilled, wondering if her eyesight might be failing. Swiping rain from her face, she blinked several times, her gaze sweeping up and down the alley.

Empty, the men who had made her life miserable gone, vanished, as if they'd never existed. Settling a hand over her slightly rounded stomach, she sent up a quick prayer. Maddy didn't wait to consider her next move, pushing up before reaching into the open barrel and grabbing the small satchel she'd dropped inside.

Securing the cloak around her, holding it together with one hand, the satchel in the other, she took one more look around, listening. Hearing nothing except the incessant drubbing of the rain, Maddy stepped out of the shadows.

Heart pounding, chest tight, she marshaled all the courage left in her shattered spirit and ran.

Chapter One

Circle M Ranch
June 1866

"Fletch, you're driving them the wrong way." Bram MacLaren laughed from atop his horse, as did his cousin, Camden, who sat beside him on his gelding. Fletcher MacLaren yelled something back, causing both to laugh harder.

"Do you think the lad knows the uncles want the calves in the north pasture, not the south?" Camden asked.

Bram shook his head. "Nae. He's no idea what we're shouting about."

"The lad's mind isn't on his work. Hasn't been since we delivered the herd to Sacramento." Resting his arms on the saddlehorn, he leaned forward. "Since Maddy left town."

"And whose fault was it the lass left?"

"Fletch's, and he knows it. We'll not be reminding him of it, Bram. The lad needs to get his head straight and forget the lass." Straightening, he lightly kicked Duke, his palomino gelding, riding toward Fletcher.

"Ach," Bram growled, following.

Drawing close to Fletcher and the two ranch hands with him, Camden waved his hand for him to hold up. "The uncles want them moved north, lad."

Reining up, Fletcher glanced around, getting his bearings. "North?"

Chuckling, Camden nodded. "Aye. Come on, lad. We'll get you there."

Letting his cousin take over directing the ranch hands, Fletcher held back, following along as he'd been doing for weeks. Ever since returning from Settlers Valley to drive the family's combined herd to Sacramento, he'd felt out of place, somehow disconnected from the people who'd always been so critical in his life.

He'd left Circle M, been gone for weeks helping his cousin, Blaine, at the family's new ranchlands near Settlers Valley. When the uncles had requested a volunteer to help Blaine, Fletcher didn't hesitate. At first, he'd seen the absence as an opportunity to put distance between himself and the woman he'd spent way too much time with over the previous weeks. A woman he knew he'd never have beyond their stolen time in her room at Buckie's Castle.

She'd become an obsession, a passion he couldn't allow to grow. Leaving Circle M seemed the easiest way to make the break. Fletcher had scribbled a brief note, telling her he wouldn't return to Buckie's when he got back to town, enclosed some money, and asked Bram to deliver the message. Within a few miles of leaving for Settlers Valley, he'd regretted the decision.

Now she was gone. Not just from Buckie's, but from Conviction.

Camden rode up beside him. "It's Saturday, Fletch. Bram and I've been thinking of cleaning up and riding to town. Come with us."

He'd avoided going to town since coming home, using every possible excuse without naming the real reason. As absurd as it seemed, riding to Conviction, knowing she wouldn't be there to welcome him, held no appeal.

When he didn't answer, Camden persisted. "You've got to get over Maddy sometime, Fletch. It'll be easier if you go to Buckie's, have some drinks, maybe spend some time with one of the other lasses. It's like being bucked off a horse, lad. They throw you off, you get back on."

Bram had ridden up beside them, approval on his features at Camden's words. He'd been thinking the same for weeks. The fact Fletcher had yet to object had both thinking he might ride in with them.

Without answering, Fletcher glanced between the two, shaking his head. "We've got a long day ahead of us, lads."

Bram and Camden didn't protest when their cousin rode off, leaving them to do whatever they wanted. Fletcher didn't care.

Pushing Domino into a gallop, he reined away, heading toward the river. He knew they wouldn't follow. Over the years, the entire MacLaren clan learned if Fletcher needed space, he'd head straight for a spot he'd found not long after they'd started the ranch.

Handsome, smart, and charming, he'd attracted women, young and old, since turning fourteen. His cousins joked about it, but as they got older, they'd become accustomed to Fletcher acting as bait, the person who drew women to them.

Even with the feminine attention and respect of his family, Fletcher required more solitary time than anyone, except Sean. Sometimes, the two rode out together, saying little, simply sharing a quiet space by the river. With Sean in Scotland to attend veterinary school, Fletcher now made the short trip alone. He'd already made the journey at least half a dozen times since coming back.

Reining Domino along the winding trail, his tight muscles began to relax. As always happened, his mood improved at the sight of the rippling, clear water, the way the river pooled into eddies. He and Sean had spent more than one afternoon fishing for trout in this spot.

Sliding to the ground, he dropped the reins, lowering himself next to the river's edge. Pulling up his knees, he draped his arms over them, staring at the water.

For the first time in weeks, he seriously thought about accepting Camden's invitation to visit Buckie's. He could use a night of whiskey and cards, even if he wasn't ready to visit the upstairs. It might be a good, long time before he had the desire to take the stairs knowing Maddy wouldn't be there to greet him.

Maddy stared at herself in the mirror, a tentative grin tipping up the corners of her mouth. She'd taken extra time with her golden blonde hair, adding a yellow ribbon she'd splurged on at Maloney's, the local mercantile.

Smoothing hands down her cotton dress, she turned in a circle, trying to quell her growing dread. Almost three months had passed since she'd last been with Fletcher. The doctor in San Francisco guessed their baby to be eight to ten weeks along. It would be several more weeks before anyone would notice.

Rubbing a hand over the small swell in her stomach, Maddy couldn't help a trembling smile. She'd loved Fletcher and she loved their unborn child. Shaking off the spark of fear, knowing she and the babe would face life alone, she blew out a reassuring breath.

In a few minutes, she'd have to leave for her meeting with the manager of the newest hotel and restaurant a couple streets away from the boardinghouse. They'd lost two employees in the last week, providing an opportunity Maddy hadn't expected.

Taking a deep breath, she settled a bonnet over her hair and grabbed her reticule. A few minutes later, she strolled along the boardwalk, her destination the next street over. Spotting the building not far ahead, she placed a hand on her stomach, doing her best to ignore the fluttering sensations.

Opening the front door, Maddy bit the inside of her mouth as she scanned the room, seeing a woman huddled over a stack of papers at a table in the back of the dining room. Squaring her shoulders, she headed straight for her.

"Miss Suzette Gasnier?"

Looking up, a smile spread across the woman's face. "Yes. And you are?"

"Madeleine Leigh. I'm here about a job."

Leaning back in the chair, Suzette set down the pencil, her gaze scanning Maddy from her head to her clean, well-fitting cotton dress, finally moving to her scuffed boots. Not a pair of women's walking boots, but the type worn by wranglers and ranch hands. Suzette stifled a chuckle.

"I'm looking for servers for the noon and supper meals. Do you have experience?"

Hope sprang in Maddy's heart. "Yes, ma'am. I worked at the Parker Hill Restaurant in San Francisco for two months."

"I've been to it. When did you leave?"

"A week ago."

Suzette lifted a brow. "My understanding is the Parker is a good place to work. Did they let you go?"

Maddy twisted her hands together. She refused to tell anyone the real reason she left. If it cost her a job here, she'd find something else. "No. I, uh...had to leave."

Pushing her chair back, Suzette stood, walking around the table. Stopping a foot away, she crossed her arms, studying Maddy. "Are you running from the law?"

Her jaw clenched. "No, ma'am." *Although the people tracking me are.*

Suzette's eyes narrowed. "I don't need trouble here, Miss Leigh."

"I won't be bringing you any, Miss Gasnier." Maddy prayed that was true.

"Where do you live?"

"At Baker's. It's down the street from the Gold Dust."

A slight grin lifted Suzette's mouth. "Yes, I know it." Dropping her arms, she walked back to her chair, resting a hand on the back. "I need you to start tonight. Be here at four o'clock. Dark skirt and white blouse."

Maddy's initial joy turned to dread. "I'm sorry, but I don't own either."

"Come with me." Suzette took purposeful strides to the back, walking through an open doorway to a storage room. Opening the door, she pointed to a rack of clothes. "Pick your size. You're responsible for cleaning them, and you only get one set." Glancing down at Maddy's shoes, she shook her head. "Do you have anything other than boots?"

"Yes, ma'am."

"Black?"

Maddy nodded.

"Wear them." Suzette held out her hand. "Congratulations, Miss Leigh. You are now an employee of the Feather River Restaurant."

Maddy felt like skipping back to the boardinghouse, the excitement of obtaining the job of her dreams almost overtaking her common sense. A respectable position, one she'd be proud to tell people, unlike the one she held at Buckie's Castle.

She shuddered, remembering the evenings she'd applied thick makeup, wore tight dresses, sweeping her hair into an alluring style guaranteed to garner the attention of the men who frequented the saloon. During her time at Buckie's, there'd been just one man she wanted to notice her, and he had—every night for weeks.

Then she'd been given his note. Months later, the familiar pain still shot through her. The next day, Maddy packed, taking the stage to San Francisco, leaving Fletcher, and the men who tracked her, behind.

Another mistake, but not as monumental as the one she'd made by falling in love with Fletcher MacLaren—a man who'd believed her to be just another saloon whore, a woman who sold her body for money. She swallowed the familiar ball of pain, knowing she'd never given him any reason to believe otherwise. Something Maddy would always regret.

Walking the last few yards to Baker's, she smiled. Her job at Buckie's and love for Fletcher were firmly where they should be...in the past. Refusing to dwell on her mistakes, she decided this was a day to celebrate. Unfortunately, a celebration would have to wait. In two hours, she'd step back into the Feather River Hotel and Restaurant and start over one more time.

Circle M Ranch

"Are you certain you heard the lad right?" Bram's eyes had grown wide at Camden's announcement. They stood on the porch, waiting for their cousin to appear.

"Aye. Fletch told me at supper he's coming with us to Buckie's." Before Bram could respond, Camden held up a hand. "Two rounds of whiskey and a few hands of cards. Nothing more."

Bram grinned. "I'll be happy with whatever time the lad decides to spend in town. Getting him off the ranch for a few hours will do Fletch good. Where is he?"

"Decided to change his boots. He'll meet us at the barn."

"What's taking you lads so long?" Fletch stood outside the barn, hands on his hips. He didn't wear a smile, but it wasn't a frown, either. "Domino is already saddled. I'm waiting for you miscreants."

Scrambling down the steps, they walked toward him. "How'd you get past us?" Camden asked, shooting him a confused look as he and Bram headed into the barn.

Fletcher didn't answer, his thoughts already moving to Buckie's and what it would be like to enter without the anticipation of seeing Maddy. He'd left Conviction to put distance between them, stayed away from the saloon women in Settlers Valley because he couldn't forget her.

Now he'd be going to the place where they'd shared so much, and not just time in her bed.

He missed their lovemaking. Even more, he missed their long talks, her throaty, unrestrained laugh, the pleasure he saw on her face whenever she spotted him from the top of the stairs. His chest squeezed at all the memories.

"You ready?" Bram led Bullet out of the barn, followed a moment later by Camden holding the reins of Duke.

Fletcher shook his head. The expectation of spending an evening at Buckie's no longer held any appeal. "I'm thinking I'll stay here tonight, lads."

"No, you're not. You're coming with us, even if you don't stay long." Bram clasped his cousin's shoulder. "We're ready to leave, lad, and you need some time away from the ranch."

"How long has it been since you've taken time to relax, play cards, and have a few drinks?" Camden swung into Duke's saddle, glancing down at him.

Fletcher thought back over the last few months. "Since the last time I saw Maddy."

"Hell, lad. That's way too long for any man. Saddle up, Fletch. It's time you put the lass behind you."

A spark of guilt flashed through him at his cousins' hopeful expressions. Letting out a resigned breath, he mounted, reining Domino toward town. Shoving aside his reservations, he shot his cousins a tight smile.

"Last one to the fence buys the first round." Fletcher kicked his sorrel gelding into a swift gallop, a surprised laugh bursting from his lungs at the shocked expressions he left behind.

Chapter Two

Conviction

The nervous sensations Maddy fought earlier subsided somewhat with each new table of diners. She'd arrived early and read through the menu several times, memorizing each item.

Picking up the latest order, she carried the plates into the dining room, setting them before two men. One, an older, distinguished gentleman with thinning, dark hair and trim mustache with strands of silver. The second man was younger, his thick, dark brown hair streaked with gold. What grabbed Maddy's attention were his startling green eyes—eyes focused on her.

The older man inhaled, a grin tugging at the corners of his mouth. "This smells wonderful, my dear."

"I'm sure you'll enjoy it. Is there anything else I can get you?" She glanced between the two, surprised at the intense stare from the younger man.

"You look familiar. I'm Bayard Donahue. Have we met?" His gaze never left hers.

Panic gripped her. Bay Donahue, the gunfighter her uncle had mentioned several times. Maddy remembered him joining them in their camp, sitting across the campfire. Perhaps he recognized her from the life she'd been forced to lead before journeying across country to Conviction.

Uncomfortable with his penetrating scrutiny, she shook her head. "I don't believe so. I'm Madeleine Leigh. It's nice to meet you, Mr. Donahue."

Bay raised a brow, nodding toward the other man. "This is August Fielder. We have a law practice in town."

Maddy hoped Bay didn't notice the brief spark of confusion at his mention of being an attorney. Had he put away his guns to practice law?

August stood, making a slight bow. "It's a pleasure to meet you, Miss Leigh."

Maddy forced a slight grin. "Mr. Fielder. Well, I'll let you two get back to your supper. Please let me know if I can get you anything else."

She returned to the back where Suzette stood, her gaze moving over the crowded dining room, her face a neutral mask. It wasn't a big space, holding fifteen tables, every one full this evening.

"I see you've met August Fielder and Bay Donahue."

"Yes, ma'am." Maddy wondered if her boss knew of Bay's past. If not, she wouldn't be the one to tell her.

Suzette glanced at her. "Both are good to know. They're also the owners, along with the MacLarens, of the hotel and restaurant."

Maddy's breath caught. "The MacLarens?"

"You probably haven't been in town long enough to hear of them."

Maddy didn't comment.

"They're the largest landowners in the area. They often partner with August and Bay in business ventures."

"Have you known Mr. Fielder and Mr. Donahue long?"

Suzette hesitated a moment, not meeting Maddy's gaze. "I met August when I arrived in town to take this job. I've known Bay quite a bit longer."

Biting her lip, Maddy asked something she probably shouldn't have. "Are you and Bay—"

"No." The response was immediate and final. "You should probably check your tables."

Knowing she'd been dismissed, Maddy nodded. "Yes, ma'am."

Suzette watched her walk away, wishing she'd never mentioned August and Bay. Especially Bay. Her mouth went dry, palms dampening each time he came into the hotel or took a meal at the restaurant. Given their history, she hated her reaction to him and the pain she'd caused. Suzette knew he loathed her.

At one time, they'd loved each other with a frightening intensity, consuming them both. They'd been happy. At least *she* had been. Happier than she'd ever been in her life, looking forward to a lifetime with Bay.

It had all come crashing down one hot, sultry afternoon when a stranger rode into town, making demands of her and following them with threats. Suzette had been forced to make a difficult, life-altering decision. The ramifications had been horrific.

Sucking in a shaky breath, she tore her gaze away from Bay, but not before he'd spotted her staring. Suzette flinched at the disgust in his eyes. It was a sentiment she knew well, as she felt the same about herself.

Straightening her back, Suzette lifted her chin, assuming the haughty posture she'd perfected to disguise the pain and humiliation, which had become her constant companions. As much as she wanted to deny it, she deserved every ounce of loathing—Bay's and her own.

"Another round, Frankie." Bram raised his empty glass at Buckie's bartender.

"One more drink and I'm done, lads." Fletcher tightened his grip around the saloon girl's waist before dropping his arm to concentrate on the cards in his hand. She'd been insistent in tempting him to follow her upstairs. He'd rejected each offer, satisfied with an evening of cards and whiskey.

"I don't know how you do it, Fletch. You've got the darnedest luck I've ever seen." Camden tossed down his cards, taking a sip from the full glass. "A couple more rounds like the last few and I'll be done for the night."

"Ach, this is a good lesson for you, lad. You've had too many nights when you've walked away the winner."

Bram held up his glass, tilting it toward Camden before emptying it down his throat.

Fletcher's mouth twisted into a sardonic grin at his cousins' conversation. Since arriving, his gaze continued to sweep to the stairs, throat tightening when he didn't see what he sought. He sobered at the thought he'd never again see Maddy's smile, watch as she descended the stairs, her gaze locked on his.

Regret lay heavy on his chest, making it hard to draw a breath. If only he'd held off asking Bram to deliver the message. But he hadn't, and it was much too late to correct his mistake.

Feeling fingers thread through his hair, he jerked. One of the older girls stood next to him, an expectant gaze on her face.

"Come upstairs with me, Fletch. I'll make you forget all about Maddy."

His stomach roiled, a deep pain growing in his chest. Catching her wrist, he drew it away from his head as he cleared his throat. "Not tonight, lass."

"Come on, Fletch. We've got a full day ahead of us tomorrow." Camden's chair scraped against the wood floor as he stood. "You ready, Bram?"

"Aye." He extricated himself from the girl on his lap. Flashing her a smile, he joined Camden at the door.

They waited as Fletcher tossed back the last of his whiskey before taking one more look over his shoulder at the stairs. Drawing in a breath, he started for the door, then stopped. Stalking to the bar, he got Frankie's attention.

"What do you need, Fletch?"

"Do you remember a girl named Maddy?"

A knowing grin tipped the man's lips. "Sure do. I think she might've been sweet on you."

Fletcher's eyes widened before he snorted. "Me and all the other men she entertained."

Frankie's brows furrowed. "Other men? Hell, Fletch. I thought you knew. You're the only man Maddy ever had up in her room."

His features stilled, eyes sparking with disbelief. "That can't be."

"Well, it is." Frankie lifted a hand to a man yelling for another drink. "She left not long after you rode to Settlers Valley." He turned to walk away, stopping at Fletcher's question.

"Do you know where she went?"

"Heard she took the stage to San Francisco."

Maddy wiped down the last of the tables, taking one more look around before heading to the back. She felt good. It had been a long first day, busier than she expected, and quite enlightening.

Learning Bay Donahue lived in Conviction had been a shock. Maddy couldn't imagine the gunslinger she'd heard so much about hanging up his guns to be a lawyer. She remembered him as young, charming, and handsome. Not much had changed, other than Bay being a few years older with deeper lines around his mouth and eyes.

Maddy thought of Suzette's face when she spoke of him. Her expression gave Maddy pause, making her wonder if there was something between them.

"You did a good job tonight, Madeleine." Suzette stopped next to her. "I have you working the next four days. Any problem with that?"

Maddy shook her head. "No, ma'am. I already saw the schedule. If anyone can't work a shift, get word to me at Baker's and I'll come in."

"I will. See you tomorrow." Suzette left her, walking back into the kitchen.

Tying on her bonnet, Maddy left by a side door. It hadn't occurred to her until this moment how far she had to walk in the dark to get to the boardinghouse. The only lights were those peeking out from inside buildings where someone still worked.

Reaching the main street, she let out a relieved breath at the bright lights coming from the Gold Dust, Buckie's, and the other saloons. Letting her gaze wander to Buckie's, a bittersweet memory washed over her.

Deep laughter echoed down the street as three men stepped out of the saloon. A gasp left her lips, breath stalling when the tallest of the three turned toward her. A hand flew to her throat.

Fletcher.

She wanted to run to him, throw her arms around his neck and never let go. Instead, she stepped back into the shadows. If he'd wanted her, intended to return, Fletcher never would have written the note.

Clearly, he had returned, discovered she'd left town, and now felt safe visiting Buckie's. She wondered which of the women he'd spent his time with tonight. A sharp pain almost buckled her knees.

Closing her eyes, she turned away when the three rode past, certain he couldn't see her on the darkened boardwalk. Hearing the receding horses, she shifted, watching as they disappeared down the trail to Circle M.

An intense ache squeezed her chest, forcing Maddy to lower herself onto a nearby bench. Taking slow, deep breaths, she braced herself against the wall of the building, resting her hand on her stomach.

Her mind raced. She hadn't expected to see him again so soon, and certainly not coming out of Buckie's. It might not have hurt so much if she'd seen him leave Lucky's or one of the other saloons. For some reason, seeing him walk out of Buckie's cut like a blade to her chest.

Swallowing the pain, she stood, sucking in a ragged breath. She didn't remember walking to the boardinghouse, climbing up the stairs, or entering her room. Sitting on her bed in the dark, Maddy didn't attempt to wipe away the tears streaming down her face. Choking back the sobs, she curled into a ball, allowing sleep to claim her.

Groaning at the bright morning sun streaming through her window, Maddy rubbed her face. She wondered at her puffy eyes and thick throat before remembering who she'd seen the night before.

Angry at allowing herself to wallow in self-pity, Maddy forced herself out of bed, determined to push Fletcher firmly and completely from her heart. He'd left her behind months ago. Now she had to do the same with him.

Performing her morning ablutions, she slipped into a yellow day dress, tying the bonnet under her chin. She ate a quick breakfast before starting her short list of errands.

Maloney's would have a lantern, ribbons for her hair, and socks. Crossing the street, she stopped at an office with a sign next to the door. *Fielder and Donahue Law Offices.* It surprised her how she'd never noticed it before.

Moving on, she noticed the gunsmith shop. In the rush to pack, she'd forgotten her six-shooter at the boardinghouse in San Francisco. It had to be replaced as soon as she earned enough money. For now, all her coin went to paying for her room at Baker's and buying the few necessities she required.

Arriving at Maloney's, she pushed open the door, her progress stalling at the sight of Bram standing at the counter. Backing outside, she closed the door, hurrying past the jail, another restaurant, and Lucky's, another of the saloons in Conviction.

Spotting the same bench she'd taken refuge on the night before, Maddy sat down, tired at the rapid pace she'd set to flee Bram. He hadn't noticed her.

Placing a shaky hand on her stomach, she rubbed the slight mound, glad the sickness of the first few weeks had subsided. At least three months. That was how long Maddy believed she'd been carrying Fletcher's child.

"Good morning, Miss Leigh."

She startled at the deep, crisp voice, turning to see Bay standing by the bench. "Oh, good morning, Mr. Donahue." Maddy started to rise, staying put when he placed a hand on her shoulder.

"Please, stay where you are." His gaze moved over her, stopping on the spot where a hand rested on what appeared to be a protruding belly. He didn't say a word, lifting his eyes to meet hers. "Will you be working at the restaurant this evening?"

Noticing where his gaze had landed, Maddy moved her hand away from her stomach, straightening on the bench. "Yes, I am. Will you and Mr. Fielder be returning for supper?"

"Not tonight. I'll be bringing a guest with me on Saturday."

"Then I'll look forward to seeing you, Mr. Donahue."

Bay studied her a moment, as if trying to remember something. Maddy hoped he hadn't begun to piece together where they'd met in the past. It had been a while and she'd been dressed in pants, a loose jacket, and hat. She held her breath, gripping her hands in her lap.

Touching the brim of his hat, he nodded. "Have a good day, Miss Leigh."

Watching him make his way down the boardwalk, she let out a relieved breath. The next moment, Bram stepped out of the mercantile, and seeing Bay, waited to greet him. After a few minutes, Bram mounted his horse, riding past without noticing her, and Bay entered his office.

Closing her eyes, Maddy swallowed the knot of dread, promising herself to be more careful in the future.

Chapter Three

San Francisco

Ex-Union Colonel Wallace "Dob" Colbert stared out the window of the rundown hotel, anger rolling through him. Almost two weeks had passed since they'd spotted Maddy in a crowded restaurant, followed her to the boardinghouse, and chased her into a dark alley. As luck ran, he'd believed she'd used up all hers. Dob had been wrong, the same as he had since she'd fled their camp in Kansas.

The pouring rain and her small stature gave Maddy an unanticipated advantage. She could curl inside places not big enough for most people. Dob also knew she carried a gun—the six-shooter her father had given her for her tenth birthday. Most girls received dolls, dresses, or hair ribbons. Maddy received a gun and been taught how to use it.

"We need money, Colonel."

Dob didn't turn away from the window to look at his lieutenant. Ross Sheehan served under him during the war, then afterward when they'd ridden off to start another kind of fighting. Battles they controlled, always won, and filled their pockets with money. Besides his closest friend, ex-Captain Lew Quick, he trusted Ross more than any of the other men.

"Pick a bank and we'll make a plan."

"Already have, sir. It's a small bank a few blocks from here. We rob it when they close on Friday. There are only two people who stay until closing. *Two*, sir."

"Have you spoken with Lew about this?"

Ross nodded. "He agrees with going in on Friday. We leave town right afterward."

Dob turned to him. "And go where?"

"The captain thinks we should backtrack. Ride through Oakland, Martinez, and if she's not in either of those, ride back to Sacramento. Lew doesn't think she'd go back to Conviction."

Dob rubbed his chin, turning back to the window. "Oakland and Martinez. If we don't find her, we'll make a decision where else to go."

He didn't agree with Lew about Conviction. If it were his decision, the gang would return to someplace she'd already fled, believing the raiders wouldn't show a second time. He knew Maddy had somehow learned they'd found her in Conviction. She'd bolted, leaving town within a day of their arrival. For now, they'd start with the two towns closer to San Francisco. If they didn't find her, they'd ride straight to Conviction.

Circle M

Reining Domino to a stop, Fletcher leaned forward, scanning the horizon for the missing cattle. Camden and a few other men searched the gullies to the east while he and Bram checked those to the west.

He focused on his work, doing all he could to forget Maddy, even though he knew it was a futile effort. After Frankie told him she'd left for San Francisco, Fletcher had thought of following, meaning to find her in a city where people went to lose themselves in a sea of unremarkable faces. He didn't have the skills or knowledge of the large city to locate her.

After several nights without sleep, pondering his options, sanity prevailed. His family needed him at Circle M, and Maddy hated him. Those reasons didn't prevent him from hiring someone to find her for him, and he knew just the man to ask for advice—his brother-in-law, Sam Covington.

"It's Saturday. Are you interested in another evening in town, lad?"

Fletcher hadn't heard Bram approach. Another night at Buckie's held no appeal, but heading to Conviction did. Fletcher's sister, Jinny, and her husband, Sam, lived in town, making it easier to fulfill Sam's duties as one of Brodie MacLaren's deputies.

"I'll ride in with you, but I need to talk with Sam."

Bram nodded, as if he understood.

"I'm thinking of trying to find Maddy."

Again, Bram nodded, remaining silent.

"Sam used to work for Pinkerton. He might know of someone I can hire to find her."

Resting his arms on the saddlehorn, Bram leaned forward, staring out at the vast pastureland. "You've got to be doing what's best for you, lad. If locating the lass is what you need, I'd say it's time to be confronting your demons."

Fletcher's expression didn't change. "Demons?"

Shifting, Bram sent him an almost bored look. "Aye, lad. Demons. The beasts biting at your heels since you returned to the ranch. I never thought the note was a good idea. Seems to me you need to see Maddy in person, get her out of your heart for good."

Fletcher's gaze hardened. "The lass isn't in my heart."

Bram straightened in the saddle, his lips twitching. "If that's what you want to believe, lad."

Nostrils flaring enough for his cousin to notice, he shook his head. "Do you still want to ride in with me?"

This time, Bram threw back his head and laughed. "I'm definitely going to be riding in with you, lad. I won't be missing hearing you explain it all to Sam." Kicking Bullet with a light touch, he rode off, not stopping at Fletcher's shout.

Conviction

Maddy's mouth dropped open at the beautiful woman entering the restaurant on the arm of Bay Donahue. She'd never seen her before, but the woman may have moved into town during Maddy's brief stay in San Francisco.

When the two stood for several moments without being greeted, she shot a quick glance at Suzette. Her boss stared at the couple, her normally serene face pinched, as if in distress.

"Would you like me to seat them?"

Suzette startled, turning her attention to Maddy. She should refuse the offer. Bay would notice the slight, and as her boss, she needed to be more cautious about her actions.

"If you wouldn't mind, Madeleine, I'd appreciate it."

"I don't mind at all. I'm certain you have meals to check on in the kitchen." Maddy glanced over her shoulder, hoping Suzette would take the hint.

Blinking at Maddy's accurate perception, she nodded, turned, and walked toward the kitchen. Waiting until Suzette had disappeared through the door, she picked up two handwritten menus.

Walking to the front, she glanced around the well-appointed room, proud Suzette had hired her to serve those who could afford a more expensive fare. With the agreement of the MacLarens, August and Bay had patterned the restaurant after the exclusive ones they'd visited back east. They'd done an excellent job.

"Good evening, Mr. Donahue. May I show you to your table?" She lifted a brow.

Bay didn't move. "Is Miss Gasnier unavailable to seat us tonight?"

"I'm afraid she's talking to the chef. Of course, if you'd prefer to wait for her to finish..."

He glanced toward the kitchen, jaw tightening. "No. We'll be seated now."

Leading the way, Maddy showed them to his normal table in an alcove designed for more private conversations.

"Here you are." She waited until Bay seated his guest and sat down himself before handing them the menus. "Will you be ordering wine tonight?"

"The red from New York, please."

Nodding, she left them alone to fetch the wine, and check on Suzette. Maddy had seen the agony on her boss's face. She knew the crack in Suzette's normally tranquil demeanor had been caused by Bay's appearance with the beautiful woman.

"He's been seated and ordered the red wine, Suzette."

When she turned to Maddy, she'd steeled her features, the pain gone. "Thank you. Did he, um...ask about me?"

"He did. I told him you were in the kitchen, which you were." Maddy grinned before leaving to get the wine. When she returned to the dining room, her gaze lit on two couples at the front. Suzette spoke to them, laughing at something one of them had said. As she seated them, Maddy poured the wine for Bay and his guest before taking their orders.

Walking to the kitchen to place the orders, she noticed the two couples had been seated in her area. Picking up menus, Maddy headed to their table.

"Good evening." Handing each a menu, she clasped her hands in front of her. "Will you be having wine tonight?"

One of the men shook his head. "No wine tonight, lass."

The Scottish brogue, the use of lass, stilled her motions. Her breath hitched. She didn't have to ask to know these were MacLarens.

"I don't believe we've seen you here before, lass. I'm Ewan MacLaren. This is my wife, Lorna, my brother, Ian, and his wife, Gail."

She instantly recognized the names, knowing the man who spoke was Fletcher's father. Doing her best to hide the curiosity at standing so close to her baby's grandparents, she tore her gaze away, not wanting to feel anything for these people. Fletcher hadn't wanted to see her again, so she felt certain his family wouldn't want her, or the baby, in their lives.

"It's a pleasure to meet all of you. I'm Madeleine Leigh." She swallowed, offering a shaky smile. "May I get you something to drink while you decide what you want to order?"

Ewan glanced around the table, then back at Maddy. "We already know what we want. The lasses will be having tea. Ian and I want your fine whiskey. We'll all be ordering the roast duck." Ewan smiled at her stunned expression. "We have the same every time we come in, lass."

She allowed a grin to tug at her mouth. "Yes, sir. I'll let the cook know and bring your drinks."

"Madeleine..." Her name rolled off Ewan's tongue. "Does anyone ever call you Maddy?"

The question startled her, causing the pencil to slip from her shaky fingers. Bending down to pick it up, she pursed her lips, not wanting to answer.

"Um...no. My mother always called me by my full name."

"A lovely name it is, lass." This came from Ewan's wife, Lorna.

Feeling an odd sense of longing at the sincerity in their voices, she cleared her throat. "I'd best get to the kitchen or you'll be waiting until midnight." She left, rushing at a faster pace than necessary, hoping no one noticed her unease. Putting in the order, she rested a hand on her stomach.

"Are you feeling all right, Madeleine?"

Dropping her hand, her brow crinkled at Suzette's question. "Yes, I'm fine. It's busy on Saturdays."

Chuckling, her boss glanced around the full dining room. "I forgot you hadn't worked a Saturday. Yes, they are always busy, which means it's hard to become bored. It appears you've met the MacLarens."

"Yes, I did."

"They're a wonderful and fascinating family. Those four come into the restaurant at least twice a month."

Maddy bit her lip, losing the battle to not ask the question burning in her gut. "What of the others in the family? Do they come in often?"

"Some do, but not often. They tend to eat at the Gold Dust or one of the other restaurants in town." Scanning the dining room once more, Suzette's gaze lit on Bay and his guest, pain flashing in her eyes before she could conceal it.

"Do you know the woman with Mr. Donahue?" Maddy winced, wishing she'd kept her mouth closed. She could see Suzette's hands clasped in front of her, the grip so tight her knuckles had turned white. The sadness on her face broke Maddy's heart.

She shrugged, forcing a smile. "No, I don't. He's always entertaining a different woman." Suzette let out a resigned breath. "I need to check the kitchen."

Maddy watched her leave, noting the similarities between her and Suzette, wondering how long it took to mend a broken heart.

Fletcher, Bram, and Camden sat in Sam's study, nursing whiskey after a huge supper. Jinny, Fletcher's sister and Sam's wife, had made enough to feed the entire MacLaren clan, then shooed them from the kitchen when they'd offered to clean up. Robbie, their young son, played upstairs with his grandfather, Thomas Covington.

"Do you want to tell me what brought you three here on a Saturday night? I'm certain you'd rather be at

Buckie's or Lucky's." Sam sipped the whiskey, glancing at them over the rim of his glass.

Fletcher raised a brow. "Can't we ride in for a visit with you and Jinny?"

"You know you're welcome anytime. I just get the sense there's more to you coming by than a family supper. Why don't you tell me what you want?"

Tossing back the whiskey in his glass, Fletcher poured himself more. "I'm looking for someone and want to hire a private investigator."

A knowing expression crossed Sam's face. He'd been a Union spy during the war, then hired on with the Pinkerton Detective Agency, arriving in Conviction as part of an assignment.

"Do you have any idea where this person might be, Fletch?"

He nodded. "The last I heard, the lass had gone to San Francisco soon after I left for Settlers Valley."

Sam tapped a finger on his desk. "A woman, huh? Tell me the entire story."

Shooting a quick glance at Bram and Camden, Fletcher rubbed his chin. "Her name is Maddy. I was, uh...seeing the lass for several weeks before I left."

"Ah, the girl at Buckie's."

Fletcher's eyes widened, a ball of dread forming in his stomach. "Do you know the lass?"

Sam shook his head. "Not the way you mean. I heard about her from Brodie."

Jaw clenching, he worked to control his temper at the mention of his older brother, the sheriff in Conviction. "From Brodie?"

Picking up the bottle, Sam poured himself another glass of whiskey. "All of you know not much gets past him. He told me you were seeing a woman at Buckie's, how Ewan and Ian were concerned about the amount of time you were spending in town. I figured that was why they sent you to Settlers Valley. To get you away from her." Fletcher's scowl had Sam chuckling. "Was I wrong?"

Blowing out a frustrated breath, Fletcher shook his head. "I volunteered to go."

Leaning forward, Sam rested his arms on the desk. "If you left to get away from her, why try to find her now?"

Standing, Fletcher walked to the window, looking out to a cloudless night. Scrubbing a hand down his face, he turned back toward them. "I've been asking myself the same since returning to Circle M." Resting fisted hands on his hips, he stared at the floor, shaking his head. "The lass..." He let out a shaky breath. "I can't get Maddy out of my mind."

"What do you plan to do once you find her, Fletch? Are you going to bring Maddy back here? Marry her?"

Fletcher speared a trembling hand through his hair, his face twisted in anguish. "The lass is a saloon girl, Sam." Even as he said the words, uncertainty rolled through him. He remembered Frankie's words.

Other men? Hell, Fletch. I thought you knew. You're the only man Maddy ever had up in her room.

"Do you honestly believe your parents will care? You may not be giving Ewan and Lorna enough credit." Sam felt he knew his in-laws well enough to understand their enormous capacity to accept others without judgment. "They love you and they'll love whatever woman you choose. What you need to decide is what you plan to do if she's found, Fletch. No sense spending the money if all you want is to satisfy your curiosity."

Muttering a curse, he lowered himself into a chair. It was a good question, a fair question, one he couldn't answer. "I don't know."

The room grew silent, broken when Bram spoke. "You don't have to be deciding tonight, lad. Sam is right. You need to be knowing what you'll do if Maddy is found." He looked at Sam. "Once Fletch decides, will you help him find the lass?"

"I'll do whatever I can."

Bram and Camden stood, setting down their empty glasses. "Come on, lad. You've some decisions to make."

Chapter Four

Carson City, Nevada

Austin DeBell studied the cards in his hand, peeking over the top to gauge the expressions on the other men at the table. The cards were good. A winning hand, assuming he could draw in the others to increase his winnings.

"You've got the damnedest luck, stranger." A wiry man with a three day stubble and cigar hanging from his mouth eyed him from across the table. "Not sure I want to hand you any more money." He groused a little more before throwing down his cards. Pulling his small pile of winnings toward him, the man stood. "See you around." He eyed Austin as if he meant it as more than at the card table.

A few more hands and the others at the table either grabbed a girl and headed upstairs or left the saloon. Austin didn't mind. He'd accomplished what brought him to Carson City. Through casual, carefully worded questions, he'd learned what he needed and would ride out in the morning.

Lifting the bottle, he topped off his drink, tossing it back in one smooth movement. His throat worked, the liquid burning its way down. The war ended over a year ago, taking with it the dreams he'd held of building a new, independent nation. Disillusioned and bone-tired, the ex-Confederate captain rode away from the devastation of Atlanta with no intention of ever returning.

Movement next to him caught his attention. A woman of undeterminable age, her dark hair piled into a fancy twist, sat next to him, an empty glass in her hand.

"Buy a girl a drink?" She nodded at the bottle before him.

"Help yourself." Austin's gaze flickered over her as she filled her glass, setting it down before taking a sip.

She leaned toward him, her voice lowering. "I hear you're asking questions about a group of riders."

"Friends of mine."

Hearing his slight Southern accent, her brows rose, a corner of her mouth tipping up in skepticism. "Friends, huh? Hard to believe those ex-Union soldiers who rode through here would consider you a friend." Lifting her glass, she took a small sip.

Austin's gaze narrowed, his respect for the woman increasing. "I've stopped questioning what I see. Dob Colbert and I met in Kansas. He asked me to ride along, but I had other priorities at the time." He lifted a brow, hoping she read more into the gesture than it meant.

"What changed?" Her tongue glided around the rim of the glass.

"Time and money. I need more of each and Dob might be the man to help me find both." He didn't explain the money he'd get from bringing in the gang would provide him enough time to figure out what he wanted to do next in his life. "Do you know them?"

Her gaze shot to the bar before returning to meet his. "Dob and his men rode through here about a month ago. I spent a little time with him." She glanced up the stairs as further explanation. "They were on their way to Sacramento, but he also talked about a small town north. Conviction, I believe." Finishing the whiskey, she picked up the bottle to fill her glass a second time.

He didn't care how much of the alcohol she drank. Her information was better than what he'd learned so far. "How many rode with him?"

She shrugged. "Six, maybe seven. All real hard looking with short tempers. The sheriff hauled a couple to jail after they drew guns on a table of local ranch hands." She cocked her head. "You sure these are the men you're looking for?"

Rubbing his chin, Austin's upper lip curled. "Darlin', those sound exactly like the men I'm looking for."

Settling her arms on the table, she propped her chin on a fisted hand. "Has what I told you been helpful?"

Reaching into his pocket, Austin took out some bills, setting them on the table. Her eyes widened, a slow grin spreading across her face.

"If you want to spend some time upstairs, I'll consider it included." She nodded at the bills.

Swallowing the last of his whiskey, he pushed the bottle toward her. "Although I appreciate the offer, sweetheart, I've got other plans." Standing, he didn't say another word as he strolled to the door and walked out.

Standing on the boardwalk of Nevada's state capital, Austin pulled a tintype from a pocket, studying the faces. He'd bought it from a man in Kansas after the gang rode out. Seven men and a girl. Dob Colbert, Lew Quick, and Ross Sheehan were the men who'd offered him a place in their gang. They were the three he wanted. The three who matched faces and descriptions on the wanted posters he kept tucked in a pocket.

Austin had learned more men had joined the gang and the girl no longer rode with them. He couldn't help wondering what had happened to her.

Thinking back, Austin kicked himself for not taking the offer. Then kicked himself again, remembering the fear on the girl's face. He hoped to remedy both mistakes.

Conviction

Bay lay in bed, hands behind his head, the woman he'd taken to supper sleeping in the bedroom next to his. It was a sick game that he'd tired of long ago.

He enjoyed the women's company, respected them, and didn't mind spending money for supper and the theater. They always ended up in the bedroom next to his, never in his bed. No matter how alluring, not one enticed him. The only woman who did slept a few houses

41

away and would never grace his bed or be held in his arms again.

Tonight had been particularly tiring. He'd paid for the actress to travel from San Francisco to visit him for two days. Bay had met her a month before on a trip to the large city on the Pacific, taking a chance she'd be a good companion. Instead, he found her to be narcissistic, able to talk about little except clothes, makeup, and the stage. She'd be leaving on tomorrow's steamboat, and it couldn't come soon enough.

Tossing off the covers, Bay slipped into pants and a shirt. Taking the stairs to the first floor, he entered the study, heading straight to the decanter. Maybe a drink would help him rid his thoughts of Suzette, erase the image of the only woman he'd ever loved. A sardonic smile crossed his lips as he poured a drink. Whiskey hadn't helped before. Bay hoped it would tonight.

Maddy moaned, gripping her stomach while pulling her knees up to relieve the ache. Opening her eyes to slits, she winced at the bright sunlight streaming through the thin curtains hanging over her only window.

Placing a hand to her mouth, she threw off the covers, jumping up to slide the bedpan from under the bed. Dropping to her knees, she bent over.

"Morning sickness," she spit out before losing the contents of her stomach.

When the nausea passed, Maddy twisted so she could sit on the floor, her back resting against the bed.

She wiped the moisture off her face with her nightgown, feeling a slight chill pass through her.

"When will this end?" It was a silly question she'd asked herself every morning. So far, the answer remained elusive.

A month had passed since she'd started at the hotel restaurant. Maddy loved the work and the people. The generous wage added to the savings in a jar hidden in a drawer. Soon, she'd have enough to buy the used crib she found at the back of a shop in Chinatown. It hadn't been for sale, but the owner's eyes sparkled when she'd asked about it. They'd agreed on a price, the man offering to deliver it to the boardinghouse once she earned enough to make the payment. Each day brought that moment closer and closer.

Sucking in a breath, she blew it out before sliding the pan back under the bed. Pushing up, she settled a hand on her stomach, mouth twisting into a grim smile.

Her biggest problem now wasn't the morning sickness. Five more months. The roundness of her belly had increased enough for anyone who looked to know the cause. The fact she was pregnant and alone scared her, but not enough to regret keeping the baby. She'd never regret having Fletcher's child.

Splashing water on her face, she brushed her hair, twisting it on top of her head. Slipping into a blue cotton dress, she left her room, praying Mrs. Baker still had food left from breakfast.

Stepping into the kitchen, she breathed a sigh of relief seeing her at the stove.

Henrietta Baker glanced up at her approach. "I wondered where you were this morning, Miss Leigh." Her gaze moved down, a brow raising. "I can make you eggs and toast. Will that be enough?"

"That would be wonderful. Can I help with anything?"

Henrietta let her gaze move over Maddy again, wrestling with a difficult decision. "Why don't you pour us each a cup of coffee. You can eat in here."

A few minutes later, she set a plate of eggs and toast in front of her, sitting down next to her. Picking up the cup, Henrietta blew across the coffee before taking a sip. She waited long enough for Maddy to get a few bites of food in her stomach, then set down her cup.

"How far along are you? I'm guessing about four months."

Maddy dropped her fork on the plate, hand shaking. Staring down, she did her best to control the dread at Henrietta's question, surprised her landlord had noticed. No one else had detected the increased roundness.

"Four months." She stared at the food, her appetite vanishing.

"You aren't married, are you, dear?"

Sucking in an unsteady breath, she shook her head, not looking up. "No, ma'am."

A few beats passed before Henrietta huffed. "I don't allow pregnant, unmarried women in my boardinghouse. And I don't allow children."

Maddy's chest hurt, throat closing. She knew this could happen, hoping it wouldn't. "How much time do I have before I must leave?"

Lifting her cup, Henrietta took another sip, struggling with an answer. "Do you know who the father is?"

Maddy's head snapped up. "Yes, ma'am."

Her expression and voice hardened. "And he doesn't want to take responsibility for the child?"

Closing her eyes, she searched for the right answer, knowing there was just one. "He doesn't know."

"Why not?" The incredulous tone didn't surprise Maddy.

She fought the moisture forming in her eyes. Lately, she'd been succumbing to tears more and more. It was frustrating to a woman who never allowed herself to cry or wallow in self-pity. Misery washed through her, wrapping around her heart, clouding her thoughts.

Henrietta leaned toward her. "Miss Leigh?"

Swiping at the tears, she sniffed. "I'm sorry, Mrs. Baker." Starting to stand, she stopped when Henrietta placed a hand on her arm.

"Sit down and finish eating. I'm assuming you've been losing too much of what you eat. You'll need all the food you can keep down."

The tears started again as Maddy picked up her fork, her grip tight so it wouldn't shake. "I'm not very hungry."

"Well, that's my fault. I shouldn't have said anything until you'd eaten everything on your plate." The chair scraped against the floor as she stood. "I'm getting more coffee. You need to eat."

Scooping up a small amount of the eggs, Maddy chewed, all taste gone. Taking another bite, she swallowed it down with coffee. After a while, she gave up, setting down the fork.

Henrietta picked up the plate, setting it in the sink before sitting back down. "Now, I want you to tell me all about the man who doesn't know you're carrying his baby."

Circle M

Fletcher swung back into the saddle of the wild mustang, determined to stay on this time. He'd been thrown twice, and in his mind, that was two times too many.

"Stay on, Fletch." Bram stood on the last rail of the fence, his arms resting over the top slat.

"You've got him, lad." Camden watched from his spot by the gate.

"How's he doing?" Quinn asked, coming to stand next to his younger brother, Bram.

He grinned. "Fourth one so far this morning."

Quinn stared into the corral. "Who lit a fire under the lad?"

Bram didn't answer. The reason was Fletcher's to tell, and he doubted the explanation would come anytime soon.

Fletcher stayed with the mustang as it quieted, not allowing himself to relax as he guided the horse around the corral. Several minutes passed, then a few more before he reined up, sliding to the ground.

"Are you done now, lad?" Camden took the reins, holding the horse while Fletcher removed the saddle.

Quinn clasped a hand on Fletcher's shoulder. "Aunt Lorna sent me to bring you lads inside. She, Aunt Gail, and Emma have food ready."

"I'll be coming in a few minutes." Fletcher carried the saddle and bridle into the barn, needing a few minutes alone. For three weeks, he'd been struggling on what to do about Maddy, trying to make a decision about hiring a private investigator. Each day brought him closer to speaking with Sam again, giving him approval.

Once she'd been found, he'd figure out what to do next. Fletcher no longer doubted how much he cared for Maddy. Having her in his bed wasn't enough. He needed to discover if they could have more, if he could love her, make her a permanent part of his life.

Soon, Fletcher would need to sit down with his da and ma, tell them about Maddy, and pray they'd accept his choice to see her again.

Walking out of the barn, he brushed the dirt and straw from his clothes, took off his hat, and shook his head. Looking up, his brows furrowed at the sight of Bram's brothers, plus Colin and Thane, riding up, their faces grim.

"What's wrong, lads?" Fletcher met them as they slid from their saddles.

"We're missing six horses. They were in the southern corral earlier. Now they're gone."

Fletcher mumbled a curse. "I'll saddle Domino."

Colin shook his head. "Nae. Let's speak with Ewan and Ian first."

Fletcher looked back toward the southern corral. They'd built it less than four hundred yards from the MacLaren ranch houses, close enough they could see it from Ian's porch.

"They're all inside." Fletcher nodded toward Ewan's house.

Thane grabbed the reins of Colin's horse. "You lads go inside and explain. I'll wait here."

He didn't wait long. Within minutes, most of the men hurried from the house, saddled their horses, and rode to the corral. Splitting up, they looked for tracks, regrouping when it became obvious the horses had been herded south toward another spread the MacLarens had purchased when Widow Evanston wanted to move to San Francisco.

Approaching the ranch, Colin raised his hand for them to slow. Motioning for a group to ride to the left, another to the right, he rode straight ahead with a few men. Ten minutes later, they regrouped near the house, which had been the victim of a fire months before.

"They aren't here." Bram barked out a curse, frustration and anger in his voice.

Colin looked around, his jaw tightening. "We know someone opened the gate. Where would they go?"

Fletcher shifted in the saddle, twisting to look in all directions. "They could be anywhere. Rustling six horses is easy. Hell, they could be partway to Sacramento or Nevada by now."

"Lads. You need to see this." Quinn motioned for them to join him on the other side of the burnt down barn. "You'll not be liking what I've found."

Riding toward him, they slowed when he pointed to a mound of dirt and rocks.

"What is it, Quinn?" Colin slid from his horse, handing Thane the reins. Kicking aside the rocks and some of the dirt, he cursed. "Who is it?"

Quinn shook his head, staring at the body as the others formed a circle around the mound of dirt. "We'll be needing to dig the lad out. Maybe one of us will recognize who it is."

It took ten minutes to uncover the body. He lay face down, arms tucked under him, boots still on, and hat a foot away. The gunbelt still hung from his hips. Quinn and Colin turned him over.

"Anyone recognize him?" Bram asked, staring down at the body.

No one answered, all continuing to scan the prone form.

Fletcher leaned down, pushing aside the coat. "Ah hell." When he moved aside, they all saw the badge. Kneeling beside him, Fletcher read the engraving. "U.S. Marshal."

Chapter Five

Conviction

Brodie MacLaren stalked out to the wagon holding the body of a U.S. Marshal and drew back the blanket. Staring at the body, studying the face, he shook his head before glancing at Fletcher and Quinn.

"I've gotten nothing about a marshal missing in this area." He blew out an angry breath. "I'll send a telegram with a description to their headquarters. I'll be needing you to take him to the undertaker when I'm done."

Fletcher stepped next to him, his gaze moving over the body. "We'll be staying as long as you need us, lad. He was covered in dirt and rocks. I'd be thinking he's been dead several days."

Brodie nodded. "I'm thinking the same." He took a longer look before heading to the telegraph office. Stopping, he glanced over his shoulder at his brother. "Fletch, come with me. Quinn, do you mind staying with the wagon?"

Quinn leaned against it. "Nae. You lads go ahead."

The Western Union office stood at the end of the street, just past the law office of Fielder and Donahue. Ira Greene stood behind the counter, his glasses perched on the tip of his nose. Looking up, he set down his pencil.

"Sheriff, Fletch. What can I do for you?"

Brodie stepped to the counter. "I'm needing to send a telegram to the Marshal's office in San Francisco. We found a body. He's wearing the badge of a U.S. Marshal. I'll be waiting for a response."

Ira's mouth opened, then closed before he grabbed his pad. Scribbling down the message, he sat down, punching the keys. "If you want, I can bring the reply to you as soon as it comes in, Sheriff."

Brodie shook his head. "Nae, Ira. This is important. I'll be waiting."

Fletcher stood at the window, both hands shoved in his pockets, looking across the street at the boardinghouse. Not paying much attention to the conversation behind him, he thought of the body and the missing horses, wondering if they might be connected.

His gaze moved to an older man walking out of Baker's, noting the tattered suit and not much more. Then his eyes lit on a slender figure in a blue dress, a simple bonnet tied under her chin. She glanced at the street, her hand raised to help shield the sun. Looking both ways, she crossed, skirting around a wagon and two riders before stepping onto the boardwalk. As she got closer, Fletcher stilled.

"What the..." He started for the door. "I'll be right back, Brodie." Rushing outside, he glanced down the street, his gaze darting from one woman to another, searching for the blue dress. He caught a glimpse near the Merchant Bank. "Maddy!"

If the woman heard, she didn't respond. Fletcher started running, brushing past pedestrians, focusing on the last place he'd seen her. By the time he'd reached the jail, he'd lost sight of her. He began to retrace his steps, looking into every shop he passed, not seeing her.

Taking off his hat, he slapped it against his leg, cursing.

"Fletcher MacLaren. You watch your language."

He winced, recognizing an older woman a few feet away. "Ach, I'm sorry, ma'am. Did you see a woman walk by wearing a bonnet and blue dress?"

Glaring at him, she shook her head. "No, I haven't. And I hope you weren't cursing because of a woman."

"Uh, no, ma'am." The lie rolled easily off his lips. He touched a finger to the brim of his hat. "Have a good day, ma'am."

He waited a minute until she'd moved on, then made a circle, searching up and down the street. *Where did the lass go?* he thought, frustration gripping him. Fletcher *knew* he'd seen Maddy, would bet his life on it, but she'd vanished as quickly as she'd appeared.

Sucking in a breath, his gaze landed on the boardinghouse. She'd come out of Baker's. Heading back to the telegraph office, he shoved open the door. "Brodie, I'm needing to go to Baker's. I'll be coming right back."

"If I'm not here, I'll be at the jail, lad."

Raising a hand in acknowledgment, Fletcher ran across the street, bursting inside. Mrs. Baker stood at one of the dining room tables. Spinning at the sound of the door flying open, Henrietta glared at him, crossing her arms.

"Fletcher MacLaren."

He came to an abrupt halt, taken aback by the disapproving glower on her face. "Good afternoon, Mrs. Baker." Clearing his throat, he took a step closer.

"What do you want?"

Stopping, he blinked, wondering what he'd done to anger the older lady. "I saw a woman walk out of here a few minutes ago. Blue dress and bonnet. The lass walked up the street, but I lost sight of her. I wondered if you might know who she is."

Henrietta's gaze narrowed on him, her mouth set in a thin line. "Yes, I know who you mean."

He swallowed, realizing this wasn't going to be as easy as he first thought. "Would you be knowing her name, Mrs. Baker?"

She took several steps forward, stopping a couple feet away. "I usually keep the names of my boarders private. Why do you want to know, Fletcher?"

Inwardly groaning, he shifted his stance, beginning to feel foolish. "The lass is a friend of mine."

Henrietta tilted her head to the side, her arms crossed over her ample chest. She quirked a brow. "A friend?"

Fletcher felt like squirming under her scrutiny. "Aye."

"All right. What is your *friend's* name?"

"Maddy."

Henrietta knew her as Madeleine Leigh, but the nickname made sense. "Do you have a last name, Fletcher?"

Feeling his frustration grow, he shook his head. "Nae. I never asked the lass." He saw her eyes spark with disapproval at his answer.

Henrietta let out an annoyed snort. "Well, I'll give her your name. If she remembers you, I'll get word to you through Brodie."

Fletcher didn't want to wait. It had already been too long. "Do you know when she'll be coming back?"

"You are *not* going to wait here for her, young man. If she knows who you are, I'll let Brodie know." Henrietta arched a brow when he didn't make any move to leave. "Is there something else, Fletcher?"

A momentary flash of defeat rolled through him. Gritting his teeth, he pushed it away, his determination returning. "Nae, Mrs. Baker. I'll be letting Brodie know you'll be getting a message to him. Thank you." He turned to leave, stopping at her clipped words.

"Only if she agrees to see you."

Swallowing, he nodded. "Yes, ma'am."

Stepping outside, Fletcher settled fisted hands on his hips, looking up and down the street. Glancing at the law offices of August and Bay, he briefly thought of sitting in their parlor to wait for Maddy's return. Glancing behind him, he discarded the idea. As steady as a sentinel, Henrietta Baker's hard gaze narrowed on his, lips twisted, almost daring him to do something to anger her. He couldn't afford to provoke his one connection to Maddy.

Finishing her walk, Maddy drew in a deep breath as she approached the boardinghouse. She loved this time alone, enjoying the activity on the main street and warm breeze wafting across her face before having to change clothes to start her shift at the restaurant.

When she'd left the boardinghouse, Maddy chastised herself for divulging the details of her pregnancy to Mrs. Baker. But once she started, stopping wasn't possible. She'd spoken of it to no one until today, and the fact her landlord listened without interrupting encouraged Maddy to continue. Somehow, recounting the story provided a relief she hadn't expected. When finished, Mrs. Baker considered what she'd heard before saying she could stay at the boardinghouse for another month or two, until her condition became obvious to everyone.

During her walk, a relived grin slid up the corners of Maddy's mouth as she thought of the conversation before the need to stay vigilant sobered her. She didn't need to cross paths with any of the MacLaren men, taking the chance one would recognize her.

Today, luck wasn't with her.

Twice, she'd avoided coming across MacLaren men. Once when Brodie walked down the boardwalk toward the jail, and the other time she passed Quinn as he stood next to a wagon.

At least Fletcher hadn't come to town with them, she thought, continuing her slow pace. An instant later, she glanced across the street and her breath caught. Fletcher walked out of the gunsmith shop, long strides taking him in the opposite direction.

Avoiding him, she turned to stare through the window of the Gold Dust Hotel, groaning when the diners at the table inside startled. Giving them an apologetic shrug, she glanced over her shoulder. Fletcher stood by the wagon, talking with Quinn. Wasting no time, she hurried to the boardinghouse and rushed inside, sucking in gulps of air to calm her racing heart.

Taking a quick glance outside, she turned, startled to see Henrietta behind her.

"Are you all right, Miss Leigh?"

Placing a hand over her chest, she nodded. "Yes, I'm fine, Mrs. Baker. I, um..." She took another shaky breath, straightening. "I'd better get to my room and change for work." Giving Mrs. Baker an embarrassed grin, she started toward the stairs.

"There was a man in here looking for you today."

Maddy stopped, her body going rigid before she shifted back around. "A man?"

Henrietta nodded, motioning for Maddy to follow her to a table. "Sit down and I'll tell you about it."

She took a seat, unable to stop herself from glancing at the window to the street outside. Catching her lower lip between her teeth, Maddy tried to relax.

"He came in not long after you left this morning. He'd seen you leave and thought he recognized you."

"Did he give you his name?"

Henrietta nodded. "It was Fletcher MacLaren, your baby's father."

Maddy shook her head for what had to be the tenth time, unable to focus on the diners in the restaurant. She'd already mixed up two orders, delivering meals to the wrong tables. Embarrassed, she apologized, correcting her mistake, vowing to do a better job the rest of the night.

Learning Fletcher searched for her didn't provide the comfort she'd expected. For so long, she'd hoped, prayed he'd return from Settlers Valley and look for her. It was a ridiculous notion. The morning after Bram delivered Fletcher's message, she'd packed, taking the stagecoach to San Francisco.

It had been the first week of her job at Parker Hill when Maddy suspected she carried Fletcher's baby. Two weeks later, the full impact of the situation settled in, along with the panic filling every day since.

"You have another table, Madeleine." Suzette nodded toward four men. Returning her gaze to Maddy, she studied her face. "Are you all right? You don't look as if you feel well."

She turned away before Suzette's scrutiny moved to her stomach. Having her boss suspect her secret would be devastating. The job would disappear, along with her ability to support the baby.

"I'm fine. A little tired, nothing more."

Lifting a brow, Suzette's skepticism faded. "All right...for now. If you are ill, I need to know."

"Of course."

The curl in Maddy's stomach tightened and didn't fade during the night. Besides Suzette's probing questions, the bloating in her stomach increased. And despite loosening the top two buttons on her skirt, it was miserably uncomfortable, making it hard to draw a breath at times.

By closing, exhaustion rolled off her in waves. Misery dogged her on the trip back to the boardinghouse, knowing she'd have to speak with Suzette soon. Maddy didn't know what she'd do if she lost the job as well as her lodging.

Topping off the wonderful thoughts, she knew Fletcher would be coming back to Baker's. She and Henrietta had agreed to say nothing to Brodie, ignoring Fletcher's visit as if it hadn't happened. Both knew the decision would gain them a small amount of time and nothing more. The MacLarens may be upstanding citizens, but when seeking information or going after what they wanted, they were relentless.

Maddy had no doubt Fletcher wanted to find her. He wouldn't have gone to the trouble of speaking with Henrietta if he didn't. She also believed he'd walk away the instant he learned of the baby. He had no intention of offering more than sharing time in her bed, and would never believe he'd been the only man to cross her threshold since she arrived in Conviction.

Taking the last weary steps into the boardinghouse, she crept up the stairs, not caring to draw attention to herself. Tomorrow, she'd stay inside, rest, and hope Fletcher made no further attempts to find her.

Circle M

"It was Maddy. I'm certain of it." Fletcher paced inside the barn, accomplishing nothing except growing more agitated with each breath. Stopping, he glanced at Bram and Camden, both leaning against stalls, not commenting. "I should ride to Baker's tonight, see if the lass is still there."

"It's after ten, lad. Baker's will be locked, and you don't want to face the old woman's wrath if you wake her. She's a tyrant during the day. No telling what she's like at this hour." Bram bent down, picking up a piece of straw, twisting it between his fingers.

Camden began coiling a length of rope, considering all Fletcher had told them. "Wait a couple days to see if she gets word to Brodie. If not, we'll all be riding to town to find the lass. Did you speak with Frankie at Buckie's?"

Fletcher continued pacing. "Aye. He hasn't seen the lass since the morning she left for San Francisco." He scrubbed a hand down his face. "Ach. I'm tired of going in circles on this. I need to find the lass."

Bram raised a brow. "We've a need to ride to town in two days for supplies. We'll talk to Mrs. Baker again, take turns watching the boardinghouse if she won't speak of Maddy. The lass will have to leave sometime. When she does, one of us will be waiting."

Camden placed the coiled rope over a hook. "It's a good plan, Bram."

Fletcher shook his head. "I don't want to wait so long."

"Be patient, Fletch. You've not seen the lass in months. Waiting two days is nothing if she's the lass you want." Tossing the bent piece of straw aside, Bram straightened. "But you'd best be making sure she's who you want. You'll not be going back on this once you claim her. Have you spoken to Ewan and Lorna, told them of the lass?"

Fletcher pressed his lips together, a vein pulsing in his neck. "Nae."

"Then you've tomorrow to explain of your intentions," Bram said.

"And tell them of the lass's background." Camden walked to him, placing a hand on his shoulder. "It's not something you can keep from them, Fletch."

A rueful grin crossed his face. "I'll be telling them once I find the lass. Maddy and I have things to say, an agreement to reach."

Bram raised a brow. "An agreement, Fletch?"

"Aye."

Camden cocked his head. "Will you be explaining this agreement?"

"Only to Maddy. It's between the lass and me." He refused to voice the doubts he still harbored about Maddy and other men. Frankie had been firm in his comment about Fletcher being the only man she allowed in her bed. Still...

Bram let out a breath. "You'll do what you must, lad. Whatever you decide, I'll be with you on it."

"As will I." Camden grinned. "I'll also be saying this is going to be interesting."

Fletcher's eyes crinkled. "Aye, lads. Perhaps more interesting than I'd expected." *Or wanted,* he thought as they left the barn.

Chapter Six

Martinez

Dob tossed back another glass of whiskey, cursing his luck. They'd spent days in Oakland looking for Maddy without success. He'd been sure she'd be in Martinez, working in a restaurant or maybe a saloon, wherever she could to put food in her stomach. After three days, they'd come up with nothing.

"I say we consider riding to Sacramento. The girl would flee someplace with plentiful work and large enough for her to disappear." Lew Quick sipped his drink, taking it slow in sharp contrast to Dob.

An excellent leader with a talent for picking good men, he had two flaws—alcohol and a short, cruel temper. Lew had seen it enough times to keep his distance when Dob's mood deteriorated beyond recovery. Tonight may be one of those times.

Grabbing the bottle, Dob filled his glass for the fourth time, draining it in one gulp. Wiping an arm across his mouth, he focused red eyes on Lew.

"She has the damnedest luck. Anyone else and we would've already buried her somewhere and been on our way." Picking up the bottle, he poured a full measure. "If the wench didn't know so much..." Dob shook his head, as if trying to clear it.

Lew's mouth twisted in disgust. "But she does. Maddy knew when she ran off it was a death sentence."

"And I'm more than ready to oblige."

"She could be all the way into Utah by now, Colonel." Taking another sip, Lew looked around, seeing no one watching them. "On her way back to the hideout. If she gets there before us..." Lew raised a brow. "What would stop her from cleaning us out?"

Dob blew out a strong string of curses. "Her life would be worthless if she stole from us."

Lew let out a mirthless chuckle. "It's worthless now, and she knows it. She may believe there's nothing to lose. What worries me is her stealing our money before she talks to the law. We won't be safe anywhere."

Shaking his head, Dob's jaw hardened. "She's not heading back to Kansas. Maddy's still around here somewhere."

"How do you know?"

Dob shot him a shrewd glance. "The girl's out of money, no horse, nothing. She'd never be able to make the trip to Kansas before starving." Snorting, he poured another glass of whiskey, his movements slowing. "We'll ride to Sacramento tomorrow. If she's not there, we head to Conviction. There was something about how the bartender spoke of her."

Lew's brows furrowed. "Frankie, right?"

"Yeah. Makes me think they're friends. I'm certain he'd protect Maddy if she returned."

Emptying his glass, Lew pushed the bottle out of Dob's reach, motioning to the bartender to take it away. "Are you ready to ride out?"

Scrubbing a hand down his face, Dob stepped away from the bar. "Let's go. We need to take care of that girl and get on to more important business."

Conviction

"Where are you headed in such a hurry?" Bram grabbed two coiled ropes, tossing one to Camden. They'd finished supper, making a decision to stay at the ranch. A rare occurrence on a Saturday night.

Fletcher didn't look at either one of them as he swung into Domino's saddle. "It's been two days." He didn't say more, knowing those words explained everything.

"Wait a few minutes for Camden and me to get our horses. We'll be riding in with you." Bram settled the two lengths of rope back on hooks.

Fletcher scowled at his cousins. "I'll not be waiting long for you."

Shrugging, Camden moved to the back door of the barn, whistling for Duke. Bram did the same for Bullet. Five minutes later, both horses were saddled, their riders settled on top.

"You miscreants ready now?" Fletcher didn't wait for them to answer before kicking Domino enough to leave them behind. Heading toward town, he ignored their laughter and gibes as they caught up with him.

"What do you plan to do once we reach town, lad?"

"I'm riding straight to the boardinghouse. Mrs. Baker will be there, and I'll be finding a way to get her to tell me about Maddy."

Bram chuckled. "Then you'll be needing our support. That woman could kill a bear with one look."

"All I'm looking for is information, lad. Don't be doing anything to anger her."

A broad grin spread across Bram's face as he pushed his hat off his forehead. "I'd never be thinking of making her mad, Fletch."

By the look in his eyes, Fletcher didn't believe it. "I mean it, Bram. You, too, Cam. I'm needing information on Maddy, and she'll not give it to me if you two make her spitting mad."

The three fell into a comfortable silence. No one spoke, even as they rode down the street, passing the jail, mercantile, and Gold Dust, before reining up at Baker's.

Sliding to the ground, Fletcher tossed the reins over the rail, not sparing his cousins a glance as he stepped onto the boardwalk and opened the door. As expected, the dining room sat empty, supper being over for at least an hour.

"Mrs. Baker?"

"Coming."

An instant later, Henrietta walked out from the kitchen, her features hardening when she spotted him. "Fletcher. What can I do for you?"

He took a couple steps toward her. "I'm here to speak with Maddy. Now, you can tell me where she is, or I'll sit outside until she shows up. Doesn't matter if it's an hour or a few days." Crossing his arms, Fletcher's unyielding gaze met hers. "It's your decision."

Features pinched, she huffed out a breath, indecision crossing her face.

"Take your time, Mrs. Baker. I'll sit down over there." He moved toward a chair near the door. That was the first time he realized Bram and Camden stood a couple feet behind him.

"Wait." Henrietta pursed her lips, sucking in a deep breath. "You don't deserve that girl, Fletcher."

His brows furrowed. "Aye, probably not."

"She's been through a lot and there's more to come. If you're here to make her life worse, you're wasting your time. I'll not let you hurt her any further."

His bravado floundered. "Hurt her?"

"Yes." Henrietta lifted her chin. "Is that why you're here? To make things harder for her?"

Confusion flashed through him. "Nae. I'd never want to hurt the lass."

Cold eyes studied him, narrowing the slightest bit as she came to a decision. "Maddy's working right now and you aren't going to bother her. She needs the job, and—"

Fletcher held up a hand. "Where?"

"I won't tell you that. I'm serious when I say she needs the job. It's not a place you walk into and cause a scene."

His brows drew together on a grimace. "What kind of place is it?"

"As I already said, I'll not tell you where she's working. You're welcome to wait, but Maddy's going to be real tired by the time she gets back. If you want a civil conversation, it would be best for you to come back in the morning."

Fletcher raised a brow. "So you have time to warn the lass?"

"I won't lie to you. I'm going to tell her you were here tonight and will be back to speak with her in the morning. I'll also encourage her to meet with you. Maddy has a mind of her own, so I can't guarantee she'll be here."

Rubbing the back of his neck, Fletcher thought of Henrietta's suggestion. He preferred waiting until she returned that evening, but he also didn't want to spook her or have their conversation when she was exhausted.

"I'll be coming back tomorrow morning, Mrs. Baker. Please let Maddy know it's important."

She wagged a finger at him. "You just make certain you're here, Fletcher MacLaren."

"You don't have to worry." He touched the brim of his hat. "Thank you, Mrs. Baker."

"I need to speak with you before you leave tonight, Madeleine." Suzette's tone and stern gaze didn't brook any argument. "Let me know when you're finished."

Maddy felt the blood drain from her face, stomach tightening. "All right. It shouldn't be much longer." Returning to the dining room, she strained to think of what Suzette might want to say, every possibility scaring her. The restaurant wasn't busy enough and Suzette needed to cut staff. She wasn't doing a good enough job. Customers had complained about her.

Not one explanation made her feel any better.

Finishing her work, Maddy let out a resigned breath. She couldn't put off the discussion with Suzette any longer.

"I'm finished."

A small smile tipped the corners of Suzette's lips. "Wonderful. Let's go over there." She headed toward a table, sliding onto a seat, motioning for Maddy to join her. "How are you feeling tonight?"

The question surprised her. "A little tired as always, but otherwise fine."

Suzette studied her, tilting her head to the side as she considered her next words. She'd been planning this discussion for several evenings, but the opportunity hadn't presented itself until tonight. She could see Maddy's lower lip tremble, the way the young woman clasped her hands in her lap. Best to get this over with and let her get back to the boardinghouse. Resting her hands on the table, Suzette's features softened.

"How far along are you, Madeleine?"

A shocked gasp passed through Maddy's lips before she could stop it. Feeling heat creep up her face, she began to tremble.

"Madeleine, there's no need to be afraid to tell me. I promise, no matter what you're thinking, we'll work something out. Right now, I need you to answer some questions, and I expect complete honesty."

Swallowing, Maddy felt herself nod.

Suzette's voice softened. "All right. Let's start once more. It's obvious, at least to me, you're pregnant. How far along are you?"

"A little over five months."

Suzette gave a slow nod. "You aren't married, are you?"

The question stung. Misery coursed through her. "No, ma'am. The father doesn't know there's a baby."

"I see." But Suzette didn't understand. "Why haven't you told him?"

Shoulders slumping, her eyes misted. Frequent tears and rapid mood changes came more often. Until tonight, she'd been able to hide them from most people.

"He wouldn't want the baby. And I'm certain his family wouldn't want me as a part of their lives."

A brow lifting, Suzette's gaze narrowed. "Why wouldn't they want you or the baby? You're a wonderful young woman, Madeleine. I'd think they would be proud to accept you."

A bitter laugh escaped, her gaze focusing on anything other than the woman next to her. "There are things you don't know about me. If he and his family found out, well..."

Suzette placed a hand on Maddy's arm. "You can't know that, Madeleine. Maybe you're right, but you might be wrong."

Shaking her head, Maddy lowered her gaze to stare at her lap where her hands were still clasped together. "Right now, it's not as important as other decisions I need to make."

"What decisions would those be?"

Biting her lower lip, Maddy blew out a slow breath. "Where to live. When Mrs. Baker discovered my condition, she gave me two weeks to find another place. I have two more days and haven't found a place I can afford."

Suzette gave a curt nod. "All right. That's one problem. What else?"

Maddy snorted. "Clothes. I've let mine out as much as possible and don't have enough money to buy new ones *and* find a place to live." She glanced up, worry etched on her face. "It's all so much more difficult than I expected."

Suzette gave a humorless chuckle. "Well, perhaps there is something I can offer."

"Offer?"

"You may not know, but I have a three bedroom home on the street behind us. The rooms aren't large, but they're comfortable and I only use one of them. I'd be happy to allow you to live with me until you find other accommodations."

Maddy's jaw opened, a slight sound of surprise escaping. "You'd do that for me?"

Shrugging, Suzette gave an abrupt nod. "It's something I'm able to offer. You'd buy your own food, but I wouldn't expect you to pay for the lodging. That way, you might be able to save enough for clothes and whatever else you need for the baby."

"But why?" She whispered the words, still not believing the offer.

Letting out a tired breath, Suzette stared down at Maddy's stomach. "Let's just say I have an idea how you feel. I wish someone would've helped me back then, but there was no one." Her voice cracked on the last. She gave a quick shake of her head, shoving away the memory. "I don't want you going through what I did. So, what do you think, Maddy?"

"What about my job?"

"There are tricks we can do with clothing so no one will notice, at least for a while. At some point, you won't be able to hide the pregnancy, no matter what we do. For now, you can stay, work as many hours as you want, and I'll help deflect any questions. Have you seen Doc Vickery or Doc Tilden?"

Maddy shook her head. "I saw a doctor in San Francisco before coming back here, but not since."

Suzette's brows drew together. "Back here? I didn't know you had ever been in Conviction before now."

Wincing at the slip, Maddy began to rock back and forth in the chair. "I lived here a few months before leaving for San Francisco."

"So the father lives here? I'll know if you lie to me, Madeleine."

Letting out a breath, she nodded. "Yes. The father lives near Conviction."

Suzette caught the difference in meaning between living in Conviction versus near the town, but she'd keep it to herself for now. Whoever it was, he was most likely a rancher. Her mind automatically moved to the most prominent family in the area. Again, she'd keep the thought to herself.

Setting both hands on the table, Suzette pushed up. "Why don't we move your belongings to my house tomorrow? You don't work until late afternoon, and I'll have time to help."

Maddy's eyes brightened for the first time since their talk began. "That would be, well...wonderful." She stood, a tentative smile forming.

"If you don't have much, I'll drive my buggy to the boardinghouse."

"Only clothes."

"Excellent. Will eleven be all right?"

Still not believing her good fortune, Maddy nodded. "Yes."

"Well, I'm exhausted. I'll see you in the morning, Madeleine." Suzette walked away, stopping at Maddy's words.

"Thank you, Suzette. I, well...I'll owe you a great deal."

Turning, Suzette shook her head. "You'll owe me nothing. I feel privileged being able to help you. Plus, I do hope to convince you to give the father a chance. You never know what will happen unless you take a risk."

Biting her lower lip, Maddy nodded. She couldn't think of Fletcher right now. Instead, she allowed herself a few minutes of mental celebration at finding a place to live and keeping her job. Two things she thought beyond her reach.

Chapter Seven

Circle M

"Saddle your horse, Fletch. We're missing over thirty head from the north pasture." Colin hurried into the barn, grabbing his saddle and tack. "The uncles are wanting all of us searching. With the murder of that U.S. Marshal, we have to be ready for anything."

Camden followed Colin into the barn, not missing the dour expression on Fletcher's face. "Sorry, lad." Camden clasped his cousin on the shoulder. "You'll have to be riding out later today or tomorrow to see the lass."

Shaking off the disappointment, Fletcher cinched Domino's saddle, swinging on top of the gelding. "This is important. We can't be letting men get away with stealing our cattle. I'll have time to talk with Maddy after we find them." Reining his horse around, he rode out of the barn, a combination of irritation and anger motivating him.

Bram swung into the saddle, catching up with him. "Brodie told Colin another U.S. Marshal is missing and presumed dead. That makes two killed out of the San Francisco division. Both were hunting a gang of rustlers who escaped before trial. I'm hoping we won't be finding another body today."

Fletcher tightened his grip on the reins. "Aye. We've no use for murderers. Rustlers are bad enough, but killing a man..." A muscle in his jaw twitched.

"Lads!" Camden galloped toward them, waving. "Uncle Ewan wants the three of us to head northeast toward the river. Colin and Quinn are leading a group of lads northwest. The uncles are riding due west toward the gully."

Fletcher's brow rose. "Just Da and Uncle Ian?"

Camden nodded. "Aye."

"They should have more lads with them. If they're ambushed..." Fletcher didn't finish, reining Domino around to hunt down his da and uncle.

"Fletch, wait up." Bram rode toward him, followed by Camden. "They've made their decision about who rides where. You'll be slowing up the search by riding after them."

"He's right, lad." Camden scanned the horizon, seeing no sign of his uncles. "Your da and Ian can take care of themselves."

Forcing away a grimace, Fletcher followed his gaze. He knew the two were right, but he'd never forgotten how their fathers, Angus and Gillis, had been murdered while away from the ranch. No one had been there to help them, and the two oldest MacLarens were now gone. But his father wasn't, and Fletcher felt the need to protect him and his uncle.

"They'll be fine, Fletch. You need to trust them." Bram knew what bothered Fletcher. It was a fear his cousin would have to work through on his own.

Scrubbing a hand down his face, he forced his attention away from the direction his da and uncle rode. "Aye, you're right, Bram. We'd best go. If we've any luck, we'll be finding the cattle in time for me to ride to Conviction tonight."

Fletcher thought of Maddy, knowing Mrs. Baker would've told her of his visit the night before. He wanted to ride to her, meet her as he'd promised he would. He needed to explain the note Bram delivered to her, try to get Maddy to understand his doubts. Fletcher didn't know if he loved her, but he did know he cared a great deal. He hoped that would be enough.

His first obligation would always be to his family, and right now, they needed him more than Maddy.

Conviction

Eyes wide, mouth slack, Maddy walked through Suzette's house, still not believing her boss's generosity. She'd expected a small house with three bedrooms. Well, there were three bedrooms, but the house was large and elegant with beautiful furniture.

Each bedroom had been decorated in a different color. She'd been given the one in various shades of yellow, one of her favorite colors. To say it took her breath away would've been a vast understatement. It was the most stunning bedroom she'd ever seen.

"Will it be all right, Madeleine?" Suzette stood behind her, looking past Maddy into the room.

"Oh, it's more than all right. It's wonderful." She carried her old, battered satchel into the room, setting it on the bed. It had served her well since racing out of Kansas and away from the horror of the men who'd held her a virtual prisoner since her father died. The rest of what she owned had been stuffed into a sack Mrs. Baker provided. Maddy would grab it from the buggy once her heart began to settle from the elegance around her.

"You said the rooms were small."

An apologetic smile slipped the corners of Suzette's mouth upward. "The last house we..." She cleared her throat. "The last house I lived in was much larger."

"Well, this is the grandest bedroom I've ever seen. It must be four times the size of any I've slept in." She ran a hand along the coverlet on the bed.

Suzette stepped next to her. "I do know how you feel. My life didn't start out like this." She swept a hand around the room. "It's taken many years and even more setbacks to achieve the small amount of success I have now."

She wouldn't tell Maddy the house came as part of her wages for managing the hotel and restaurant. The confidential agreement had been arranged by August Fielder, with the approval of the MacLarens, after she'd already accepted an impressive sum for her services.

Suzette still didn't have the entire story of how August had found her and decided she'd be the perfect person to run the new business. Someday, she'd ask. For now, Suzette intended to do everything possible to make the hotel and restaurant an unqualified success.

"I'll give you a chance to get organized and rest before preparing for your shift at the restaurant. Please let me know if there's anything you need." Slipping into the hallway, Suzette closed the door behind her.

Maddy turned in a circle, taking in the wardrobe, dresser, settee, desk, and chair upholstered in a beautiful, flowered brocade. Walking to it, she sat down, pulling it up to the desk. She imagined herself penning a letter to her father, telling him of her adventures the last year, leaving out her current condition.

"My current condition," Maddy whispered to herself, sadness washing through her. She'd felt a combination of relief and disappointment when Fletcher didn't arrive as he'd promised Henrietta. Perhaps the woman had misunderstood, although Maddy doubted it. She remembered everything, retrieving bits and pieces from her memory whenever most advantageous to Henrietta.

Maddy's first reaction when learning Fletcher had returned to the boardinghouse was dread, followed by terror. She recalled settling both hands on her stomach, rubbing the growing fullness, scared for the baby and how Fletcher would take the news.

Twisting and turning all night, Maddy wrestled with what to tell the man she loved only a little less than the life growing inside her. Some nights, the urge to seek him out, run into his arms, overwhelmed her. So far, she'd been able to squelch the ridiculous notion.

Maddy couldn't decide if the best approach would be to tell Fletcher the truth or lie, assure him the baby wasn't his. She'd always hated lies and those who told them. After a lifetime of being honest, she found it unsettling to lie about something as important as the parentage of a child. *Their* child.

Sitting in the beautiful bedroom, Maddy let out a resigned breath. Fletcher hadn't shown this morning, and perhaps never would. Maybe his family had sent him back to Settlers Valley. Or, once he confirmed her residence at the boardinghouse, he'd decided seeing her again held no appeal. The latter made the most sense.

Regardless, Mrs. Baker had promised not to divulge Maddy's new residence to anyone, including Fletcher. With Suzette's house located well off the main street, there was every likelihood they might never see each other again, never have the conversation Maddy knew he deserved but she didn't want to voice.

The thought of his response to her situation caused a sharp pain in the area of her heart. She knew he'd question the baby's parentage, wonder how a saloon girl could be certain of the father. As far as he knew, she entertained other men. Maddy had never done anything to make him think otherwise, which she now regretted.

He'd been the only man to share her bed, and she relied on Frankie to keep her secret from everyone, including Fletcher.

She shuddered at the thought of one other man, the person who'd dishonored her, ruining Maddy for a decent marriage. After all this time, there were still days she couldn't get the vile smell, the disgusting touch of him out of her mind.

Fletcher's gentle ministrations and soothing words had helped diminish the bad memories, and he'd never even realized it. He'd come to her bed believing her nothing more than a saloon girl, offering favors to those who paid. Although she'd never lied, Maddy hadn't told him the truth, either. She wasn't what he thought, and now the results of her silence were hers to carry.

Standing, she forced herself to shove aside the thoughts haunting her and focus on the new life Suzette offered.

Circle M

"How long do you think the body's been here?" Fletcher stared at the tattered remains of another U.S. Marshal, shocked they'd found two bodies in such a short time. Pulling the bandana over his nose, he kneeled, checking the man's pockets, finding nothing except the badge still pinned to his shirt.

Camden knelt beside him, his bandana also covering his nose. "Brodie said nothing to me of another lawman being out in this area. I'd rather we found the cattle than this."

Tossing a blanket on the ground, Bram frowned. "Aye. It may be the lads rode together, then split up. Still, it's not explaining why no one told Brodie of another missing marshal."

Camden and Fletcher each took a side of the blanket, spreading it out next to the body. The three worked in silence, rolling the body inside before securing it over the saddle of Bram's horse. Fletcher and Camden mounted their horses, Fletcher reaching out a hand for Bram to swing up behind him.

Camden led the way home, holding the reins of Bram's horse, glancing back at the others. "We'll need to be riding into town with the body."

"Aye. It should be done tonight." Anxious to speak with Maddy, Fletcher had planned to ride to Conviction anyway.

"We'll be riding in with you, lad," Bram said from behind him. "Unless Ewan or Ian order otherwise."

Camden looked over his shoulder. "They'll be wanting to get the body to town, lad. I don't think they'll be asking us to stay at the ranch."

Approaching the ranch, the lack of activity caught their attention. Fletcher let out a breath, wishing they weren't the first to arrive. "It appears the other lads haven't returned."

Camden led them to a corral at the far end of the compound, wanting to keep the body away from as many of the family as possible. "We'll need to be leaving the body outside somewhere."

Fletcher pointed to an area behind a stack of firewood. "Over there. We'll need a tarpaulin. I don't want the young bairns to get curious and investigate."

"I'll get the tarpaulin." Bram slid off Bullet, heading for the closest of four barns. Emerging, he caught sight of a group of riders coming from the north. Ewan and Ian led the group, Colin, Quinn, and the others following behind. Waving, he waited until they reined next to him.

Ewan nodded toward Fletcher and Camden. "What did you find?"

"Another body. A U.S. Marshal."

Ewan, along with several others, cursed. "You'll need to be taking him to town tonight."

Bram began walking toward the body. "Cam, Fletch, and I'll be taking him to Brodie. He'll want to know right away. Did you find the cattle?"

Ewan's lips curled, a scowl marring his normally calm features. "Nae. Colin and Quinn found tracks, following them until they disappeared when the rustlers took them across the river. We've had horses and cattle stolen. We cannot lose any more."

Colin and Quinn reined next to Ewan, following Bram to where Fletcher and Camden laid the body.

"Thane is getting the wagon ready," Colin said, his voice sharp with anger. "That makes three lawmen dead. Two on our land. The other several miles south of here."

Quinn's mouth twisted in disgust. "Three lads we know of. There could be more. Who knows how many they sent out to find the escaped outlaws."

Ewan sent a hard glare at Colin and Quinn. "You lads need to remember they could still be around here. You'll not be going out with less than three in a group."

Rubbing the stubble on his chin, Colin watched as Thane stopped the wagon next to the body. "Aye, Uncle Ewan. I'll be having the lads bring the cattle closer until we know what's happening. We've a smaller herd since driving so many to Sacramento."

Quinn's attention focused on his brother, Bram. "We'll be needing all the lads here, watching the herd. And I want Thane with us. The younger ones, Kenzie, Clint, Banner, Chrissy, and Alana, can keep watch on the horses so Bram, Fletcher, and Camden can be with the cattle."

Colin pressed his lips together, frowning. "With those three gone, we'll be putting off the horse breaking for a time."

Quinn shrugged. "Aye, but it can't be helped. We've got rustlers stealing our cattle and horses and killing lawmen on our property. Brodie doesn't have enough deputies to help. It's up to us. I'll talk to the lads and let them know to ride right back after they deliver the body to town. We can't have them going out and drinking tonight. They need to get back before dark."

The others knew what he meant. With the rustlers still close by, anyone riding after dark put themselves in danger. Men who'd kill a lawman wouldn't hesitate to kill anyone else.

Conviction

Fletcher's jaw clenched, his shoulders tight as the three rode to town. Quinn's orders had been clear. They were to deliver the body to Brodie, explain what was happening at the ranch, and ride back before the sun set. He knew the instructions were meant to keep them safe. Still, he didn't like it. The order meant there'd be no time to visit the boardinghouse and speak to Maddy.

He thought of writing her a note, asking Brodie to deliver it to Mrs. Baker. The idea was discarded right away. Brodie would have questions, and Fletcher had no intention of explaining himself to his older brother.

Bram stopped the wagon in front of the jail, the scene eerily similar to when they'd brought the first body to town. Camden dismounted and looked around before going inside. A moment later, Brodie and Sam walked out, their faces grim.

Pulling back the tarpaulin, Brodie grimaced. "Where'd you find him?"

Fletcher described the location, the stolen cattle, reminding Brodie they'd never found the missing horses. "We can't be letting them steal more animals or kill anyone else."

The cords in Brodie's neck tightened. "Aye. I don't have enough deputies to help, but I might be able to ride out."

Fletcher shook his head. "Nae. You're needed here. I'm just telling you none of the family will be riding to town until we've taken care of the danger."

Another pang of disappointment flashed through him. He'd have to find a way to get to town and speak with Maddy, even if it went against Quinn's instructions. The family hierarchy was clear. Orders from Colin or Quinn were to be taken as if they came directly from Ewan or Ian. Going against them would mean bringing their wrath down on Fletcher, but especially his father, Ewan.

It wasn't that he didn't care about his family and their concern for each member. He did, but he needed to see Maddy, explain his reasons for leaving and asking Bram to deliver his message. Plus, he needed to learn why she'd returned from San Francisco. Fletcher couldn't deny he hoped a large part of her decision had to do with him. Knowing she lived at Baker's brought an urgency he hadn't felt when considering hiring a private investigator.

Fletcher stared down the street, his gaze landing on the boardinghouse, a strange excitement claiming him. Maddy lived less than a hundred feet away. Soon, she'd be within his grasp, and it couldn't come too soon.

Chapter Eight

Circle M

A week had passed since they'd taken the second body to town and he'd missed his chance to see Maddy. Fletcher couldn't wait any longer.

There'd been no more missing cattle, no more stolen horses. Fletcher, Bram, and Camden took turns staying behind to break and train horses while the others guarded the herd. Soon, they hoped to return to their normal routine.

They had a buyer in Sacramento with an open order for fifteen horses. The loss of six set them back a couple weeks. The inability to continue breaking and training set them back even more. Now they had a chance to catch up and Fletcher saw an opportunity to see Maddy. He wouldn't waste it staying another night at the ranch.

"If you're determined to do this, we'll be riding with you, lad." Bram grabbed a bridle.

"Nae. I'll be going alone. It's been quiet, but it doesn't mean the rustlers have left the area. I'll not be shorting the family three men."

Camden crossed his arms. "Your da is going to be furious when he learns you've ridden to town, Fletch."

Tightening Domino's cinch, he grabbed the reins. "Aye, and that's another reason you lads are staying here. I'll not be having you in trouble because of me."

An amused smile tilted one corner of Bram's mouth. "Do you know what you'll be saying to the lass when you see her?"

Swinging into the saddle, Fletcher shook his head. "Not yet. I'll be thinking on it the entire ride to town, though."

Face sobering, Bram walked toward him. "You be careful, lad. We'll not be wanting to hear any bad news."

Camden stepped next to Bram. "Are you sure you're wanting to go alone, Fletch? I'm not feeling good about us staying behind."

"I'm sure, lad." He reined Domino around, riding out the back door of the barn, through the corral, and toward the trail so no one would spot him.

"We'll be making some excuse so no one comes looking for you," Bram called out.

Fletcher raised a hand in acknowledgment, not looking back.

Conviction

Her body sagged in exhaustion. More than normal at this time of night. Maddy had been working a mere two hours of the full six, wanting nothing more than a long nap.

During the last week, her stomach seemed to double in size, her skirt becoming too tight. Suzette had given her a larger size six days earlier, but Maddy already needed a bigger one. Same with the white blouse. Soon, there'd be no way to hide her condition. When that happened, Suzette might no longer be able to keep Maddy at the restaurant, and cleaning rooms would be difficult.

If she weren't so underweight when she got pregnant, she may have been able to conceal it longer. The fact she hadn't been able to gain weight for almost six months didn't help.

"I'm seating August and Bay at their usual table." Suzette nodded to the back corner, knowing it meant Maddy would be serving them.

Dread sliced through her at serving two of the owners of the Feather River Hotel and Restaurant. Men who, if they paid close attention, would figure out her situation and direct Suzette to end her employment. Lifting her chin, she walked to their table.

"Good evening, gentlemen. Will you be having wine tonight?"

August grinned. "Good evening, Madeleine. You look lovely tonight."

His compliment surprised her, giving her a renewed sense of confidence. "Thank you, Mr. Fielder." She shot a quick glance at Bay, noticing his attention on Suzette, who stood across the room, talking to a table of men.

"I'll have a whiskey tonight." August lifted the menu, scanning tonight's offerings.

"Mr. Donahue?"

Pulling his gaze away from Suzette, Bay didn't smile. "Whiskey. A double."

"I'll leave you to read the menu while I get your drinks."

Walking away, she let out a shaky breath. Even though August made a nice comment about her appearance, neither man really looked at her. If they had, she doubted either could miss the growing swell of her stomach.

Pouring their drinks, Maddy scanned the other tables, seeing no need to walk by them before delivering the whiskeys to August and Bay. That was when she saw it again—Bay's gaze locked on Suzette, a look she couldn't quite define on his face. Loss or hurt perhaps, but she couldn't be certain.

"I'll take these to them, Madeleine."

Maddy's eyes widened at Suzette. "Are you sure? I have time before I need to check with my other tables."

She held out her hands. "I'm certain."

Holding out the glasses, Maddy watched as her boss made her way to the corner table, noticing Suzette's back straighten with each step. Believing a history existed between Bay and her, Maddy's respect for her boss rose.

One day, she'd find the courage to ask Suzette about it.

Tossing Domino's reins over the rail, Fletcher did his best to brush trail dust off his clothes. Removing his hat, he pushed open the door of Baker's, hesitating an instant when Henrietta's dark gaze landed on him. Clearing his throat, Fletcher continued forward.

"Good evening, Mrs. Baker."

Lifting a brow, she leaned a hand on the counter, the other fisted on her waist. "Fletcher."

Fingering the brim of his hat, he sucked in a breath. "Is Maddy here?"

"No."

"Working tonight?"

Henrietta smirked, seeming to enjoy Fletcher's discomfort. "I wouldn't know. She doesn't live here anymore." At the look of shock on his face, she chuckled.

"Where'd the lass go?"

Pushing away from the counter, she smirked. "Sorry, but you had your chance."

Blowing out a frustrated breath, Fletcher took a step closer. "Rustlers stole some cattle. I was needed at the ranch and couldn't leave until now."

"Yes, I heard about the problems you're having, including the two bodies found at your place, and I'm sorry about it. Still, I'm not letting you know where that girl is. She has enough going on and doesn't need a *friend* who I suspect isn't one."

Furrowing his brows, he cocked his head. "Isn't one what?"

"I'm not certain you're a real friend to her, Fletcher. She's a wonderful girl with a good heart. Something tells me you may have something to do with the sadness she carries with her."

Shifting his feet in discomfort, he began rolling the brim of his hat in his hands. "That's why I need to be seeing her, Mrs. Baker. Can you at least be telling me if the lass is still in town?"

Letting out an uncertain breath, she crossed her arms. "She is, but that's all I'm going to say."

Realizing he wouldn't get any more out of the dour widow, he thanked Henrietta and left. Stepping outside, Fletcher looked up and down the boardwalk, his gaze moving to the other side of the street. The thick cloud cover created a darkness that didn't help his search.

At least he knew Maddy hadn't left Conviction, which also meant she still had a job somewhere in town. A voice inside him insisted he wouldn't find her at one of the saloons. Those women didn't rent rooms at a boardinghouse, saving money by living where they worked.

Removing his hat, Fletcher scratched his head, his mind sorting through the possibilities. He'd already decided she didn't work days, which meant he wouldn't find her at the mercantile or similar business. She knew how to serve drinks, make people comfortable with her quick smile and easy laugh. Maybe she had a job at one of the growing number of restaurants. He had no idea where to start, but he couldn't stand there any longer doing nothing.

Settling the hat back on his head, he grabbed Domino's reins, swinging into the saddle in one smooth motion. Riding down the street, he stopped in front of the Gold Dust. Leaning down, he peered through the window, watching for a few minutes before satisfying himself Maddy wasn't inside.

Moving on, he passed two more restaurants, doing the same as he'd done outside the Gold Dust. Reaching the end of the street, he shot a quick look at Brodie's house, knowing his brother and his wife, Maggie, were inside with their young son, Shaun. For a shocked moment, Fletcher felt a pang of jealousy. Not because of Brodie's happiness. In amazement, he realized he wanted what his brother had—a wife, children, his own family.

Knowing he'd find a few more restaurants on the next street, he continued, believing the search to be a complete waste of time. Still, he couldn't bring himself to ride home. Fletcher simply couldn't give up—not yet.

Maddy leaned against the wall dividing the dining room from the kitchen, her body aching and weary. It had been busier than expected for the middle of the week. A good kind of busy, as it kept her mind on work and not Fletcher.

Ever since Mrs. Baker told her of his visit, Maddy couldn't get him out of her thoughts. Of course, she'd never been able to rid him from her mind. Not when she carried his baby. Not when she'd always love him.

"You look exhausted. The place is almost empty. You should go on home." Suzette stood next to Maddy, looking as fresh as she did when leaving the house before noon.

"You don't look tired at all. What is your secret?"

Suzette chuckled. "I've been doing this a long time. After a while, you get used to it. I'm as tired as you, Madeleine."

Brows furrowing, she took a careful look at her boss, for the first time seeing the dark circles under her eyes, the pronounced lines on her face. Maddy wondered how she hadn't noticed them before.

"I can help until you're ready to leave."

"Not necessary. I'll be here quite a bit longer. You go on, Madeleine."

Twisting her mouth into a grimace, she nodded. "All right. I'll see you tomorrow."

It didn't take long for Maddy to gather her belongings. Stepping out the back door, she drew the shawl around her. Even in late summer, nights could be cool, sending a chill through her.

She could see Suzette's house from the back stoop of the restaurant. Sam and Jinny, Fletcher's sister, lived in the house next door, August's house to their right, and Bay's home at the end of the block. Maddy couldn't remember a time she lived in what some would consider a respectable neighborhood. Resting a hand on her stomach, she rubbed slow circles, a small smile tilting one corner of her mouth. Her life was far from perfect, but as close as it'd been in a long time.

Taking the three steps to the street, her head whipped to the right at the sound of a horse's whinny. A hand flew to her throat, breath hitching. The silhouette of the cowboy atop the horse looked exactly like Fletcher. And he was staring straight at her.

Fletcher's mouth went dry. A hundred yards away, a woman stood outside the hotel and restaurant, a shawl drawn around her shoulders. He watched her head swivel toward him, a hand fly to her throat. If the clouds hadn't parted, allowing a sliver of moonlight to illuminate the street, he might not have seen her.

He hadn't been certain when he'd first seen her profile. When she turned toward him, Fletcher knew with certainty who stared at him.

Maddy.

Raising a hand, it stalled midair when she turned and hurried away. Surprised, he didn't move for several seconds, frozen in place, watching her disappear between two houses. He knew one belonged to his sister, Jinny, and her husband, Sam. August lived on this side, but Fletcher didn't know who lived in the house on the other side.

Gently kicking Domino, he followed her, determined not to let her get away. Reining up next to Jinny's place, he looked down the open space between the two houses, certain of the path Maddy had taken.

Fletcher had no doubt she recognized him, the knowledge bringing a wave of frustration. He didn't know why she fled, almost as if she feared him. Not once had he ever threatened her, raised a hand in anger. He'd never hurt a woman—not ever.

Their many nights together had consisted of frequent rounds of lovemaking, talking, and lighthearted teasing. From the start, they'd been comfortable, as if they'd been intimate for years. Then he'd left, losing so much more than he imagined.

The sound of a door slamming brought his attention to the back of the house next to Jinny's. He expected to see the soft glow of a lantern inside. After a few minutes, seeing nothing, he reined Domino to the other side of the house. Still nothing.

Sliding to the ground, he tossed the reins over a rail. Fletcher's gut told him Maddy had disappeared inside this house. He walked up the steps, his nerve faltering when he stopped at the front door. Inhaling a deep breath, he lifted a hand and knocked.

Chapter Nine

Maddy stood in the parlor, arms wrapped around her waist. The knock reverberated through the quiet space, the sound causing her to shudder. Or perhaps it was the man on the other side of the door who made her body tremble and heart pound.

She knew Fletcher stood on the other side, could almost see the anger and confusion on his face. When the pounding stopped, Maddy thought he'd left. To her surprise, she didn't feel the anticipated relief. After a few more moments, he knocked again, louder this time.

Resigned to the inevitable, she forced herself forward, taking slow steps to the door. A knot formed in her stomach. Looking down, Maddy once again pulled the shawl around her, doing what she could to hide the obvious. Stretching out her hand, she gripped the doorknob, took a deep breath, and pulled the door open.

For several long moments, they stared at each other, neither saying a word. She trembled at the way his hard gaze moved over her, slowing briefly on her stomach before raising to her face. To her surprise, his expression didn't change, even if his gray eyes darkened to a color she hadn't seen before. The continued silence did nothing to calm the growing knot in her stomach. She just wanted him to say something...anything. Licking her lips, the corners of her mouth slid into a shaky smile.

"Hello, Fletcher." She winced, feeling her face pale at the tremor in her voice.

He didn't answer. Instead, he took a step forward, sliding his hand behind her neck, lowering his head to kiss her.

At first, she didn't respond, surprised at the action. The feel of his warm lips broke through her resistance. Maddy lifted her hands, resting them on his shoulders as he deepened the kiss. She didn't know how much time passed before he raised his mouth from hers.

"Hello, Maddy." He touched her lips with his once more before dropping his hold. "May I come inside?"

The haze lifted enough for her to take a quick glimpse behind him, realizing if anyone was on the street, they'd see them. She stepped aside.

"Of course."

Closing the door after he entered, she clasped her hands together, confused and scared. Maddy needed to tell him about the baby, let him know she didn't expect him to marry her, even if it was exactly what she wanted.

Removing his hat, Fletcher continued into the parlor, his gaze taking in the beautiful furniture, before turning back toward her. "Is this yours?"

Her brows drew together before his meaning became clear. "The house belongs to Suzette Gasnier. She's my boss at the restaurant."

He cocked his head. "The restaurant in the Feather River Hotel?"

Biting her lip, she nodded. "Yes. I work five or six evenings a week. If needed, I also work afternoons." He continued to stare at her, not replying. "If you want, I can make coffee..." Maddy's voice trailed off, her chest squeezing.

He shook his head. "I don't need coffee, lass. Do you have time to talk? I've things I need to say to you."

Her heart stalled, courage slipping. She wondered if he planned to tell her he'd met someone and was marrying. Or maybe he was leaving for Settlers Valley again. Maddy gave herself a mental shake. Neither of those made sense. The way he'd searched for her, kissed her, refuted both.

She indicated chairs a few feet away. "All right. I have something to tell you, too."

They sat across from each other, Fletcher leaning forward, resting his arms on his thighs. He locked intent eyes on hers. "You go first, lass."

Her heart tripped. She'd always loved the way he called her lass, sometimes lassie. "Are you sure? Because—"

He held up his hand to stop her. "I am, lass." Fletcher sat back, stretching out his long legs, setting his hat aside. "What I have to say can wait."

Looking at the hands clasped tightly in her lap, her courage began to wane. She hadn't expected to see him tonight or this week or even this month. When he didn't appear as Mrs. Baker had mentioned, Maddy decided he didn't care enough to ride into town to see her. Yet here he was, his expectant gaze locked on hers.

When she didn't talk, he tilted his head, an encouraging grin on his face. "Well, lass?"

Mouth going dry, a lump in her throat, Maddy fought the urge to rest a hand on her stomach. Glancing down, she adjusted her shawl. In a few minutes, she wouldn't need the disguise—at least not in front of Fletcher.

"I, um...I..." She couldn't get the words out, her throat tight, the same as her chest. Sucking in a shaky breath, she looked away.

Standing, Fletcher moved to the chair beside her, reaching out and resting a hand on top of hers. A frown deepened the lines on his face. He squeezed her hand.

"What is it, lass?" Lifting his other hand, he gripped her chin, tipping it toward him. His eyes widened at the tears he saw. His voice thickened. "Tell me."

She pushed away her fear, blinking several times. "You remember how many times we slept together?"

"I remember everything, lass." He dropped his grip on her chin.

Biting her lip, she nodded. "Well, one of those times, we, um..." She pulled away the shawl, displaying the swell of her stomach.

Fletcher's jaw dropped, the color draining from his face. He worked to breathe as his mind strained to comprehend the sight before him. After a couple minutes, he shifted in the chair, his attention still on her stomach.

"You're having a wee bairn."

Her throat tightened. *"We're* having a baby, Fletcher."

Jumping up, he strode away, scrubbing a hand down his face. Setting fisted hands on his hips, he lowered his head, staring at the floor. A minute passed, then another as he absorbed what he thought she meant. Whipping around, his hard glare leveled on her, voice inflexible.

"So you're saying the bairn is mine?"

Maddy gasped, a hand going to her mouth. Breath coming in uneven gulps, she blinked away the sudden moisture in her eyes and stood. Legs wobbly, she couldn't meet his gaze, the pain too great to respond right away.

Lifting her chin, Maddy straightened her back, walking straight to him. Steeling her voice, she met his gaze. "Yes."

She didn't wait for a response, walking to the stairs.

"Maddy, wait."

She didn't. Instead, she hurried upstairs, not looking back as he continued to call for her.

Blowing out a breath, Fletcher slammed a palm down on the bannister. Reining in his anger, he fought the doubt rolling through him. He lowered himself onto one of the stairs, resting his feet on the bottom stair, covering his face with his hands.

He'd always fought his growing attraction to Maddy, riding to Buckie's every night to be with her. Fletcher had hated the thought she'd entertained other men when he wasn't there. Hated he couldn't do anything about it. He remembered telling himself picking the life of a saloon girl had been Maddy's choice. It hadn't been forced upon her. She'd wanted it, at least that was what she'd always told him when they'd spent time in bed talking. Maddy had never once mentioned not being with other men. Fletcher never thought to ask, knowing he wouldn't want to hear the answer.

With all she'd told him, how could he take her word the baby was his? The only doubt came from what Frankie had told him.

"Hell, Fletch. I thought you knew. You're the only man Maddy ever had up in her room."

Groaning, he wondered if it could be true. Was he the only one?

So lost in his thoughts, he didn't hear the front door open and close.

"Fletcher?"

He lifted his head to see Suzette staring at him, eyes laced with confusion. Standing, he stepped to the floor. "Good evening, Miss Gasnier."

"What are you doing here?" She glanced up the stairs. "Is Maddy all right?"

Fletcher shook his head. "I don't know. The lass told me about the bairn, and I, well...I didn't respond too well."

She cocked her head, eyes sharp with concern. "Maddy talked to you about the baby? Why would she talk to *you*?"

It was Fletcher's turn to look confused. "She says the bairn is mine."

Sacramento

Dob Colbert paid for the ammunition and picked up the boxes. Stepping outside, he stuffed his purchase into saddlebags, looking back to the boardwalk to see Lew approach. "Anything?"

"We've been here a week, Colonel. There's no sign of Maddy. We've searched every saloon, restaurant, and boardinghouse. The gal isn't here." Lew rubbed the back of his neck. "I think it's time we moved on to Conviction."

"Maybe." Dob stepped onto the boardwalk, glancing around to confirm they were alone. "There's someone I want you to meet."

"Who?"

"A man I met at the saloon last night. He's riding with a group of men and they're looking for a few others. I'm supposed to see him again tonight."

Lew pursed his lips. "How do you know we can trust him? Could be he's luring us into some kind of trap. Maybe he's a lawman."

"That's why you and Ross are coming with me tonight. I want both of you there, ask questions. Afterward, we'll make a decision."

Lew crossed his arms, frowning. "What about Maddy?"

Dob snorted. "We aren't giving up our search for her. She knows too much about our past and can identify us. Doesn't stop us from talking about this other opportunity."

Blowing out a ragged breath, Lew glanced around again, making certain no one could hear them. "What is it this man wants to talk about?"

Chuckling, Dob clasped him on the shoulder, a conspiratorial tilt on his lips. "He's in the cattle business."

Circle M

Fletcher worked to calm the wild mustang, the chore soothing him, giving his mind something else to think about. For two days, he couldn't pull his thoughts from Maddy and what he'd learned. He needed to ride back to town and get her to speak with him. First, he had to be certain his control wouldn't falter, scare her into running.

Suzette asked few questions when she'd found him in her home, and couldn't hide her surprise at learning Maddy believed him to be the father. Fletcher had gotten the impression she had no idea of Maddy's background before working at the hotel restaurant, and he wouldn't be the one to tell her. How did you tell someone her friend once worked as a saloon girl, offering paid favors to whatever man could pay.

Muttering a curse, he stopped working with the horse, drawing in a shuddering breath. The thought of Maddy with other men set off a stream of unexpected emotions. Or perhaps not so unexpected.

"Are you finished with him, lad?" Bram moved toward Fletcher, a watchful eye on the horse.

Letting out a resigned breath, he held out the rope. "Aye. My mind isn't on it today."

Bram took the rope from him. "You've not said what happened with the lass." He led the horse to a small corral, removed the halter, and let the animal loose. Shutting the gate, he turned back to Fletcher. "You've been surly and distant since returning from town. What happened after you found Maddy?"

Looking around, Fletcher nodded to the barn. "Not out here. Come on."

Stalking to the barn, he scanned the interior, making certain no one still worked inside. Pacing back and forth in front of a stall, he rubbed his forehead, staring at the ground.

"She's pregnant."

Other than a murmured curse, Bram didn't respond.

"The lass says it's mine."

"Sonofabitch," Bram snarled. Seeing the confusion on Fletcher's face, he took a step toward him. "Are you believing her?"

He closed his eyes. "I don't know what to believe."

"Where's the lass living?"

"With Suzette Gasnier. She works at the restaurant in the Feather River Hotel." A ghost of a smile appeared. "The lass looks good, Bram."

"Ach. You'd say that if she had no hair and was covered in mud." Bram choked out a laugh at Fletcher's disgusted expression. "You've wanted the lass since the first night you saw her at Buckie's. It's been over eight months and you still can't forget her." Bram seemed to think as he rubbed his chin. "If the bairn's yours, the lass would be about five months along."

Leaning against a stall, he shrugged. "By the look of her, seems right."

Bram's voice rose. "She's a saloon girl, Fletch. It could be anyone's."

Pinching the bridge of his nose, he nodded. "Aye."

"I've been looking for you two." Camden strolled into the barn, coming to an abrupt halt at the serious looks on his cousins' faces. "What is it, lads?"

Bram's mouth drew into a thin line and he shook his head.

Camden took a couple steps forward. "Fletch?"

Scrubbing both hands down his face, he let himself slide to the ground. Fletcher rested his arms on bent knees, his gaze meeting Camden's.

"Maddy's with child."

Camden's jaw dropped, eyes almost bulging from their sockets. "Is it yours?"

"Hell if I know, Cam. It could be." Fletcher stared into the distance, his eyes vacant. "The lass says it is."

Camden walked over, sitting on the ground next to him. A moment later, Bram joined them. No one spoke for long minutes. When the silence grew too heavy, Camden picked up a clod of dirt, sending it across the barn.

"How would you even know, lad? The lass is a saloon girl."

Fletcher glared at him. "I know what the lass is."

"Ach, don't be daft, lad. You know what I'm saying. Maddy is a bonny lass, and we all know she has feelings for you—at least she did before you left for Settlers Valley. It's just, how would you be knowing for certain the bairn is yours?" Camden threw another clod of dirt across the barn, watching it disintegrate against the wall. "Where'd you find her?"

Fletcher explained how he'd found her, where she lived and worked. "Suzette returned to the house before I left. She knew of Maddy's condition, but nothing about the father."

Bram watched as Camden shot another hard ball of dirt across the barn. "You know she manages the hotel and restaurant and that our family is partners with August and Bay. Will she be saying anything?"

Fletcher shook his head. "Nae. She says it's Maddy's business, and mine, if I..." His voice faded on a groan.

"If you decide the bairn is yours?" Bram asked.

"Aye."

Silence once again settled over the three, each searching for an answer, coming up with little. To their knowledge, this hadn't happened in the family before. Maddy's past profession didn't help.

"If she's the lass you want, your da and ma will accept her. They'll not be judging her for carrying your bairn." Bram glanced toward the entrance at the sound of voices.

"Ah hell," Fletcher groaned, seeing Colin and Quinn walk inside. "Could this be getting any worse?"

Stopping before them, Colin stared down at the three. "There'd best be a good reason you lads are taking up space on the ground instead of working." Placing fisted hands on his hips, he waited. "Well?"

Sucking in a breath, making no move to stand, Fletcher looked up, his features tight and grim.

"Maddy's back in town. The lass is pregnant." Fletcher glanced between Colin and Quinn. "She says the bairn is mine."

Chapter Ten

Conviction

Maddy sat at her bedroom window, staring out at nothing in particular. She'd been doing more of this, moping around with little energy since seeing Fletcher for the first time in months. He looked good. Better than good. His handsome features and dear face brought back all the desire she'd tried to forget. She now realized getting over Fletcher MacLaren would be much more difficult than Maddy anticipated.

Closing her eyes, she recalled all the times they'd sat in her bed, him with a hand on her thigh while she'd stroke fingers along his cheek, jaw, and down his neck. He was so incredibly handsome it broke her heart. Letting him burrow his way into her heart had been a mistake.

Even if she had no idea how she'd handle being a single woman with a child, Maddy didn't regret the life growing inside her. She already loved the baby.

Unconsciously settling a hand on her stomach, she winced at the horror on Fletcher's face when he learned of the baby. She knew he doubted the parentage. At first, his uncertainty angered her. Thinking about it over the last two days, lying awake at night and coming to understand his distrust, Maddy recognized she'd expected too much of him.

Paying to spend almost every night with Maddy didn't eliminate Fletcher's belief she was no more than a saloon girl. A whore who sold her body for money. She'd done little to convince him otherwise, sharing nothing of her past or how she'd come to work at Buckie's.

Falling in love with him had taken no effort at all. It happened a little each night as he made sweet love to her, staying to hold her until almost dawn. He'd never spoken of love or a future. Still, she allowed herself to dream of a life with Fletcher, helping him on the MacLaren ranch, having the family she'd always prayed for.

An icy slap of reality destroyed her dreams the night Bram delivered Fletcher's note. It had been cold and heartless. Until then, she never would've used those words to describe him. He'd thanked her for all the good times.

Good times.

She still felt the pain.

"Madeleine."

She startled at Suzette's voice. "Coming." Standing, Maddy forced a smile when she opened the door. "Sorry. I was daydreaming."

Suzette gave an understanding nod. "I wonder if you might have a few minutes."

Maddy's brows furrowed. "Of course. What do you need?"

"Oh, I don't need anything. I have tea prepared downstairs and hoped you'd share it with me."

A relieved smile broke across her face. "I'd love to."

Making their way into the parlor, Maddy took a seat on the settee while Suzette poured tea into two cups.

"Afternoon tea may seem a somewhat silly habit, but it's one I've come to love." She looked at Maddy. "Would you like some sugar or cream?"

"May I have both?"

"Of course." Suzette added them to the cup, handing it and a spoon to Maddy. "I once met an elderly English woman at a hotel where I worked. She told me all about her love of tea, explaining the right and wrong way to prepare it, the types of sandwiches or pastries a hostess would offer. I became quite interested, determined to learn as much as possible about the tradition. Over time, the hotel began offering an afternoon tea." She chuckled. "It was very popular."

Waiting until Suzette prepared her own cup and sat down, Maddy took a sip, savoring the warm drink. "I haven't had tea in a long time. This is wonderful."

"I'm so glad you like it." Suzette settled back in her chair. "Now, tell me how you are feeling?"

Maddy's fingers tensed on the cup. "Tired, but that seems to be normal right now."

"We haven't had a chance to talk about this, but when I came home the other night, Fletcher MacLaren was in the house. He seemed quite, well...agitated." Suzette leaned forward, her voice full of concern. "When I asked him why he was here, Fletcher said you'd told him he's the father of the baby. Is that correct?"

Maddy glanced away, shifting in her seat. She didn't want to discuss the other night, the baby, and especially Fletcher. Suzette's support and friendship meant too much to ignore her concern.

"Yes." She turned an uncomfortable gaze to Suzette, taking another sip of tea.

"I see. How did you meet him?"

Misery flashed in Maddy's eyes before she stared down into her cup. "I haven't been exactly truthful about my past, Suzette. It's something I'm not proud of, but it can't be changed."

"Do you want to tell me about it?"

Eyes shadowing, her hands trembled. When she spoke, her voice wavered. "I first came to Conviction the end of last year. I've known Frankie, the bartender at Buckie's, since we were children. He helped me get a job as one of the, the…"

She bit her lower lip, eyes tearing. Setting down the cup, she swiped at the moisture, grateful Suzette didn't push her. After a while, Maddy regained a little of her composure.

"The agreement was I'd serve drinks, talk to the customers, but not be required to take men upstairs. After a few weeks, I met Fletcher. He captivated me so much, I eventually took him upstairs. Fletcher was the only man I invited to my room." Clasping hands in her lap, she cleared her throat. "He came in almost every night, played cards and drank whiskey before we'd go upstairs. Fletcher paid for all my time, not leaving until almost dawn. Frankie cautioned me to be careful, saying a MacLaren would never marry a saloon girl and Fletcher would have a hard time believing I didn't share my bed with other men." Her voice broke on the last. Drawing in a shaky breath, she forced out the rest. "Instead of taking Frankie's advice, I fell in love with Fletcher, allowed myself to dream of a future with him. One night, Bram and Camden brought me a note from him. He thanked me for all the good times, but he'd left for Settlers Valley and didn't plan to come back to Buckie's when he returned to Conviction." Watery eyes locked on Suzette. "It was over."

Leaning forward, Suzette placed a hand on Maddy's arm, allowing her to take all the time she needed before continuing.

Brushing away tears, Maddy clasped her hands together again. "I left for San Francisco the next morning. Without Fletcher, I couldn't stay, knowing I'd never see him again. A few weeks later, I realized I carried his baby."

"Is that why you came back to Conviction?"

Maddy nodded. "I had no other place to go and hoped he might, well...maybe he would want to know. I don't expect him to marry me, but..."

Suzette's eyes softened. "You hoped he'd offer."

A bitter chuckle burst from her lips. "A silly fantasy. He doesn't even believe the baby is his. And why would he? I never said or did anything to make him think otherwise."

"You've had months to accept the pregnancy. Fletcher's had a few days. I don't know him well, but from what I've learned about the MacLarens, they're men of honor. If he believes the child is his, he'll do what's right." She squeezed Maddy's arm. "You have to tell him the truth about your job at Buckie's."

Even though she knew Suzette was right, old uncertainties gripped her. What if he didn't believe her? She couldn't bear seeing doubt and regret in his eyes. Maddy needed to see passion and desire on his face, what she'd always experienced when he used to visit her at Buckie's. She feared the hungry craving she'd anticipated may be gone forever, replaced with revulsion and disdain. If he walked away again, Maddy didn't think she would survive. At least not emotionally.

"Would you like me to send a message to him, saying you need to speak with him?"

Maddy's gaze snapped to Suzette's. "No." Her chest heaved. "I mean, he needs to come on his own because he wants to learn more."

Studying her a moment, Suzette nodded. "I understand. Let me know if you change your mind. Would you like more tea?"

Shaking her head, Maddy stood. "I'd like to go upstairs and rest before going to the restaurant. Thank you for the tea, and the conversation."

Walking up the stairs, a wave of guilt flashed through her knowing she hadn't told Suzette the entire truth. Not of the men following her, what they'd do when they found her, or the reason she'd fled Kansas so many months before. She didn't want to think of the horror that would arise if they learned she'd come to Conviction.

And she wasn't ready to face a future without Fletcher.

Circle M

Standing in the barn, Fletcher stared at the house where his father, Ewan, worked in his office. His cousins had encouraged him to speak with him, get his thoughts on Maddy and what he'd learned. At first, he'd thought they were right.

An hour after his cousins left the barn, he still hesitated, unconvinced talking to his father before seeing Maddy again was wise. He had questions, important ones, before he faced his da, a man who'd insist on answers before offering advice.

Emerging into a clear afternoon, he observed Bram and Camden working the same horse Fletcher had half-heartedly attempted to train earlier. They appeared to be making progress, a lot more than he'd achieved with his mind preoccupied with Maddy and the baby.

Taking long strides to the corral, he watched a few more minutes until Bram saw him and handed the rope to Camden.

"Have you made a decision, Fletch?"

Mouth forming a thin line, he nodded. "I'll be riding to town when I'm done here. Speaking with Da will have to wait until I've more information from Maddy." Removing his hat, he shredded fingers through his hair. "The lass seems convinced I'm the bairn's da. How could she be so certain? I've not seen her in months. Any of the men she'd been with could be the da."

Pushing his hat off his forehead, Bram considered what he knew. "Don't be getting angry before you hear me out, lad."

Fletcher's brow furrowed. Crossing his arms, he leaned a shoulder against one of the rails, waiting. "What are you thinking?"

"I'm not certain Maddy is what she seems. Something about the lass doesn't make sense."

Fletcher had thought the same, but his brain was too cluttered with images of her swollen belly to think clearly. "What are you trying to say, Bram?"

"None of us ever saw the lass take another lad upstairs. Ranch hands I've played cards with swear she served drinks and nothing more. Until she met you, Fletch. Afterward, you were the *only* one she'd allow to accompany her to the second floor. The lads were pretty vocal about it." Bram gave him an unsettling look. "According to Frankie, Maddy left town the morning after I gave her your note."

"The lad seems to know a good deal about her."

"Aye, Fletch, he does. I'm thinking there's even more Frankie knows." Shifting toward Camden, he grimaced

116

when the horse reared back, almost clipping his cousin on the way down. "Watch yourself, Cam!" Bram shook his head, looking back at Fletcher. "I'll be riding in with you. You talk with Maddy and I'll be visiting Frankie." Lips twisting in a wry manner, he locked his gaze on his cousin. "Do you love the lass?"

Scrubbing a hand down his face, Fletcher shrugged. He'd asked himself the same question for months, ever since leaving for Settlers Valley and continuing upon his return. The answer still confounded him. There was one thing he knew with certainty.

"If I'm convinced the bairn's mine, I'll be marrying the lass whether I love her or not."

Bram studied his face a long time before nodding. "Aye, lad. I know you will."

Conviction

Maddy felt a good deal better after taking a short nap. Not great, but much more rested than after speaking with Suzette. Explaining her relationship with Fletcher had been difficult and painful.

Relationship.

She wondered if he'd ever thought of them being together or if he just considered her a mere convenience, someone to satisfy his needs. Reminding herself of his terse note, she couldn't fool herself any longer. Fletcher had seen her as no more than the soiled dove he perceived her to be, never looking further, never asking questions to satisfy his curiosity.

Their long talks consisted of stories of their childhood and little more. His had always been entertaining, generating laughter she hadn't experienced in years. Fletcher helped her forget her past, the humiliations she'd endured, providing a joy she hadn't known since well before leaving Kansas.

After putting up her hair, Maddy slipped into her chemise, skirt, and blouse, then slid into her black shoes. She had fifteen minutes to cross the short distance to the restaurant. Unlike the last few days, she looked forward to the job, not feeling the distress dogging her since Fletcher's visit.

As had become a habit, she placed her right hand on the bannister, left hand on her stomach while descending the stairs. Suzette left mid-morning, the same as every day. Maddy didn't know how the woman kept up the torturous pace of managing both the hotel and restaurant. Even with an assistant manager, the job consumed her, leaving Suzette little room for a life beyond work.

Grabbing a shawl, Maddy opened the door, giving a slight yelp at seeing Bay on the stoop. "Mr. Donahue. You startled me."

He removed his hat. "Apologies, Madeleine." His gaze moved over her, stopping on her stomach. "Are you all right?"

"I'm fine. Um, Suzette isn't here. She left for the hotel several hours ago."

"Actually, I came by to speak with you. Do you have a few minutes before you leave?"

Glancing behind her into the house, Maddy hesitated a moment. "There's no one else here. I'm not certain..." Her voice trailed off when she saw understanding register on Bay's face.

"This won't take long. We can stand in the entry and leave the door open."

"Well, I suppose that would be all right."

Opening the door wide, she moved a few feet inside. He followed, making certain anyone who looked inside would have no doubt they were involved in no more than conversation.

"I'll get right to it. I need to know if you're with child, Madeleine."

She felt the blood drain from her face, her body swaying enough for Bay to reach out and steady her. Tilting his head, he didn't let go until certain she wouldn't faint.

"It seems my question surprised you."

Maddy nodded, fear forming a knot in her stomach. "Well, yes. It did."

He lifted a brow. "Well?"

Resigned, she let out a stuttering breath. "Yes, I am, Mr. Donahue."

"Is that why you're living with Suzette?"

Maddy felt her body begin to tremble, her hopes of continuing at the restaurant dissolving. "Yes, it is. Mrs. Baker doesn't allow unmarried women in my condition to live at her boardinghouse. Suzette learned of it and offered me a room here." Searching for courage, she lifted her chin. "Was that wrong of her?"

Ignoring the question, Bay continued. "You realize working at the restaurant more than a few more weeks isn't possible."

Swallowing her distress, she nodded. "Yes, sir."

"How would you feel about taking a job in the kitchen when the time comes for you to move from the dining room?"

Eyes widening, a wary smile appeared. "I'd love to work in the kitchen."

Bay almost chuckled at her enthusiasm. "It's hard work, harder than in the dining room, but it would conceal your condition a little longer."

"I don't mind hard work."

Satisfied, he nodded. "I'll speak with Suzette today." Clearing his throat, Bay opened his mouth to ask something else when the sound of boots pounding up the steps stopped him.

Looking through the open doorway, Maddy's breath caught at the sight of Fletcher moving toward her.

Chapter Eleven

Fletcher's steps faltered, seeing Bay standing inside with Maddy. Glancing between the two, his features hardened. "It seems I should be coming back another time."

"No need, Fletch." Bay held out his hand, which Fletcher grasped. "I wanted to speak with Madeleine about her work at the restaurant. We're finished." He looked at Maddy. "I'll let you and Suzette decide the best time to make the change."

The smile returned to her face. "Yes, sir. And thank you, Mr. Donahue."

Her excitement at not losing her job faded when her gaze moved from Bay's retreating back to Fletcher. Chest tightening, her face clouded with unease.

"Hello, Maddy." He glanced behind him, making certain no one could overhear. "Would you be having time to talk?"

Hesitating, she shook her head. "I'm sorry, but I'm on my way to the restaurant."

As if he didn't hear her, Fletcher took a step closer. "I've questions, lass, and I'll not be leaving until I have answers."

"I know you need answers, but I can't lose my job." She heard the panic creep into her voice. "Please, Fletcher. I need the money for the baby."

His expression clouded in anger. "Is the bairn mine?"

She stiffened, ignoring her humiliation. "Yes."

"How can you be sure?"

Maddy shuddered, but refused to let his anger cower her. "I've been with two men. One who forced me long before I came to Conviction. The other one is you, Fletcher MacLaren."

Pushing past him, she didn't stop when he called after her, but came to an abrupt halt when he grabbed her arm, forcing her to look at him. Tears formed in her eyes as she tried to break his hold.

"Stop fighting me, Maddy." He pulled her close, wrapping his arms around her. His throat tightened on the sound of her sobs. Rubbing a hand in circles over her back, he let her cry, ignoring those who moved past them. "We'll be working this out, lass." He relaxed when he felt her arms wrap around his waist.

Looking past her at the restaurant, he saw Suzette walking toward them. Her curious features turned to a hostile stare as she came closer.

"What have you done to her, Fletcher?"

Tightening his hold, he whispered in Maddy's ear before facing Suzette. "I came for answers."

Settling fisted hands on her waist, she glared at him. "And did you get them?"

"Not all of them, but it's a start." Kissing Maddy's temple, he loosened his hold. Using the pad of his thumb, he wiped tears from her face. "Are you going to be all right, lass?"

Sniffling, she nodded, dropping her arms from around his waist. "I'll be fine."

"I'll be waiting for you when you're finished tonight. What you told me was a fine start, but I need to know more of it, Maddy. I need to know all you've been keeping from me."

"Madeleine won't be working past seven tonight. You're welcome to talk in the house." She offered a conspiratorial expression to Fletcher. "You're going to need the privacy."

Maddy's eyes flashed with concern. "But what will people think if Fletcher and I are in your house alone?"

Suzette moved closer. "I know you don't want to hear this, but a good number of people already saw what happened out here between you and Fletcher." She patted Maddy's arm. "The fact some already suspect you're with child, well...I believe being in the house with him won't be a problem. But if you'd rather wait, Fletcher can come over after I'm finished tonight."

Chewing her lower lip, Maddy shook her head. "You're right, Suzette. Fletcher and I will talk when I finish tonight." Her voice trembled, causing Fletcher to draw her back to him.

"I'll be seeing you later tonight, lass."

"Do you want some whiskey, Fletch?" Brodie sipped his coffee, holding baby Shaun while his wife, Maggie, finished with supper.

"Nae. Coffee is fine. I need to be having my mind clear tonight." Fletcher watched his older brother and his family, feeling the normal pang of wanting, the same as he always felt when around Colin and Sarah, Quinn and Emma, and Sam and Jinny. So many members of the family had married in the last few years, and all were happy, content. He wanted the same, but only if it happened with the right woman.

Brodie settled Shaun on his lap. "Do you think Maddy is telling you the truth, lad?"

Stretching out his legs, Fletcher stared across the room, looking at nothing in particular. "I don't know. The lass was upset when she answered me, so I'm not sure how much truth was in it."

He'd shared what Maddy had told him, leaving nothing out. If it was true, and the baby was his, he'd do what was right.

Somehow, Fletcher knew she kept other secrets and he meant to learn every one of them before making a final decision on how much of his heart he'd offer. A marriage to legitimize a child was one thing, and he was prepared to go forward with one. It wasn't what he wanted, but he'd not shirk his responsibility. Giving his heart to Maddy was something else, a decision Fletcher still had to make.

"What's her full name?"

Fletcher's mouth twisted. "Madeleine..." He thought another moment, realizing he still didn't know her last name. "I'll ask the lass when I see her tonight. I do know she's from Kansas."

"Get as much as you can, Fletch. Her da's name, ma's name, the town where the lass was born. I'll be asking Sam for help and send telegrams to her hometown. Maybe someone will remember her."

A stab of guilt moved through him. "Maddy will be angry if she learns what you're doing."

Brodie let out an unremorseful chuckle. "I'll not be caring too much what she thinks. My concern is for you, lad, and the type of woman who might be joining the family."

The front door flew open, crashing against the wall. "We're hoping you've not eaten everything without us." Bram walked inside, followed by a more reserved Camden.

"Bram MacLaren. You march right back out there and enter as a civilized gentleman." Maggie moved toward him as she spoke, the large spoon in her hand cutting through the air.

"Ach, Maggie, sweetheart. I meant no harm."

She glared at him, doing her best not to laugh. "Out with you."

"And don't you be calling my wife sweetheart," Brodie barked out, grimacing when Shaun began to cry.

Maggie looked at her husband before focusing her wrath on Bram. "Now see what you've done."

Fletcher knew better than to jump between his sister-in-law and anyone. She might seem quiet and reserved, but give her cause and she'd transform into a formidable opponent. One you didn't want to cross.

Holding his hands in the air, Bram bowed before stepping back outside. Knocking, he waited until Maggie invited him inside.

Sweeping his hat off his head, he bowed. "Well, good evening to you all. Did you save any supper for Camden and me?"

Laughing, Maggie motioned them to chairs at the table. "Sit down, you miscreants, before you hurt yourselves."

Camden clasped Fletcher on the shoulder as they all sat. "Did you speak with her, lad?"

"Aye. Did you two talk with Frankie?"

Camden nodded. "Aye, we did."

Bram rested his arms on the table. "The lad knows quite a bit about the fair lassie."

Fletcher wanted to groan. Rubbing a hand on the back of his neck, he gestured for Bram to continue.

"Tell us what the lass said first, lad." Bram reached into the basket on the table, quickly removing a biscuit while Maggie had her back to him.

He'd already repeated Maddy's confession to Brodie. Fletcher had no desire to share the same intimate details with Bram and Camden.

"I'll be meeting the lass after she's done at work. Tell me what you learned from Frankie."

Shrugging, Bram sat back in his chair. "She's from Abilene. That's where Frankie met her. He said her da was a Union colonel during the war."

"An uncle was also a colonel," Camden added. "Her da and ma are dead, but the uncle is still alive."

Brodie shifted Shaun to his other arm. "Where's the uncle now?"

Camden shrugged. "Frankie didn't say anything more before it got real busy."

"Did he tell you Maddy's last name?" Fletcher asked.

Bram's brows lifted. "The lass may be carrying your bairn and you don't know her last name?"

Pushing away from the table, Fletcher stood. "I need to be meeting Maddy."

"Not until you've eaten." Maggie set a plate of stew in front of him. She glared at Bram. "Leave him alone. He's got enough on his mind without you making him feel worse."

Lowering himself back down, Fletcher ate in silence, thinking of what his cousins had learned. Looking up, he lifted a brow. "Did Frankie say if she has any brothers or sisters?"

Camden glanced at Bram, who shook his head. "Nae. We can go back after supper and see what else the lad is willing to share," Camden offered.

Brodie rubbed his chin while rocking Shaun in his other arm. "Fletch, you still need to be getting her last name and her da's first name from the lass. With what

Bram and Cam learned, Sam and I'll be able to find out more about her."

Other than a brisk nod, Fletcher didn't respond. He didn't do much more than move his food around the plate before standing again. Letting out a resigned breath, he shoved the chair back under the table.

"This isn't how I expected my life to go."

Maggie tossed down a towel, walking to him. Placing her hands on his shoulders, she looked up at him. "You're a good man, Fletcher, and a good judge of character. If you like Maddy, I'm sure it's because she's a good woman. We all fall on hard times, especially women. We do what we must to survive." They all knew the hardships Maggie faced, including kidnapping and spending time in jail, before falling in love with Brodie. "If you love the girl, so will the rest of the family. My instincts tell me if Maddy says the child is yours, then it is. *You* just need to learn enough about her to believe it. If it's all true, no one doubts what a good father you'll be."

Giving Maggie a peck on the cheek, he nodded at the others before walking out. He did believe he'd make a good father. Fletcher was less certain of the type of husband he'd be.

Maddy couldn't control the waves of nausea rolling through her. She knew it had nothing to do with the baby. Her horrible mood and sour stomach were all due to Fletcher MacLaren and the talk they were to have when she stepped out the back door.

She'd promised herself to tell him everything, the entire sad tale of her family and her life after leaving Kansas. Some of it might be hard for him to hear. It would also be difficult for her to voice aloud. Frankie knew much of it, but even he didn't know everything.

"Are you going to be all right talking to Fletcher by yourself?"

Maddy hadn't heard Suzette come to stand beside her. Straightening, her mouth twisted into a grim smile.

"I'll be fine. He'd never hurt me or intentionally upset me. Fletch is a good man. I'm sure it's hard for him to learn the woman he believed to be nothing more than a saloon whore is someone very different."

"And carrying his child," Suzette added.

Maddy sucked in a weary breath. "Yes. He needs answers. I hope to give him all he needs to finally believe the life we made is a part of him."

"If you need me—"

Maddy held up her hand. "Thank you, but I'll be fine. In fact, I'll be glad to put it all behind me. Once Fletcher knows, he can make whatever decision is best for him. Then I'll know what my baby and I will face as a future."

"If he accepts what you have to say, Fletch won't walk away from you. Something tells me you already know that, Maddy."

Pursing her lips, she turned toward the back door, wanting to believe what Suzette said. Squaring her shoulders, Maddy pushed open the door, her gaze landing on Fletcher standing at the bottom of the steps.

He draped an arm around her shoulders, neither speaking as they walked back to Suzette's. Once inside, he followed her into the parlor, turning up several lamps.

"Do you want me to make coffee?"

Fletcher shook his head. "Nae, lass." He sat on the sofa, patting the spot beside him. "Come sit by me."

Hesitating a moment, she worried her bottom lip.

"I'll not bite you, lass. Unless you want me to." When he smiled, it felt as if he'd opened the heavens for her.

Lowering herself next to him, she studied his much too handsome face, remembering the times she'd held it in the palms of her hands before kissing his lips. He was all she wanted, now and forever, and she couldn't help herself from praying he'd believe what she had to say.

Reaching over, Fletcher picked up one of her hands, clasping it between his larger ones.

"You know, lass, I don't know your last name."

"You never asked."

Fletcher felt a pang of guilt at how he'd never thought of asking. She must think him a selfish prig to never be curious about her life the way she'd been about his.

"I'm asking now, lass."

Sucking in a breath, she closed her eyes for an instant, praying for strength. "My last name is Colbert. My father was Byron Colbert, and my uncle is—"

"Dob Colbert," he interrupted, blowing out a disbelieving breath. "The Colbert gang." Fletcher wondered if it could get much worse. Later, he'd realize it did.

Chapter Twelve

Standing, Fletcher paced to a window, staring into the dark sky littered with stars. Scrubbing a hand down his face, he couldn't help questioning what else he didn't know about Maddy, admitting it was doubtless a lot.

Would he also discover the woman was a liar, someone who'd tell a man she carried his baby when it belonged to another? The idea stung.

Being from Kansas made sense, knowing her father was part of the Colbert gang. Not just a part, but one of its leaders. Even those living in the far west had heard of the group who terrorized towns after the war ended. His da had told him the difference between the Colberts and other guerillas was the men in their gang were northerners, not from the south. It didn't make any difference to Fletcher. Being from the north or south didn't make one group of murderers better or worse than the others. They were all killers, men Fletcher hoped never came to Conviction.

Turning, he crossed his arms. He stared at Maddy a long time before his questioning gaze bored into hers.

"Why *did* you come to Conviction?"

Wrapping both arms around her stomach, she thought of the truth. A group of horrible men—murderers, rapists, and kidnappers—searched for her with no intention of letting her get away again. A shiver ran through Maddy. Nausea almost doubled her over at the thought of what the men would do to her once they learned of the baby.

"Their life wasn't what I wanted. My father and mother were already dead…" A lump she always tried to ignore formed in her throat, closing it. Maddy shut her eyes, squeezing them until the image of her father's lifeless body vanished. From experience, she knew it wouldn't leave her for long. Neither his body nor the image of her mother's, both bleeding out, would ever be erased from her memory.

"They've been gone almost two years." She didn't want to talk about her sweet, kind mother, a woman who'd stood behind her husband, even when the horrors of the war changed him into a man no one recognized. Sometime, far in the future, she'd tell Fletcher about the woman who gave birth to her and an older brother Maddy hadn't seen in years.

Fletcher didn't change his stance, presenting a somewhat menacing pose, features distrustful. "How did he die?"

The look on his face told Maddy he wasn't going to accept anything she said with ease. She'd learned trust played a huge role in the MacLaren family. Broken, it might never be given a second time.

"He was murdered by, um…" She swallowed. "One of the men in the gang murdered him." She could see her answer didn't make sense. "His brother ordered the killing."

"Dob?"

Maddy nodded. "They didn't get along. My father was older, but Dob started the gang, so he became the leader. He selected all the men, and they were loyal to him." Her watery gaze met his. "My father was a good man, Fletcher. The war changed him. When he returned home, Father seemed lost, had a hard time completing his regular chores." Stifling a sob, she refused to look away. "He didn't deserve what Dob did to him."

Although it almost killed him, Fletcher refused to go to her, draw Maddy into his arms. He couldn't let himself forget there were still too many questions needing answers. With what she'd already told him, Fletcher could go to Brodie, have his brother and Sam work their magic to verify if the information was true or a lie. A way for Maddy to cover her background, loosen his defenses. Until he knew she'd been truthful, he'd keep a tight grip on his trust and his heart.

"I'm sure your da didn't deserve to die, at least not at the order of his brother. You were there when it happened, lass?"

Nodding, she clasped her hands together. She ached to have Fletcher come to her, offer his arms as comfort, but understood his hesitancy. He still had doubts. Opening her palms, she rested them on her stomach.

"The baby is yours, Fletcher. Yours and mine."

The lifting of his chin, lips pressed together, gave the only indication his hard exterior might be crumbling. A full minute passed before he dropped his arms, settling into a chair several feet from Maddy.

"You still haven't told me how you ended up in Conviction, lass. Of all the towns between here and Kansas, why here and not Austin or Denver?" Fletcher thought he knew the answer, at least one of them, but needed to hear it from her.

"Do you remember Frankie, the bartender at Buckie's?"

He nodded.

"When my family moved to Kansas, we became friends. Frankie was twelve and I was ten." She stopped herself from saying her older brother and Frankie were close. No need to mention his name yet.

"Frankie was a friend?"

She cleared her throat. "He was always there when I needed a friend. After leaving Abilene, Frankie let me know where he ended up and invited me to come out. I'm sure he didn't think I'd ever do it, but..." Shrugging, a humorless smile tilted up the corners of her mouth. "I needed a change and this was the only place I knew to come."

A muscle in his jaw ticked. "So your *friend* encouraged you to take a job in a saloon?" Fletcher couldn't imagine recommending such a job to any female, certainly not one he cared about.

Straightening her back, chin jutting out, Maddy glared at him. "Frankie arranged a job so I would only be required to talk to the customers, encourage them to drink, and serve whiskey. *Nothing* more."

Fletcher choked out a disbelieving laugh, running a hand through his hair. "As you did with me?"

Intense pain sliced through Maddy, making it hard to breathe. If he'd intended to hurt her, he'd succeeded. She offered him a resolute shake of her head. "No. You were different. I..." She sucked in a breath, allowing the agonizing thump of her heart to ease. A bitter chuckle escaped her lips. "I made an exception for you."

Fletcher matched her harsh chuckle with one of his own. "Because I'm a MacLaren and you thought I'd be easy to fool?"

She couldn't hold back the gasp. Pressing a hand to her mouth, Maddy shook her head.

Ignoring the slight twinge of doubt, Fletcher continued. "Do you believe I'd be believing I'm the only lad who bedded you at Buckie's?"

Her pale face and the pain in her eyes sliced through him, but not enough to stop his next words.

"Whose bairn is it, Maddy?"

It couldn't hurt any more than if he'd kicked her in the stomach. Maddy wanted to run from the room, never look back, never be in the same space as Fletcher ever again.

She knew it would be hard for him to accept the baby as his. Few men would believe she'd worked in a saloon, not letting just any man into her bed. Fletcher had been the only one, yet he'd made it clear he'd never believe her.

Perhaps because she loved Fletcher, Maddy had let herself hope he'd accept the truth. He'd accused her of thinking him a fool. The bitter truth hit her like a slap to the face. *She* was the fool, a silly woman daring to hope for a future with the man she loved.

After all she'd lived through, the pain life had dealt her, Maddy didn't understand why she'd allowed herself to believe anything would change. Frankie had warned her, tried to prepare her for the rejection she now faced. She'd waved him off. Given time, Maddy truly believed Fletcher would accept the baby as his, accepting in his heart he'd been the only man in her bed.

As with everything else in her life, since her father left to serve the Union Army, Maddy would have to force herself to be strong. This time, it meant more than her existence. It meant doing everything she could for the safety of her baby.

Anger swelling, mixing with the pain in her heart, Maddy drew in a deep breath. She remembered the note Fletcher wrote before leaving for Settlers Valley. The trite words, flippant *thank you* for all the fun they had. These weren't the words of a man who held real feelings for a woman. The fact he'd sought her out meant little. Not with him sitting across the room, disgust in his eyes, believing she'd try to trap him into marriage.

Standing, Maddy did something she rarely allowed herself—she let her emotions take control. Walking to him, she gave no warning before drawing back her hand, landing a blow to his face, snapping his head back.

"*Get out*. Get out and don't come back." Not sparing him another glance, she turned, picking up her skirt as she walked upstairs, head held high, not allowing herself to look back.

Rubbing his face, disbelief warred with a mixture of anger and admiration as he watched her climb the stairs. Fletcher hadn't expected the blow. The intensity shocked him.

He'd never seen her angry, never heard her voice raised. He'd never witnessed the slightest bit of deceit in Maddy, not in actions or words. The pain of her strike paled when he remembered the look on her face as he'd asked who fathered the baby. As always, he'd seen no trace of deception, only dismay and regret.

By the time he recovered from the sting of her blow, realized he'd made a huge mistake, she'd left the room.

Standing, he cursed himself as a fool before following. Stopping at the bottom of the stairs, he stared up. Speaking with her in the parlor skirted the boundaries of propriety. Going to her room would cross all limits. If anyone saw him, there'd be no turning back. Marrying her would be his only option.

Fletcher chuckled. "Ach. You're going to marry the lass anyway," he mumbled, bounding up the stairs. The thought might not bring the joy he hoped, but it didn't bring the expected dread, either.

Seeing the one closed door, he moved to it, knocking. "Open the door, Maddy." When she didn't respond, he tried the knob. Locked. "Maddy, let me in, lass."

Waiting, he wondered how soon the aunts could arrange for them to marry. It wouldn't be a big wedding. Family and a few friends. The women would cook while the men brought out the chairs and tables. Emma and Sarah would make a cake, something simple and pretty, as they'd done for other family celebrations.

Celebration.

The word caught in his mind, a thread of worry tugging at him, wondering what his family would think of Maddy.

Lost in thought, he didn't know how much time had passed before he heard stirring inside the room. "Open the door, lass, or I'll be kicking it down."

Waiting another minute, he took a step back, preparing to raise his leg when the door opened, but not enough for him to see her face.

"Go away, Fletcher. There's nothing for us to talk about."

"I'll not leave until we discuss the wedding."

The door flew open, Maddy's red, puffy face twisted in disbelief and rage. "*Wedding*? You must be insane if you think for a second I'd marry you."

He held up a hand. "I know you're upset with me, lass, but—"

"Upset?" she yelled. Crossing the room, she picked up a book from the dresser. "You haven't seen upset." The book sailed through the air, missing his head by a couple inches. Grabbing another, she threw it, hitting him in the chest. "This child will not be raised by a man who doesn't want him, won't love him, and will always think of him as a burden." Looking around the room, her gaze landed on a vase. She turned toward it, not seeing Fletcher come up behind her.

Wrapping his arms around her waist, he pulled her against his chest. "Stop, lass."

Struggling, she clawed at his hands. "Let me go. I'll never marry you."

Her struggles did nothing except intensify his hold, his arms tightening like bands of iron. "You'll upset the bairn, lass. Settle down."

"I'll not settle down until you leave." Lifting her foot, she brought it down hard on his boot, feeling his grip slacken. "Curse you, Fletcher MacLaren."

"What in the world is going on?"

Dropping his arms, Fletcher took a reluctant step away from Maddy. Turning, he winced at the sight of Suzette glaring at him, hand on her waist, lips drawn into a thin line. She lifted a brow.

"What are you doing in Madeleine's bedroom, Fletcher?"

He walked to her, his features lined with distress. "The lass refuses to marry me."

"No, I won't marry you, Fletcher. And I'd appreciate it if you'd leave." The firm tone of her voice dared either of them to protest.

Stepping farther into the room, Suzette kept her voice calm and low. "You told me Fletcher is the baby's father, Madeleine. Explain to me why you won't marry him when you've already admitted how much you love him."

Fletcher stilled at the words, his chest tightening in a painful grip. Could it be possible? Did she love him?

Wrapping her arms around her stomach, Maddy shook her head. "Fletcher doesn't believe the baby is his. I won't marry a man who'll regret it. He'd only make all our lives miserable."

Suzette glanced over her shoulder at Fletcher, lifting a brow.

Leaving his arms relaxed at his sides, he shook his head. "I'd never hurt you or the bairn, lass. You'd be living at the ranch, protected, with everything you'd ever need."

Her gaze locked on his. "Do you love me, Fletcher?"

Panic ripped through him. He'd asked himself the same question so many times, coming up with nothing except he wanted her in his life and in his bed. Did this mean he loved her? Oddly enough, he did feel a thread of love for the unborn child. He just wasn't certain about Maddy.

"I care about you, lass, and I'd do my best to be a good husband and da to the wee bairn."

The slight amount of hope Maddy clung to disappeared. Refusing to let him see how much his answer hurt, she lifted her chin.

"It's a fine offer, Fletcher. I know you'd never hurt the baby, at least not intentionally. But don't you see? A marriage out of obligation will lead to more pain than never marrying at all."

He stepped closer, holding out his hand. "Lass..."

"You'd end up despising me and the child. We'd be the reason you'd never find a woman you truly loved." Maddy looked away, shaking her head. "I can't marry you, Fletcher. I won't be the cause of you hating me."

"I could never hate you or the bairn, lass. Maybe in time—"

She choked out a bitter laugh. "You can't force yourself to love me, no matter how obligated you feel."

Fletcher reached out to her, dropping his hand when she stepped away. He glanced at Suzette, a look of pure desperation on his face.

"I'll be going, Maddy." Determination gleamed in his eyes. "We aren't done, lass. We're a long way from being done."

Chapter Thirteen

Circle M

Fletcher braced his head with his hands, rubbing to relieve the throbbing ache. He'd made it home from Buckie's well after midnight, going through one bottle of whiskey, starting another before Camden ripped it from his hand. Remembering a brief scuffle before one of his cousins lifted him over their shoulder and carried him to Domino, Fletcher groaned.

"Serves you right, lad."

His eyes opened to slits at the unmistakable sound of his mother's voice. Grimacing, he closed them again, squeezing.

"Ach, you deserve a little pain for the way you came home last night. I was telling your da it must be a lassie."

Fletcher's head hurt too much to let himself be drawn into discussing a pregnant Maddy. The thought of her rekindled his need for another drink. He'd never felt this way about any woman and didn't understand why hot desire gripped him now. She was a saloon girl, someone he shouldn't trust or believe anything she said. Yet he did. The realization had been what drove Fletcher to drink enough whiskey to kill most men. Today he dealt with the lapse in judgment, producing the intense pain in his head.

"Clean up and join us downstairs for supper, lad. I'll be taking no excuses for you not being at the table. You've ten minutes."

He winced at the sound of the door slamming shut.

Fletcher heard little of what she said other than the word *supper*. He'd missed an entire day, forcing his cousins to take on his chores again. The knowledge sickened him. They'd been covering for him since before he'd left for Settlers Valley, and even now, after his return.

His cousins knew the consequences created by his nights with Maddy, the child she carried within her—a baby Fletcher knew in his heart belonged to him. Convincing his mind proved to be more difficult. He still had unanswered questions and believed, deep down, she still had secrets.

Everything inside Fletcher shouted for him to be cautious, a bitter chuckle bubbling inside him. He might not have a choice to be wary or not. Maddy already wanted nothing to do with him, refusing his offer of marriage.

Carefully sitting up, he swung his feet to the floor, standing. Slipping into last night's clothes, Fletcher took the stairs to the dining room, groaning at the sight of Camden and Bram sitting at the table with his da, ma, and younger siblings. Having to sit through their knowing looks, subtle jabs, almost caused him to head back up the stairs. If his father hadn't spotted him, he might've done it.

"Take a seat, Fletch, and we'll be starting our supper." Ewan's steely gaze swept over him, taking in the red eyes, sallow skin, and miserable expression. "Quite a night, lad?"

"Ewan," Lorna admonished, nodding at Kenzie and the twins, Clint and Banner. Fletcher's younger siblings hung on every word their older brother and parents said. They didn't need to hear explanations over the supper table.

Sliding a knowing grin at his wife, Ewan picked up the roast, taking a large piece before handing it to Fletcher. "We've a new contract for horses from the Army." He didn't miss the concern on the faces of his son, and nephews, Bram and Camden. "I've not agreed to the number. With the loss of those six, we're already behind on the current contract. You lads need to tell me what we can and can't do."

Holding the fork in front of his mouth, Fletcher's hand faltered. Mouth dry, stomach roiling at the smell of food, he set the fork down.

"Aren't you hungry, Fletch?" Kenzie's worried eyes landed on her older brother. "Bram and Cam said you were feeling sick."

"I hate being sick," Clint chimed in, Banner nodding in agreement before stuffing another huge bite of potatoes into his mouth.

Fletcher rubbed his forehead. "Aye. It's not my favorite, either."

Conversation continued, more in the background than directed at him, for which he was grateful. He knew the food taking up space on his plate would be good, but Fletcher couldn't summon even an ounce of hunger. Gratitude rippled through him when his father pushed back his chair, standing.

"You and the lads go on now, Ewan." Lorna stood, glancing at the children. "Kenzie and the laddies will be helping me with the dishes."

Ewan turned his attention to his son and nephews. "We'll be talking in the study."

Fletcher entered last, closing the door behind him, still hoping to excuse himself from further discussion on the horse contact and anything else his father meant to address. An uneasy tension clung to him as he lowered himself into one of the leather chairs.

"We'll need to be riding north or into Nevada, Uncle Ewan." Camden took the glass of whiskey Bram handed him, setting it on the nearby table. "We'll not be able to fulfill both contracts without finding more wild horses."

"I've learned of several herds between here and Sacramento." Bram stared into his glass, ignoring the liquid inside. "The three of us would be needing to go. Maybe Thane, too."

Ewan lifted a brow at Bram. "For how long?"

"Several days, unless luck is with us. If it is, two or three."

"And what would you be thinking, Fletch?"

Rubbing the heels of his hands into eyes aching from the effects of too much whiskey and regret, he rested his head against the back of the chair. He tried to forget how he'd left her the evening before, knowing she'd expected more of him. He just wasn't sure what.

Fletcher had seen her disappointment at his explanation of marrying him for the sake of the baby and a safe life on the ranch. From their late-night conversations, he already knew life on a ranch appealed to her. She'd always been interested in his stories of Circle M and his family. Fletcher remembered Maddy expressing her desire for a family of her own, eyes glassy, as if she'd been thinking of something far away.

"Fletch, lad. Did you hear me?"

Jarred to attention by his father's voice, he straightened. "Nae, Da. What did you say?"

Ewan repeated what he, Camden, and Bram discussed. Finishing, he tilted his head in question, waiting for his son's opinion.

Scrubbing a hand down his face, he stood and picked up the glass of whiskey Bram had poured earlier. Ignoring any pretense of patience, he tossed it back. A few measured steps and he stood at the window, looking out at nothing in particular.

"It's a good plan, Da. I've heard the same as Bram." Glancing at the whiskey bottle, he shook his head, as if clearing his thoughts. "There are mustang herds south of here, but north of Sacramento. The lad I spoke with said they're hiding in the hills where they've shelter in the gullies. We could be gone two days or ten, Da. Can you spare us so long?"

Standing, Ewan shoved both hands into his pockets, joining Fletcher at the window. "If you go, I need to be knowing you'll not hold the lads back. They'll not have time to nurse you each morning."

Fletcher opened his mouth to protest, closing it at the deep concern in his father's eyes. He hadn't buried himself in a bottle for months. In the past, long nights with Maddy had contributed more to his irresponsible behavior than whiskey.

Last night's journey downhill had to do with the way Maddy seemed to drift away from him, wanting his help, but not being able to accept it. At least that was the way Fletcher interpreted her declination at his proposal.

"Nae, Da. I'll not be forcing the lads to take on my work." He glanced over his shoulder at Camden and Bram. "There'll be no more miscreant behavior like last night."

Clasping him on the shoulder, Ewan came to a decision. "You lads and Thane will be riding out before sunrise."

Conviction

Dob signed his name in the register at a shabby hotel at the end of a street near the docks. Paint peeling, sign hanging down on one side, it had three roads leading from it. Perfect for getting out of town in a hurry.

He looked at Lew and Ross before nodding toward the stairs. "Get your gear upstairs, then meet me down here. We need to start searching."

A few minutes later, he stood outside in the early morning sun, ordering the men in different directions, Lew and Ross staying with him.

They'd camped outside of town the previous night, wanting to ride in at first light, ready to search for Maddy again. The woman had proven to be more than a nuisance since running from them in Kansas. The days, riding through one small town after another, had begun to fade together. Over all the miles, they'd never stopped robbing banks and stagecoaches.

Today, Dob, Lew, and Ross would be checking the two banks in town, deciding which would be best for their next strike. As with the other men, they'd watch for Maddy, hoping this would be the last stop before making a return trip to Kansas.

The journey had been profitable, earning them more money than they could've stolen in a full year in Kansas or neighboring Nebraska.

"Damn girl." Lew bit the words out, voicing the frustration all the men felt.

"We have to find her soon." Dob focused on the people around them, looking for any sign of Maddy. "The men we met in Sacramento started out the day we left there. They'll be expecting us at the meeting place in three days."

Ross shot a look at him. "Are you sure you want us to get involved with them, Colonel? Seems we have a good thing going. We've never rustled cattle or stolen horses. Sure, we can all do it, but is that what we want? Hell, I'd rather rob a stage."

Lew walked between the two, feeling the tension build. He knew never to anger the colonel. Dob's brother, Byron, had and it ended with him in a shallow grave.

He agreed with Ross. Lew hadn't been impressed with the outlaws who'd been stealing cattle and horses, selling them within days to whomever paid the most. A couple months before, the rustlers had made a mistake, ending up in jail. Not long after, they'd broken out, cutting a path by robbing, rustling, and if what Dob learned was true, killing U.S. Marshals.

Unclenching his jaw, Lew slowed his pace, reaching into his pocket for a cheroot. Stopping, he struck the lucifer against the sole of his boot, lighting the slim cigar. He assessed Dob, hoping it wasn't his day to end up at the undertaker.

"Ross has a point, Colonel. The rustlers' faces are posted all over the state. They aren't careful, take risks." He drew on the cheroot, blowing out a stream of smoke. "You've done a good job keeping us off wanted posters. Even if they know our names, they'd never be able to recognize us. Seems to me we're better off on our own, not partnering with a group of men we don't know if we can trust."

Dob stopped outside San Francisco Merchant Bank, doing his best not to draw attention as he studied the door, windows, and people walking in and out. He turned a hostile gaze toward Lew and Ross.

"I've agreed to the meeting and I won't be going back on my word. Once we get the cattle, we'll take the herd to the buyer, then start back to Kansas."

Lew finished the last of the cheroot, dropping it onto the boardwalk and grinding it out with his boot. "What of Maddy?"

"If she's here, that gal won't be leaving." Dob couldn't hide the disgust he felt each time he heard his niece's name.

Fletcher leaned forward in the saddle, kicking Domino into a gallop, keeping the mustangs in sight. He heard his cousins behind him. It wouldn't be long before they caught up, spreading out to stop the horses from breaking toward an escape.

Camden shouted to the others. "They're turning right, lads." He reined his palomino, Duke, in the same direction, letting out a loud whoop as he gained ground on the mustangs.

"Toward the gully." Bram pointed in the direction the horses ran, looking around to make certain the others saw him. He needn't have worried. His younger brother, Thane, stayed on the herd's right, Camden on their left, with Fletcher and Bram at the back, pushing the horses toward a narrow gorge with no escape.

They'd almost reached their goal when the lead horse, the herd's stallion, stopped, the other horses skidding to a halt. Snorting, he pawed at the ground, silently ordering the mares to gather behind him. As if human, the mares did what he wanted, their wide eyes skittering over the riders and back to the stallion, unsure of their next move.

Fletcher motioned for his cousins to push the horses back into the gully, blocking any path from the improvised cage. As they rode closer, the stallion reared, lashing out with his front legs, staying alight far longer than Fletcher thought possible.

Before any of them knew his intentions, the stallion dropped to the ground and charged past the men. An instant later, the mares followed, rushing toward them with a wave of power and frightened determination.

Chapter Fourteen

Fletcher whirled Domino around, yelling over his shoulder. "I'll get the stallion. Don't let the mares get away." He didn't look back, kicking his horse and giving chase.

Leaning over the saddlehorn, Fletcher focused on the stallion, urging Domino into a run. The mustang ran back in the direction they'd come, stopping on top of a hill. Turning, he faced Fletcher, snorting in anger and warning. Rearing back, he snorted again, eyes wild. Coming down, he pawed at the ground before rearing once more.

"You are a beautiful animal." Fletcher whispered the words to himself. Wrapping a hand around his rope, he checked the noose. He'd get one chance. If he missed, the stallion would run again. Fletcher would follow, but success would depend on Domino's speed and endurance.

Clucking, he slowly moved his horse toward the stallion. Spooking him would make his work harder. Getting as close as he dared, Fletcher prepared the rope.

When the stallion dropped to the ground one more time, Fletcher made his move. Swinging the rope, he said a prayer, releasing it into the air. The entire sequence took seconds, but seemed longer. He blew out a relieved breath when it sailed over the horse's head, slipping down his neck. Fletcher tightened it, giving the horse notice he'd been caught.

It took a few seconds before the stallion realized what had happened. Pinning his ears back, he squealed, a loud, high-pitched, ear-piercing scream, before he reared back. A moment later, he let loose with a deafening roar, an imposing sound indicating the stallion's furor.

Fletcher's muscles strained, sweat glistening on his face and neck. Never had he worked so hard to control a horse, but he'd never encountered such a wild, spectacular animal. Desire to take the stallion to Circle M, make him a central part of their breeding operation, solidified his determination to control the horse.

The stallion calmed, snorting before letting out a deep whinny. Rocking from one side to the other, he eyed Fletcher with unconcealed fury. One minute passed, then another. The lull was expected, a tactic Fletcher had seen many times when breaking horses. He refused to let down his guard as he waited for the stallion to make his move.

As expected and without warning, the stallion reared back again, this time with a force stronger than Fletcher anticipated. The rope almost slipped from his grasp before he tightened his hold.

Most times, he broke horses while standing on the ground. Today, he didn't dare leave the saddle. Domino had performed well, and Fletcher had full confidence in his gelding's ability to respond to his commands. This wild stallion was unlike any he and Domino had encountered.

The horse continued to rear and buck with such force, Fletcher's confidence waned. If Bram and Camden were here, their ropes around the stallion, he had no doubt they'd have him controlled with little effort. He briefly thought of his cousins, hoping they'd kept the mares secured in the gully. Fletcher suspected they had or the horses would already be upon him, their senses guiding them to their impressive leader.

Groaning, his arm and back muscles burned at the stallion's constant struggle to escape. He'd be sore for days after this fight. It would be worth it if he secured the horse for their ranch.

The matching of wills continued, Fletcher panting under the effort. He wondered how much longer he could hold out. His hands blistered more with each tug of the rope. If they weren't already, they'd be bleeding before the contest ended.

Surprising him, the rope went slack, the stallion exhaling with a loud blow. Spirits improving, Fletcher allowed his muscles to relax. This was what he'd been waiting to hear. A blow typically indicated the final stages of a horse's fight, and it couldn't come soon enough. He reminded himself not to relax his grip. In a second, the stallion could rear back, starting the battle again.

The horse moved back and forth, his angry blows changing to snorts. After another moment, the stallion whinnied, then nickered.

Fletcher swallowed, talking to the stallion. "That's the way, lad. Calm down and I'll loosen the rope." Pressing his legs into Domino's side, the gelding moved forward. Fletcher didn't allow him to go far before reining back, waiting to see if the stallion had given up.

Several more minutes passed, Fletcher watching for any sign the fight wasn't over. After fifteen minutes, he rode closer, his gaze steady on the stallion's eyes. He'd expected to see defiance. Instead, he saw defeat. It was the final indication Fletcher needed. The struggle was over.

Getting as close as he dared, Fletcher stroked Domino's neck, still watching the stallion, his comments directed to both horses.

"It's time for us to head home, laddies." Making certain no more than ten feet of rope separated him from the stallion, Fletcher reined Domino around. "Time to find the others."

Conviction

Maddy slipped into her white blouse, then stepped into the dark skirt which made up her uniform. Her hands shook, fingers uncooperative, as she worked to close the top. It seemed to take forever before she finished the chore, tucking it into the skirt.

It had been this way since she'd sent Fletcher away, refusing his suggestion they marry. *Suggestion,* she thought with a grim smile. He didn't love her, didn't want her or the baby. Still, he'd do what was right, marrying her to legitimize the child. It should've been enough, an answer to her prayers. Coming from Fletcher, it had been a slap in the face.

She didn't know what else she expected. Before he left for Settlers Valley to help Blaine with his ranch, Maddy allowed herself to believe he loved her as much as she loved him. Then she'd gotten his note. He felt no love at all. And why would he? He'd come to Buckie's for fun, which was what he'd thanked her for in the brief message. She felt the blow with the same intensity today as she had months ago. Maddy wondered if the ache would ever go away.

A knock had her opening the bedroom door, seeing Suzette in the hallway.

"I'm walking over to the hotel. Would you care to come with me?"

Maddy's eyes sparkled. "Can you wait a couple minutes? I'm almost ready."

"Of course." When Maddy opened the door farther, Suzette walked in, sitting on a chair by the window. "How are you feeling today?"

Picking up her stockings and shoes, Maddy sat on the edge of the bed. "Good, considering..." She left the remainder unsaid, knowing Suzette could fill in the rest. "I'm wondering when you think it would be best for me to move into the kitchen." When Suzette's brows furrowed, Maddy's heart sank. "Did Mr. Donahue speak to you about me changing jobs when people begin to notice my condition?"

Grimacing, Suzette shook her head. It was always the same with Bay, doing all he could to undermine her job. The reason for his antics wasn't lost on her. He wanted her gone, sooner rather than later. August hadn't brought him in on the decision to hire Suzette, not mentioning his partners, the MacLarens and Bayard Donahue, until his last telegram.

She remembered how her heart had stopped when she saw his name on the telegram. They hadn't seen each other since the worst night of her life. Even now, pain and humiliation ripped through her. Suzette still loved him, would always love Bay, but she'd ruined everything.

"Suzette?"

Blinking away the past, she turned to look at Maddy. "No, he didn't mention it. Please, tell me what he said."

She bit her lip, chest tightening. Suzette could go along with what he offered or fight it with August and Bay.

"He stopped by one day when you were still at the hotel. Mr. Donahue had figured out my condition and suggested when I reached the point where it was obvious that I move into the kitchen. He assured me he'd speak with you about it."

Seeing the uncertainty in Maddy's eyes, Suzette offered a humorless smile. "It's a good idea. I don't have any problem with you working in the kitchen, although I do hope Bay spoke to the chef about it." She chuckled, thinking about the man's temperament. "You know how he can be." As she spoke, Suzette saw Maddy's features relax. "Please don't worry about it. Do you feel you're ready to make the shift?"

Placing a hand on her stomach, Maddy considered a move into the sometimes chaotic kitchen where the chef had a habit of yelling when everything didn't go as he expected. She worried how the added anxiety would impact her. As she idly rubbed her stomach, she knew working in the kitchen would be better than not having a job at all.

"Would making the change in a couple days give you enough time to speak with the chef?"

"Plenty of time. I don't want you to worry about it, Maddy. My only request is if he yells at you, you'll tell me. The man needs to have some limits to his outbursts, after all." This time, the smile reached her eyes. "Are you ready?"

Standing, Maddy let out a relieved breath. "I am. Thank you, Suzette, for allowing me to make the change."

She set a hand on the young woman's shoulder. "It's my pleasure to be able to keep you working with me. It would be quite lonely without you in the restaurant."

Lew Quick leaned against the outside of a building, taking out a cheroot and lighting it. The day hadn't gone as planned. When they knew no more about Maddy than when they rode into town, Dob's temper had flared. He lashed out at everyone. Not unusual for the man he'd known for years.

Taking a draw on the slim cigar, Lew thought of Maddy. As always, guilt knifed through him. He knew what happened was one of the reasons she'd ridden out in the middle of the night, alone, with nothing but her tattered coat, some food, a small amount of money, and a gun.

Lew knew he should walk back to the hotel, meet the others for supper, but he needed time to himself. He didn't like the way the gang had changed over the time since Byron's death. Everyone had been stunned at Dob's decision to kill his brother, a man he professed to admire. Lew had almost ridden out the same night, and given what happened later, he regretted his decision to stay.

Taking a last draw of the cheroot, he snuffed it out on the ground. Pushing away from the building, he started to leave when his gaze landed on two women stepping out of a house across the road. Lew almost turned away, stopping when one of the women laughed, holding the rail as she descended the front steps. When she glanced up, his throat tightened. *Maddy.* After all this time, they'd finally found her.

He tucked back against the building until certain they couldn't see him, allowing his gaze to wander over her. When his eyes roamed over her stomach, his gut clenched. Maddy was pregnant.

"Sonofabitch," he ground out in a low voice.

Watching them cross the road, he leaned away from his cover long enough to see them enter the Feather River Hotel. Scrubbing a hand down his face, he murmured several more curses.

"What the hell do I do now?" He spoke to no one, needing to get the words out as a way to voice his irritation. Lew knew he couldn't tell Dob about seeing Maddy. The man wouldn't care a wit about her pregnancy. He'd kill her either way, burying her far from town before riding away without an ounce of regret.

Lew wouldn't allow Dob to hurt her, not after all the pain he'd already caused his niece. A bitter chuckle crossed his lips. The colonel didn't care if someone was a relative, close friend, or a woman he professed to care about. He'd kill any of them with little thought and no remorse.

Making a quick decision, Lew walked back to the hotel, vowing to never tell Dob what he'd seen.

South of Circle M

Bram, Camden, and Thane sat around the opening of the gully, guarding it while chewing jerky and eating hardtack. A noise behind them had each turning.

"Seems the lad found the stallion." Camden stood, the corners of his mouth sliding into a broad smile.

Cupping his mouth with both hands, he shouted. "Do you need help, Fletch?"

As he drew closer, Fletcher nodded. "More rope," he shouted back.

All three scrambled to grab the rope from their saddles before running toward him. Reining to a stop twenty yards from the entrance to the gully, Fletcher gripped the rope tighter, unwilling to let his guard down even a bit. The stallion could change his mind at any time.

The horse had picked up the scent of his herd half a mile back, becoming agitated, pulling at the rope. Fletcher needed to get more restraints around him soon before the herd began to fuss, rushing out of the gully to join him.

"What do you want us to do?" Bram checked the noose, his gaze locked on the magnificent stallion.

"I'm needing two more ropes around him, lad." Fletcher winced at the pain from the blisters. "Cam and Bram, I'll be needing your ropes around him. Thane, keep yours ready. I'm not thinking it's needed, but..." He shrugged, having no idea how many ropes would keep the stallion under control. The instant the other two ropes slid over the stallion's head and down his neck, he bucked, snorting.

"He's a braw one, Fletch." Cam held his rope, studying the incredible horse. "This stallion is what we'll be needing to grow the horse breeding."

162

"Aye. I've been thinking the same." Fletcher glanced over his shoulder at the mares. "How did you keep them in the gully when the stallion escaped?"

Camden chuckled. "Thane drew his gun, fired in the air. Stopped the herd before they breached the gully's entrance."

"The lad is growing up fast." Fletcher tugged on the rope, watching the stallion start to settle. He continued snorting, pawing at the ground, but no longer reared up or bucked. Quite a successful trip, assuming they could get the herd back to Circle M.

"We'll be needing two lads on the stallion, the other two with the herd." Camden's muscles slackened when the stallion stilled.

"Aye. I plan to be staying with the stallion. The three of you decide who rides with me and who stays with the herd."

Camden nodded at Fletcher, his mouth twisting as he thought about the trip home. "It'll be a slow trip. If we leave at dawn, we should be getting the herd to Circle M before dark. We'll be needing to keep the stallion separated and hobbled. If we don't, he'll be running within the first day."

Bram moved next to them, having heard the exchange. "I'm agreeing with Cam. This stallion will be able to jump the corral fences. If he does, the mares will stampede to follow. Hobbling is the only way to control the horse until he's broken."

Sucking in a breath, Fletcher's jaw clenched. He didn't mind hobbling for short periods, but the stallion was so stubborn, he'd need to be hobbled all the time, except when one of them worked him.

"Aye. First, we have to be getting him and the herd to Circle M. We need to be concentrating on which trail. Cam's right about leaving at sunup. If we don't, we'll not be making it to the ranch before dark. We don't want to be out with these horses after sunset."

Bram nodded. "And we'll have to be keeping watch for the rustlers. If they see us, we'll be too much of a temptation for them to ignore."

Camden glanced at the stallion again. "We can't be forgetting the dead U.S. Marshals. The rustlers aren't opposed to killing. Driving a herd is the perfect time for them to shoot us and steal the horses."

Moving the rope to his other hand, Fletcher studied the blisters. Slipping into gloves wouldn't be possible until they healed, which meant holding onto the stallion's rope all the way home.

He glanced between his cousins, not feeling the guilt he expected at the announcement he needed to make.

"I'll be needing to ride into town when we return, lads." Fletcher blew out an irritated breath. "I've got to be figuring out what to do with Maddy and the bairn."

Camden's brows rose. "You've got to be talking the lass into marrying you, Fletch. There's nothing more you need to be figuring. Wed Maddy. You can work through the rest of it afterward."

Fletcher stared into the darkening sky, agreeing with Camden. The problem wasn't the responsibility to marry. He'd already accepted his obligation.

The problem was getting Maddy to accept the inevitable. He might not fully trust her, but he respected what she'd done to keep the baby. Fletcher enjoyed her company, broad smile, and hearty laugh, so unlike the tittering sound of many young women. She was smart and a hard worker, both perfect for the role as a rancher's wife. Circle M would be a safe place for her and the child, surrounded by his family and the support they'd offer. He was offering everything he had and couldn't understand what else she expected.

Frustration didn't quite encompass what he felt. All he understood was he had to do something to get Maddy to change her mind, and he needed to do it soon.

Chapter Fifteen

Conviction

Lew finished breakfast, leaving Dob and Ross at the restaurant as he checked the repairs on his saddle. In truth, the saddlery wasn't his destination. He'd said nothing to Dob about Maddy, never intending to expose her presence in town. Lew wouldn't take part in the kidnapping and murder of a woman with child. After years with the man, he knew Dob wouldn't spare a second thought at giving such an order.

Striding down the boardwalk, he crossed the street, walking between a couple buildings. Crossing the next street, he stopped at the same spot where'd he'd seen Maddy the night before. Pulling out a cheroot, he lit it, coming to terms with what he needed to do.

A night almost two years ago crossed his mind. Considering all he'd done in his life, the mistakes he'd made, lives lost at his hand...that one night stuck with him.

Rubbing his chin, he stared at the house, still thinking of what had happened to the beautiful young woman.

Unbeknownst to Dob's men, Maddy had been standing in the shadows when he ordered his men to kill her father. Lew had backed away, disgusted at the command to murder his leader's brother, a man everyone saw as better than Dob. Better, and not as ruthless.

Putting several yards between him and the others, Lew had heard a soft sob. Taking a quick glance to his side, his stomach roiled at the sight of Maddy, tears streaming down her lovely face, both hands clutched over her mouth.

Unable to go to her without arousing Dob's suspicion, he'd watched Maddy double over, unable to control the pain at what she'd witnessed. She'd also been unable to do anything about it.

The instant she straightened, her gaze met his. He'd given her a terse nod, a signal for Maddy to run. When she'd turned away, Lew thought that would be the end of it. He'd been wrong.

The sound of laughter pulled his attention from the dark thoughts of his past. Maddy and another woman left the house, walking in the opposite direction than the previous evening. They headed toward the main street. Even in her condition, there would be little chance Dob or one of his men wouldn't recognize her.

Making a quick decision, Lew hurried to catch up, trying to think through what he planned to say. The instant she saw him, he had no doubt Maddy would panic and run. He knew there was no help for it. She needed to be warned and taken out of town, even if she fought him the entire time.

Praying she wouldn't, he closed the distance between Maddy and him. Coming alongside her before they reached the main street, he waited a moment for her to notice. It took mere seconds for her to look over at him, a slight gasp escaping her lips. In her attempt to dash away, Maddy almost tripped, Lew reaching out to steady her.

"No!" Maddy screeched.

Lew tightened his grip on her arm, wincing at the pain radiating from his shoulder when the other woman slugged him. He glanced at her, shaking his head.

"I need to speak with Maddy. It's important," he hissed when she hit him again. Grabbing Maddy's shoulders, he forced her to look at him. "Dob is here. You must get away." He slowly directed her between two buildings and out of sight.

Face paling, breath coming in rapid pants, she focused on Lew. "Dob..."

"Yes. And he won't care that you're with child, Maddy. He plans to kidnap and kill you. Trust me, he won't change his mind at learning of your condition."

"Who are you?"

He looked at the other woman, not letting go of his hold on Maddy. "Lew Quick. You?"

"Suzette Gasnier."

"Miss Gasnier, Maddy must come with me before Dob discovers her. If he gets his hands on her..." Lew swung his gaze to Maddy. "You know what he'll do." He dropped his hands, stepping away.

Suzette settled a hand on Maddy's arm. "Is Dob the man you're running from?"

Pulse racing, she nodded. "Yes. He's been chasing me since I ran away in Kansas."

Lew drew her attention back to him. "Do you have somewhere to go until Dob gives up and leaves?"

A stricken look lightened her already pale face. Maddy cast a troubled gaze at Suzette. "Do you think Fletcher might allow me to stay with him?"

Suzette's features softened, keeping her voice low. "He wants to marry you and is the father of your baby." She squeezed Maddy's arm. "I don't believe he'll have any problem with you staying at the ranch."

Sucking in a shaky breath, she looked at Lew. "There's a ranch a few miles east of here. They might let me stay there."

Lew stepped back a couple feet, his gaze sweeping the street as he'd done since giving Maddy the news about Dob. "Do you have a horse?"

Pursing her lips, she shook her head. "No."

"You can use my buggy."

"Then you'd have no transportation, Suzette."

"If I need to go someplace, I'll rent one at the livery or borrow August's. I'd take you out, but I don't have enough time before I must be at the hotel." Suzette looked at Lew. "Will you ride out with her?"

He ignored the horror in Maddy's eyes. "I won't let her go alone."

"I can go alone," she protested.

"Then how will the buggy get back to Miss Gasnier? I don't know how long Dob will stay in town. It could be a few days or a couple weeks."

Maddy understood his meaning. "Then I'll drive the buggy and you can ride alongside."

Impatience swept through him. "Fine, but we need to start soon. Every minute you stay gives Dob a chance to find you."

Trail north to Circle M

Fletcher's entire body ached, his hands bleeding from the numerous blisters. He worked hard every day, breaking and training horses. It never occurred to him catching a wild stallion would create additional pain. Even with Camden sharing the responsibility, they struggled to keep the horse from trying to escape. If he did, the mares would follow and they'd have to start all over.

Maddy's image flashed through his mind. Fletcher needed to get to Conviction, convince her to reconsider his offer of marriage. He intended to claim her and his child, no matter how long it took. First, he had to get to her. Losing the stallion and herd wasn't going to happen.

"Fletch." Camden called his name, motioning to the stallion.

His thoughts moved from Maddy to the job of getting the herd to the ranch. Turning his attention to the horse, he realized the stallion had become docile and quiet. No longer did he show the rage of being captured. The fight had disappeared.

"Can you handle him by yourself, lad?"

Camden nodded. "Aye. You help Bram and Thane."

Riding to his cousin, Fletcher handed him the rope. Relief surged through him. The loss of the rope gave his hands immediate respite from the constant pain.

"You'll be signaling me if he changes his mind, Cam."

He waved Fletcher off. "Aye. Now go help the lads."

Giving a brisk nod, he reined Domino around. Lifting a hand to Bram and Thane, he waited until the herd passed before taking a position at the back. Normally, he hated riding drag. Today, he didn't care where he rode if it meant a reprieve from handling the stallion.

His thoughts went back to Maddy and what he could do to convince her a marriage to him wouldn't be as bad as she believed. Fletcher still didn't understand what she found so repulsive. He'd offered her a life she'd never achieve as a single mother. She hadn't been rude when declining his proposal.

"Proposal."

The word didn't feel right when he spoke it aloud. Wincing, he thought back on the last time he'd seen Maddy. Instead of a proposal of marriage, he'd made an offer out of duty. Even if they'd known each other while she worked at Buckie's, Maddy had expected more from him.

The thought she'd anticipated something else confused him. They'd shared weeks of private time in her room, being intimate and talking until almost dawn. He'd grown much more attached than he'd planned.

His affection for Maddy had been the real reason he'd volunteered to help his cousin, Blaine, at the MacLaren's new ranch in Settlers Valley. It was why he'd written the terse note to her, telling her their time together was over. Guilt ripped through him when he recalled the message, understanding too late how it would affect her. He'd never meant to hurt Maddy, yet he knew he had. The note was something he had to address with her, along with the reasons marrying him wouldn't be so awful.

Tilting his face up to the clear afternoon sky, Fletcher relaxed in the saddle. If the stallion kept his current sullen behavior and the weather held, they'd make it to Circle M before sunset. They'd secure the herd and hobble the stallion, then clean up before riding to Conviction.

Tonight, he'd begin his campaign to convince Maddy marriage to him wouldn't be a miserable union. In time, he hoped it could be much more.

Circle M

Her anxiety increased as the ranch came into sight. Maddy had never been here, didn't know any of the MacLarens except Fletcher, Bram, Camden, and Brodie.

As sheriff, she knew Brodie wouldn't be at the ranch. Biting her lower lip, she prayed at least one of the others would be there.

Scanning the row of houses, she breathed in, letting it out in a slow whoosh. Passing the first house before stopping in front of the second, her chest squeezed, not sure what to do next.

"I'll help you down."

For a brief moment, she'd forgotten Lew rode beside the buggy. "Thank you."

Feeling her feet touch the ground, she dropped her hands from his shoulders, stepping away. The less contact she had with Lew the better. She'd hoped to never see him again and wondered why it had to be him saving her from Dob.

Back then, Lew had done what was forced upon him. Today, he'd found Maddy, rescuing her before doing what he'd promised—accompanying her to Circle M.

Steeling her resolve, she looked around, noting a couple men in a corral not far away.

"Do you recognize anyone?"

Licking her lips, she shook her head. "No."

"Then we'd best introduce ourselves." He stalked to the steps, noting Maddy still stood by the buggy. "Come on. I need to get back to town before Dob misses me."

The implied threat of Dob learning about her had Maddy moving to Lew, stopping next to him. "All right. I'm ready."

"It's going to be fine, Maddy."

She shot him a disbelieving glare. "How do you know that? These people don't know me, have no idea what I've been through..." Her voice trailed off, as did her courage.

"I'm guessing they don't know about the baby."

Maddy shook her head, humiliation flashing in her eyes. "Or that Fletcher is the father."

Without thought, she placed a hand on her stomach, dropping it at the sound of the door opening. A woman she recognized from the restaurant stood there. Fletcher's mother, she was certain of it.

"I thought I heard voices. May I be helping you?" An interested grin accompanied the question before her gaze moved from Maddy's face to her stomach. The grin changed to a broad smile. "You've a bairn on the way."

Swallowing, she nodded. "Yes, ma'am. Almost six months now." She glanced at Lew. "I'm Madeleine. I—"

"Ach, I know who you are, lass. You work at the Feather River Restaurant. I'm Lorna MacLaren. You've served me and my husband, Ewan." She opened the door. "You'll be coming inside and tell me why you've come."

Once inside, Maddy introduced Lew, both declining anything to drink. Settling onto a settee, she drew in another breath, desperate to find a sense of calm before explaining the reason for her visit. Lew took a seat next to her, which didn't help with her search for composure.

Lorna sat in a chair near Maddy, clasping her hands together in her lap. "Now, tell me why you're here, lass."

Clearing her throat, she found it hard to meet Lorna's gaze. How did you tell a woman the baby you carried belonged to her son? Maddy's shoulders slumped, realizing how difficult this was going to be and having no idea how to start.

"Lass, are you all right?"

She looked up into Lorna's concerned face. "I'm sorry, Mrs. MacLaren. Yes, I'm fine. I wondered if, well...is Fletcher here today?"

Her brows drew together. "Fletcher? Nae, the lad and three of his cousins went after wild horses. Are you needing to speak with Fletch?"

The slamming of the front door stopped any response. Lorna turned to see who had walked inside.

"Ewan, we have guests. This is Lew, and this is—"

"Madeleine." Ewan grinned before his eyes moved to her stomach. "Are you here to see Fletch?"

Gasping, Maddy's gaze darted between the three people in the room. Her throat tightened, another wave of uncertainty gripping her chest.

Lorna's eyes widened. "Ewan, how would you be knowing the lass is here for Fletch?"

Ewan stared at Maddy before sitting in a chair close to his wife. "This is the lass Fletcher was seeing before he left to help Blaine."

Tears began to form, Maddy doing her best not to let them fall.

Lorna's mouth dropped open. "Fletch was seeing you, lass? What would that be meaning?"

175

"Aye, love. They were seeing each other for a while. Isn't that right, lass?"

All the courage she'd fought to attain disappeared as tears began to flow down her cheeks. Covering her face with both hands, she sobbed.

Lew moved closer, putting an arm around her shoulders. She leaned into him, doing what she could to regain control. After a minute, she pulled away, brushing the moisture from her face before standing.

"I'm so sorry. I shouldn't have come."

"Sit back down, lass. Whatever it is, we'll be working it out." Ewan's stern voice had her stilling. She saw the determined, yet sympathetic look on his face, deciding to do what he asked. "Now, tell us how we can be helping you?"

"Is the bairn Fletch's?" Everyone turned to look at Lorna. "Well, is it, lass?"

She lowered her gaze to stare at her round belly. "Yes, ma'am." Looking up, she saw the doubt on Ewan's face. "It truly is Fletcher's, Mr. MacLaren. I wouldn't lie about something so important."

Lorna's features sobered. "Does the lad know about the bairn?"

Maddy swallowed. "Yes, ma'am. He asked me to marry him, but I turned him down."

Jumping to her feet, Lorna glared at her. "You said no to the lad knowing you carried his bairn?"

"You don't understand."

"No, lass, I don't." Lorna forced herself to sit back down.

Maddy stared back down at her lap, her voice cloaked in regret. "Fletch doesn't love me. I don't want him to marry me out of duty."

"Do you love the lad?"

She lifted her head at Ewan's question. A shaky breath escaped, misery on her face. "Yes, I love him. At one time, I thought he felt the same, but why would a man like him want a life with a woman who worked at Buckie's?"

Lorna slouched against the chair. "Buckie's. And what would you have been doing there?"

"Serving drinks, nothing more. The bartender, Frankie, and I grew up together. He encouraged me to come to Conviction and convinced the owner to hire me."

"And the bairn?"

Feeling her pulse race, she swiped more tears from her face. "I can't explain it. When I came downstairs one night, Fletcher, Bram, and Camden were at the bar. He turned and looked at me, and something happened. Fletch kept coming to Buckie's, never talking to any of the girls but me. I finally realized *I* was the reason he came in so often." She let out a bitter laugh. "Actually, several of the girls told me they'd never seen him pay so much attention to anyone. Frankie said the same. Though I knew it was wrong, after a while, I took him to my room." Her voice had grown increasingly low and rough.

"And the lad continued to ride into town every night." Ewan's voice held no trace of accusation. He looked at Lorna.

"The lad wouldn't have been doing that if he felt nothing for you, lass."

Maddy's surprised gaze met Lorna's. "That's what I thought until I received his note."

"Note?" Lorna asked.

She drew in an unsteady breath. "He was leaving and wrote me a note. Bram delivered it." She pursed her lips, heart clenching. "It was over. He didn't want me."

Ewan scowled. "Ach, the lad knew what he was wanting, and it was you, Maddy. I'm thinking Fletch didn't know how to tell his ma and me about his saloon lass."

She felt the color drain from her face. "But—"

"Ach, lass. If you knew Fletch better, you'd know the lad cares a great deal for you." Ewan leaned forward, resting his arms on his thighs. "Maybe the lad doesn't love you. Caring for you would be a good start to a marriage."

Lorna stood, crossing her arms. "You'll be staying with us for now, lass."

"But what about when Fletcher returns?"

Snorting, Lorna dropped her arms to her sides. "If the lad is such a dunderhead, he can be staying in the barn." She looked at Ewan, who held up his hands.

"Aye, love. If the lad can't be talking the lass into marrying him, he can be making his bed in the barn." Ewan stood, as did Lew.

Lorna grinned. "It's settled. I'll be showing you to a bedroom, lass. Would you be spending the night, Mr. Quick?"

"No, ma'am. I just wanted to be sure Maddy arrived safely."

Ewan stepped beside him. "I'll be walking you outside then. I'm hoping you'll be visiting us again, Mr. Quick."

Lew settled his hat on his head. "Wish I could, but I'll be leaving town soon." He lifted Maddy's belongings out of the buggy, carrying them up to the porch. "Thank you, Mr. MacLaren."

"For what, lad?"

"Taking Maddy in. She's a good girl...a real good girl. If she says Fletcher is the father, he is."

Bounding down the steps, he tied his horse's reins to the back of the buggy. Climbing onto the seat, he nodded at Ewan, hoping the man he'd taken an immediate liking to never learned of Lew's history. Slapping the lines, he prayed the MacLarens would take care of the young woman he'd been unable to protect in the past.

Chapter Sixteen

"We're almost home, lads." Bram lifted his hat, letting out a loud whoop as he rode alongside the herd, keeping them in a tight group.

Fletcher felt a rush of relief, more than ready to corral the herd. Camden and Bram would make sure they were fed and the stallion hobbled while he cleaned up for his trip to town. He still hadn't settled on what he would say or how he'd persuade Maddy to see him if she refused.

Staring beyond the herd toward the approaching ranch houses, he noticed a buggy taking the road back to town, wondering at the driver. The curiosity didn't last long.

The sounds of the herd prompted several MacLarens to run toward them, shouting their welcome, broad smiles on all faces. The sight of them helped settle Fletcher's growing unease at his inevitable conversation with Maddy.

Colin rode toward them, followed by Quinn, one moving to the right while the other took a position on the left, helping them keep the herd in close as they approached the corral. Coral, one of the orphans the MacLarens adopted, ran from the barn to the corral and opened the gate.

Each time Fletcher returned from travel, it surprised him at how Coral had grown into such a beautiful young woman. She'd always seemed so much younger, while in truth, only months separated their ages.

Securing the herd, Fletcher slid to the ground.

"I'll take care of him, Fletch." His younger sister, Kenzie, held out her hand, taking Domino's reins.

"Thanks, lass. I'll be needing to ride him into town tonight."

A frown crossed her face. "You'll be wanting to speak with Da about it, Fletch. He and Ma are inside with a visitor." Kenzie didn't say more before heading to the barn.

Brows furrowed, Fletcher shook his head, not allowing his sister's comment to concern him. Nodding at Bram, Camden, and Thane, he headed to the house, bounding up the front steps and opening the door.

"Da, Ma, we're back."

His brows crinkled again at the quiet. Kenzie, Clint, and Banner were outside, but he expected his parents to be in the house, his mother preparing supper. Shrugging, he hurried up the stairs, beginning to strip from his shirt as he walked.

The sound of voices stalled his steps. Before he reached his bedroom, the door to an extra room across the hall swung open. His father walked out, then his mother, both pinning him with an unrecognizable gleam in their eyes. A moment later, he knew why.

His breath caught at the woman following them out of the room.

"Maddy?" He barely got her name out before taking a step closer. When she didn't respond right away, he turned a curious gaze to his parents, dismayed when they didn't speak before walking down the stairs. Shifting back to Maddy, he held out a hand. "What are you doing here, lass?"

Not moving from her spot just outside the bedroom, she let him grasp her hand. She lifted her face to search his. "I'm sorry, Fletcher. I had no other place to go."

Conviction

Lew felt the breath seep from him under the tightening grip of Dob's strong hand around his neck. Returning near dark, he'd returned the buggy to Suzette before hurrying to the hotel. Pushing open the door to his room, he found himself shoved against a wall, the door slamming shut.

Clawing at Dob's grip, Lew summoned enough strength to slam a knee into his groin, at the same time sending a vicious punch to the man's jaw. Feeling the hold on his neck loosen, Lew pushed Dob's chest, shoving him away before kicking his knee. Toppling over, Dob's head slammed against the frame of the bed, eyes rolling back as he slid into unconsciousness.

Staring down at the colonel's inert form, Lew sucked in several deep breaths, rubbing his neck. His time with Colbert's gang had come to a sudden end.

Grabbing his saddlebags, stuffing his few belongings inside, he took one more look at Dob. He hoped never to see the deranged killer again, and prayed leaving would cut any ties to where he'd taken Maddy.

Making a sudden decision, Lew hurried from the room and out of the hotel. Tying the saddlebags behind the saddle, he mounted in one smooth motion and kicked the horse. He took a quick look behind him, leaning forward when he spotted Ross on the boardwalk, a gun pointed in his direction.

Urging the horse forward, he refused to look back, trusting Ross would make the right decision and lower the weapon. Lew had never been sure of his old friend's loyalties. Some days he seemed fine with Dob's orders. Others didn't sit well with him. Unlike Lew, Ross had never reached his limit, never made the decision to leave the gang.

As he came to the end of the street, he hesitated before taking the trail east—directly toward the MacLaren ranch.

Circle M

Unable to miss the distress on Maddy's face, Fletcher gripped both of her hands in his, squeezing. "There's no need to be fretting on it, lass. You did right by coming here."

Narrowing her gaze, she didn't answer, trying to get her trembling body under control. The instant she'd seen

Fletcher, her throat closed and body shook, the same as it had the last time he'd come to Suzette's.

Turning down his offer of marriage had been much more difficult than she'd expected. He looked so handsome, which wasn't unexpected. One look at Fletcher and her mouth would dry and heart flutter. Today wasn't any different.

He used a finger to lift her chin to meet his gaze. "I'm not angry at you being here, lass. It's good you came. It will be giving us time to talk."

The last brought a small smile. "Do you mean time to talk so you might convince me to marry you?"

He returned her smile. "Aye, Maddy. I'd been planning to ride to town tonight. You being here is much better." Fletcher heard his mother setting the dining room table. Moving a hand to her elbow, he turned her toward the stairs. "Let's be going down to supper. Afterward, we'll be taking a long walk, lass."

She lifted a brow. "Long?"

"For as long as it takes to convince you I'm who you should be marrying."

Conviction

Dob sat in a chair, wincing at the throbbing pain in his head. It came from two places—his jaw and the spot where he'd struck the bed frame. Trying to straighten his knee, he let out a string of curses. He wouldn't be going anywhere for a while.

"You ought to see a doctor, Colonel." Ross stood out of the man's reach. No one could predict when Dob would lash out. Even injured, he could build enough rage to kill a man with his bare hands.

Dob glanced at the men standing in his room. In a low, ruthless voice, his gaze stopped on Ross. "None of you worthless reprobates saw Lew ride off?"

Everyone shook their head, Ross being the only one to answer. "No, sir," he lied. "We were all spread around town searching for Maddy. How long ago did this happen? Maybe we have time to go after him."

Dob sneered, upper lip curling. "If you didn't see him leave, it would be a waste of time to search. Lew could've gone in any direction." Besides, he wanted to be there when they found them, which he didn't doubt they would. Lew knew how to get lost, but at some point, he'd lower his guard. Revenge appealed to Dob, and he'd enjoy doling it out on his former captain.

"Everyone stays here until we grab Maddy. Afterward, we'll go after Lew. But I'm warning all of you. I'll be the one to take his worthless life."

Circle M

Supper had been quiet, the conversation centering on the new horses, contracts, building an additional corral, and including more of the young women in ranch work. Bridget, Fletcher's cousin, was eighteen and ready to help with the herd. At nineteen, Coral was also

185

begging for more time helping with either the cattle or horses.

"I'm thinking it's time we let the lasses work with us. They're good riders and we could be using their skills, Da." Fletcher took another bite of venison.

"This is excellent, Mrs. MacLaren." Maddy cut a slice of meat. "You should run the kitchen at the restaurant instead of the annoying man..." Her voice faded, remembering the MacLarens were part owners of the restaurant. "I mean—"

"Ach, lass." Ewan waved a hand in the air. "I'm knowing the man's a dunderhead. August knows, too. He and Suzette are looking for a replacement."

A relieved grin tipped up the corners of her mouth. "That's wonderful news. Suzette already told me I could start working in the kitchen."

Fletcher raised a curved brow, holding back a retort. They'd be outside soon, taking a long walk as they discussed their future, including any notion she had of going back to work.

The table lapsed into normal conversation until all food had disappeared. After dessert, Fletcher stood, pulling out Maddy's chair. "We'll be taking a walk."

"Oh, no. I should help your mother with the dishes."

Lorna's mouth twisted into a wry grin. "Nonsense, lass. You should be going with Fletch. It's a beautiful night, and I'm sure you two will be having a lot to talk about. Besides, Kenzie and the laddies will be helping me."

"Thanks, Ma." Taking Maddy's hand, he helped her stand, placing a hand on the small of her back, directing her outside. Feeling her shiver, he stopped. "Are you cold, lass?"

"No, I'm fine."

She didn't feel fine. Tension rolled off her in waves, the shivers having nothing to do with the temperature and everything to do with the man next to her.

He studied her a moment before Fletcher gave a brusque nod. "We'll be walking down to the horses we brought in today."

She shuddered with excitement. "I love riding. When I arrived in Conviction, I was forced to sell my horse." Maddy pushed away the regret lancing through her stomach at the thought of selling her beautiful mare she'd owned for years. "Papa gave her to me when I turned ten. She was green, and my father let me help train her. For a while, I'd hoped to buy her back from the livery owner. It didn't work out." A gloomy expression replaced the quick look of exhilaration she'd shown a minute before.

Fletcher studied her face, not liking the pain in her eyes. "Is the mare still at the livery?"

Wrapping her arms around her waist, Maddy shook her head. "No. When I returned from San Francisco, she was gone. The livery owner said he'd sold her to a rancher who planned to give her to his daughter and use her for breeding."

With each word, the puzzle came together. Taking Maddy's hand, he changed directions.

She picked up her pace to keep up with his long strides. "Where are we going?"

"To the corral on the other side of the second barn."

They slipped into silence, Maddy observing the four large houses, four barns, and numerous corrals.

"Four brothers came west with their families, each building a house and barn." Fletcher grinned. "Everyone helped with each building, Uncle Angus's house being the largest." His hand squeezed hers. "Uncle Angus and Uncle Gillis were murdered. Colin is the oldest of Angus's lads, and Quinn is the oldest of Gillis's, so they take care of their families now. My da and Uncle Ian have the final say on what we do. Several no longer live here."

"Brodie?"

"Aye. As sheriff, the lad needs to live in town. You already know Blaine is in Settlers Valley. Heather, Quinn's oldest sister, married Caleb Stewart. They're running a ranch not far from Blaine's. My sister, Jinny, married Sam Covington, so they're in town. Sean, Uncle Ian's oldest, is in Scotland at veterinary school. The clan is no longer the same as when we arrived."

Maddy's voice held a hint of curiosity. "Better or worse?"

"Ach, lass. It depends on who you talk to."

"What do you think, Fletch?"

"The lads and lasses who left are happy. I've no issue with them leaving if it's what they wanted. From what I've seen, it is."

An ache grew in Maddy's chest. If she married Fletcher, he'd no longer be able to build the future he wanted. He'd be shackled with her and a baby, a child he hadn't accepted as his. From what Lorna said earlier, all the marriages in the past had been based on love. Maddy envied them. A marriage with Fletcher wouldn't include love, at least not from him.

Stopping by a large corral, Fletcher seemed to be searching for something. Her gaze followed his, breath catching when he pointed to a small mare. Placing a hand over her mouth, she stifled an excited scream.

"What's her name?"

"Snowflake," she whispered, unable to take her gaze from her mare.

Fletcher whistled before cupping his hands to his mouth. "Snowflake!"

The mare lifted her head. Spotting Maddy, she whinnied before trotting toward them. She whinnied twice more before stopping on the other side of the fence.

"Snowflake." Maddy moved closer, stroking the mare's nose.

Fletcher stepped next to her, placing a hand on her shoulder. "Is this your mare?" He already knew the answer. When his da had bought the horse for Kenzie, he'd been told her name was Snowflake.

She swiped at the tears on her face. "Yes. Whose horse is she?" Her voice shook.

"My sister, Kenzie. Da bought the mare for her."

"Oh."

A sharp pain pierced through Fletcher's chest at the hurt in that one word. "I'll be talking with Da and Kenzie. They'll understand."

Continuing to stroke Snowflake's nose, Maddy shook her head. "I don't want to take the horse away from Kenzie."

Settling an arm across her shoulders, Fletcher reached over the fence, running a hand down the mare's neck. "The lass won't mind. Da will get Kenzie another horse."

She slid one hand over her stomach. "I won't be able to ride until after the baby comes, which is still a few months away. Can we wait until then to say anything to Kenzie?"

He squeezed her shoulders. "Nae, lass. She and Da must be knowing right away. Trust me, you'll be getting your mare back."

Maddy hated taking away a young girl's horse. She knew how it felt to lose an animal you loved.

Leaning down, Fletcher kissed her temple. "No more fretting on this, lass. I know Kenzie, and she'll understand. So will Da. Are you ready to be continuing our walk? You'll be seeing her as much as you want, love."

She kissed the tip of Snowflake's nose. "All right." Stepping away, she took one more look at the mare before allowing Fletcher to guide her away. The horse she'd never thought to see again whinnied, bringing a grin to her lips. "Thank you, Fletch."

He didn't admit he'd do anything to see her happy. Instead of answering, he pointed to the corral on the far side of the last barn. "Luck had been with us. We found the herd sooner than we'd been expecting. All are mares. The stallion is in another corral at the other end of the first barn, near Colin's house."

"Why do you need so many?"

"Da and Uncle Ian signed contracts to supply horses to the Army. Our breeding program isn't large enough to fill the orders. We'll be keeping two or three of the mares for breeding." He rested his arms over the top rail of the corral, watching the horses graze. "We've a lot of work, lass. I want you here to see it."

Stomach twisting, she gripped her hands together. "I don't know, Fletch."

"What would you not be knowing, Maddy?"

She moved a few feet away from him, feeling her body tremble. Being near him was as dangerous now as when she'd still worked at Buckie's. Maddy felt her face flush when he turned to fix his gaze on her.

"Maddy?"

Keeping her voice calm, she straightened her spine. "I came here because men are after me, Fletch. I didn't come to agree to a marriage." She saw his nostrils flare, the pain her announcement caused.

"Who are the men after you?"

"My uncle, Dob Colbert, and the men who ride with him."

Chapter Seventeen

Fletcher didn't interrupt as Maddy explained the reason Dob wanted her. He already knew her uncle had murdered her father. Learning the outlaw planned to do the same to her sent icy waves of anger through his body.

"I'm so sorry, Fletcher. It wasn't right of me to bring this danger to your family. They've been very kind and welcoming. I believed there was nowhere else for me to go…" Her voice faded as images of Ewan and Lorna came to mind. Refusing to meet his gaze, she dipped her head. "I should leave tomorrow." The slight shimmering of tears glistened in her eyes.

He wanted to take Maddy in his arms, hold her against him until he made her understand this was exactly where she should be. Stepping to within a few inches, he lifted her chin with a finger, cupping her face in both hands.

Lowering his head, Fletcher held his breath, waiting to see if she moved away. When she didn't, he pressed his lips to hers. The kiss was slow and sensual, laden with all the pent-up desire he'd tried to forget since leaving Maddy behind.

Feeling her hands move up his arms to grasp his shoulders, Fletcher drew her closer, his arms wrapping around her back. His mouth covered hers in a hungry passion more intense than anything he'd ever experienced—except with Maddy.

Fletcher hadn't allowed himself to remember the feel of her in his arms, the intensity she put into everything. Their first few nights together had been tentative, at times faltering, as they explored, bringing each other pleasure. Tonight, her touch, the way her hands caressed his shoulders before stroking his back, almost brought him to his knees.

His lips brushed down the soft column of her neck, kissing the pulsing hollow at the base of her throat. Her soft moan made him crazy, his kisses becoming urgent, body responding to a painful degree. Raising his mouth, he stared into her eyes, glazed with passion.

"Ah, Maddy. I've missed you, lass." He grazed another kiss across her lips, feeling her tremble. "Marry me. Live with me at Circle M where we can raise our bairn together."

Stilling an instant at the mournful expression on her face, he began to stroke his hands in a soothing motion on her back.

"Do you love me, Fletcher?"

His brows furrowed, the question catching him by surprise. Unease rushed through him. He didn't know if he should lie, telling her he did love her, or let her know in the gentlest way possible he wasn't certain. Would admitting he cared about her a great deal be enough? The tightening in his chest gave him his answer. She needed the truth.

"I'm not sure. I care about you very much, Maddy." Feeling her stiffen, he rushed on. "I'll make you a good husband and be a good da to the bairn. You'll not be worrying about me straying, lass. I've no interest in any other woman."

Sliding her hands between them, she pushed on his chest, moving out of the comforting embrace. Lower lip trembling, Maddy stared up at him, collecting her courage.

"It's a very good offer, and I'm quite honored at your desire to do what you consider right. I'll not have you throw away your future on a woman you don't love. You deserve so much more than that, Fletcher."

Jaw clenching, he glared at her. "Is the bairn mine, lass?"

Jutting out her chin, she nodded. "Yes. I wouldn't lie to you about something so important."

"Are you loving someone else, Maddy?"

Pain flashed in her eyes before she shook her head. "No."

"If you left, where would you be going? Do you have family or friends who'd provide for you, care for you as I would, lass?"

Again, she shook her head. "No."

"I'm the bairn's da, Maddy. I'll not let you go, taking the bairn from me."

Blinking, a hand flew to her throat, to the exact spot Fletcher's lips had been a few minutes before. "I don't think..." She glanced away, finding it impossible to finish the sentence. He'd offered her so much—a safe place for her and their baby, a family, and respectability, something she was desperate to regain since working at Buckie's.

"You're being awfully quiet, lass. What is distressing you?"

Worrying her lower lip, a look of despair mixed with vulnerability clouded her features.

He stroked his knuckles down her cheek, his expression full of hope. Gripping her chin, he rubbed the pad of his thumb over her lower lip.

"Tell me, Maddy."

She waved her hand toward the houses and barns in a sweeping gesture. "You have a wonderful family, Fletch. You're successful and respected. Everyone north of Sacramento knows the MacLaren name." Locking her gaze with his, she shook her head, hoping he'd understand. "My uncle is an outlaw, a horrible, brutal man who is searching for me. I worked in a saloon. Few people know I only served drinks and you were the only man I invited upstairs." When Fletcher opened his mouth to respond, she touched his lips with a finger. "You must know most believe I was the same as all the other girls at Buckie's, no more than a common saloon whore. My reputation will only hurt your family, and I can't do that to them, or to you."

Fletcher waited, giving her time to say more. When she remained silent, a slight grin lifted the corners of his mouth.

"So I'm understanding you, you're saving my family embarrassment because you worked at Buckie's." He tilted his head in question.

Maddy gave a jerky nod.

"You're also not wanting to ruin my future. I'm remembering you didn't want to be standing in my way of finding a lass I might love. Do I have it right?"

Feeling heat infuse her face, she lowered her head a little, then lifted it in a questioning nod.

Reaching out, Fletcher gripped her chin, keeping her attention on him. "I'll not be meeting another lass, Maddy. You're the only one I want, and I'll never be in another's bed. As for your past, you're insulting my family by thinking them so shallow. Once I explain, they'll not be caring about you working at Buckie's, and they'll not spare a second worrying about what others think." Dropping his hand, Fletcher took a step away, giving her a little space. "I'm wanting you Maddy, you and the bairn. Stay. You'll not be regretting it."

She wanted to believe him, more than he'd ever understand. Fear more potent than the reality of Dob chasing her had kept her from accepting Fletcher's offer. She loved him so much, wanted him to love her back. Maddy didn't doubt he'd love the baby, providing a good home.

She needed to remember their child's future. Having a safe home and loving family was much more important than not gaining Fletcher's love.

Closing her eyes, she breathed in, letting it out in a slow hiss. Squaring her shoulders, she rested a hand on her stomach, raising her gaze to his. Reminding herself she was doing this for the baby, Maddy nodded.

"If you're sure this won't hurt your family."

The tightness in his features began to ease. "I am, lass."

"All right, Fletcher. I'd be honored to marry you."

Before she had a chance to draw another breath, he swept her into his arms. "Ah, lass. You'll not be regretting your decision." Burying his face in her hair, he allowed relief to drift over him. "I'll never be doing anything to make you sorry."

Wrapping her arms around his waist, she accepted his promises, trusting he'd keep them. What she prayed for, wanted to believe would still be possible, was the love he might never feel.

Lew slipped farther into the trees not far from the corral where Maddy spoke with someone he suspected to be one of the MacLarens. He hadn't met the man, but by the obvious emotion sparking between the two, he believed it was Fletcher MacLaren. The man Maddy loved, the father of her baby.

Lew couldn't hear what they were saying and didn't dare try to get any closer. He just hoped Fletcher would make her happy, be a good father, and keep her safe from Dob and his wretched plans.

He planned to camp within the boundaries of Circle M, intending to speak with Ewan the next morning. The family needed to be warned about Dob and his intention to join with another gang to raid the MacLaren's cattle and horse stock. He didn't know when, but it would be soon. Whoever stood in their way could die, and his conscience wouldn't allow him to stay silent.

Once he warned them, Lew planned to ride away, putting as much distance between himself and Dob as possible. He'd always wanted to see the Montana and Dakota territories. He planned to ride through Nevada and Utah, cutting north through Idaho before heading to Montana.

He'd heard they were always in need of lawmen in both territories. To his knowledge, he didn't appear on any wanted posters and no one knew his name. Starting over sounded good, a relief from Dob's constant search for Maddy, killing anyone who opposed him. A part of him wished Ross would ride with him, but he'd had plenty of chances to change his path and walk away from the man Lew now considered to be deranged. He understood how the atrocities of war affected a man, providing memories no one wanted to remember. Nightmares, rage, loss of decency were common within a good number of men who served for the North or South.

Lew still suffered nightmares, as did Ross and a few of the other men. Only Dob had deteriorated to a point where violence and death had become common. Killing someone almost seemed to soothe his agitation. For a few weeks afterward, he'd stay calm before the tension built again.

Right now, he knew the colonel sought revenge for the way Lew beat him before riding away. Dob would see it as a betrayal, punishable by death. The same judgment he planned for Maddy.

Warning her would soothe his guilt, as would apologizing for his part in hurting her. It may not have been his choice, but it was amazing what a man would do with a gun leveled at his head. That night, there'd been one pointed at him, another at Maddy. Lew counted it as the worst night of his life, and without having to ask, he knew she felt the same. He couldn't ride off without begging forgiveness. Whether he received it or not didn't matter as much as his attempt to get it.

From his hiding place, he watched Fletcher wrap his arms around her, pulling Maddy against his chest. Lew stiffened at the sight until Maddy circled his waist with her arms.

Not willing to take a chance of either of them hearing him move, he waited until they turned to walk back to the house. Resigned, Lew took one more look around before taking a trail to his small camp. Tomorrow, he'd talk to Ewan, speak with Maddy, then ride out of California to pursue his own dreams.

Fletcher and Maddy stood on the porch, hearing the sounds of his family inside, his siblings laughing. Putting his hands on her shoulders, he turned her to him.

"When we go inside, I'll be telling my family about the decision. Unless you're not ready, lass."

Studying his face, she lifted a hand, cupping his cheek. Her heart clenched at the look of hope on his face. "Let's tell them tonight."

Leaning down, he kissed her. He could've become lost in passion, but forced himself to pull back. "Are you ready, lass?"

Moistening her lips, she nodded. "Yes, I'm ready."

Holding her hand, he led her inside, walking straight into the front room. His da and ma sat on the settee. Ewan read a book while Lorna worked on embroidery. Kenzie sat on a chair watching Clint and Banner, sprawled on the floor, playing checkers.

Taking a quick glance at Maddy, he let out a shaky breath. "Ma, Da?" Fletcher waited until they looked up. Ewan was the first to speak.

"What are you needing, lad?"

Fletcher didn't miss the way Ewan's gaze dropped to their joined hands. "Maddy has agreed to marry me."

Lorna dropped her embroidery, jumped up, and hurried to them. Hugging her son first, she turned her attention to Maddy, a warm smile spreading across her face.

"This is bonny news." Her eyes began to water before she glanced at her husband. "Isn't this grand?"

Ewan took his time rising, allowing himself time to compose his response. In the end, he strode to Fletcher, clasping his shoulder. "Your ma is right. This is grand news."

Kenzie walked to them, hugging her brother, then Maddy, her smile infectious. "You'll be my sister."

Maddy swiped tears from her eyes, grinning at his family's acceptance. "Yes, I will."

Kenzie turned to her brothers. "Clint, Banner. Fletcher and Maddy are getting married."

Banner glanced up and nodded. Clint made a move on the checkerboard, then looked up. "That's good. I like Maddy."

"I do, too," Banner agreed, studying the board.

Lorna slipped an arm through Maddy's, turning her toward the kitchen. "Ewan, you should be taking Fletcher into your study. The lass and I will be talking in the kitchen. We've lots to plan for the wedding."

"Now, Ma?" Fletcher cocked his head at his mother.

"Aye, lad." She patted Maddy's stomach. "We've no time to waste."

Chapter Eighteen

Kenzie made certain the news traveled fast, visiting each of the three other homes early the next morning before her mother knew what she was doing. Not long afterward, the dining room in Ewan's home buzzed with activity.

Lorna decreed it had to take place the following Saturday. She hadn't even looked at Maddy when making the announcement, knowing the young woman would understand the urgency. Maddy did, but it still annoyed her. She'd run her life since leaving Kansas, never having the ability to discuss her fears or difficult decisions with anyone. Lips pursed, she kept her thoughts buried inside. She'd do nothing to offend her future mother-in-law, a woman who'd welcomed her into the MacLaren clan and in whose house Maddy would be living.

"We've a great deal of food to prepare." Kyla MacLaren, Colin's mother, looked at her daughter-in-law, Sarah. "You make such wonderful pies."

A slight smile tipped Sarah's lips upward. "I'll be happy to make several."

Lorna looked at Emma, Quinn's wife. "I know you're riding with the men a couple days a week, but would you be able to bake bread?"

Emma touched Lorna's arms. "Of course." She looked at Maddy. "I'm so pleased you're going to be a part of the family."

Forcing a smile, Maddy nodded, not sure why they'd want a pregnant woman, one who'd slept with Fletcher for weeks without benefit of marriage, to join their family.

Emma didn't notice the dismayed look on Maddy's face. "It's time someone snagged him. He's been wild long enough."

Maddy's eyes widened an instant before she caught herself. "Thank you." She knew her answer sounded weak and uncertain, but it conveyed how she felt.

"Maggie and Jinny will want to help," Lorna said to no one in particular.

Maddy recognized the names, her stomach clenching at meeting more of Fletcher's family.

Audrey, Quinn's mother, tapped her fingers on the table. "They can be bringing fried chicken and making biscuits when they arrive the day of the wedding." She looked at Lorna. "You, Kyla, and Gail can be making the roast, potatoes, and vegetables with me. Colin, Quinn, and the other lads can set up the tables and chairs."

Maddy's head began to spin as the women continued to make plans, becoming less and less sure of her role. "What can I do?"

Lorna raised a curved brow. "You'll be having plenty to do, lass. Getting fitted for your dress, going to town for slippers, ribbons, and lace. Emma will be sewing the dress and driving you to town." Lorna didn't notice the horrified expression on Maddy's face.

She didn't plan to go back to town, not until Dob gave up looking for her and rode off. Maddy looked at Emma. "Would it be all right if you rode into town without me?"

"I'd be happy to get what we need, Maddy. We'll make a list tonight."

Letting out a relieved breath, Maddy relaxed. "I'd appreciate it. Thank you, Emma." She glanced at Lorna, gratitude washing over her at all Fletcher's mother had already done for her. "I appreciate everything you're doing, Mrs. MacLaren."

Lorna reached across the table, placing a hand over Maddy's. "It's time you call me Lorna, lass."

She felt a flush of warmth. "All right...Lorna."

The sound of the front door opening drew everyone's attention. Maddy pushed up from her chair when she spotted Fletcher, her heart beginning to race.

The solemn expression on his face softened, his eyes crinkling at the corners as he sauntered closer to Maddy. A devastating grin flashed across his face, prompting a shiver to run through her.

"Good morning, lass." His deep voice caused her throat to constrict, heart to pound almost painfully. Every time she saw him, his presence affected her the same way. She supposed it always would.

Loving someone without the sentiment being returned felt as if a knife had been plunged into her chest. Maddy had to keep reminding herself the marriage would secure the baby's future, nothing more. She'd do her best to ignore her own regrets and focus on the most important person in her life. The baby.

She kept her voice even, features bland. "Good morning, Fletcher."

His eyes flashed for a moment at the formal tone, the steely resolve in her gaze. It didn't take much to understand the intent behind her calm determination. He wasn't a fool. Maddy was marrying him for the sake of the baby and expected nothing more from him. The thought should've comforted him. Instead, it caused a wave of regret. He looked at his mother.

"I'm needing to speak with Maddy."

Cupping her elbow, he felt her stiffen before guiding her outside, and down the steps toward the barn. Entering, she stopped, a breath whooshing out at the sight of Snowflake saddled and ready to ride.

"I spoke with Kenzie and Da. They've no problem finding another horse for my sister. Snowflake is yours."

She didn't look at him before pulling out of his grasp and hurrying to her horse. Stroking the mare's neck, Maddy kissed her nose. "Hello, Snowflake. It's been a long time."

The mare nickered, nuzzling her nose against Maddy's neck.

"I'm thinking she's glad to see you."

Maddy glanced up, not allowing herself to smile. She had to fight her emotions when it came to Fletcher. If not, she'd find herself growing bitter and resentful at his lack of feelings. At least their baby would be loved by them both.

"Thank you."

He narrowed his eyes at her distant tone. Fletcher didn't care for her detached manner, but there was nothing he could do about it. Not for the first time, he regretted telling Maddy he didn't love her. He should've lied, given her something to hold onto instead of dashing her hopes.

Fletcher contemplated if it would've been so awful a lie...or if it was a lie at all. He missed Maddy when they weren't together, wanted to talk with her until long into the night, wanted to hold her close while they slept. One of her brilliant smiles could improve his mood, make each day pass easier knowing he'd see her in the evening. When he'd left her behind to join Blaine in Settlers Valley, the sunlight disappeared, the easy days turning to gloomy hours and lonely nights.

Until she'd come to Circle M, he'd thought lust motivated him to spend time with her. Having Maddy at the ranch, knowing she carried his child, he accepted it was more. Fletcher wondered if it was love, if it always had been.

"Domino is already saddled. Are you feeling well enough to be taking a short ride?"

The first true smile she'd offered him in months lit her face. "I'd love to."

"You stay here, lass. I'll get your hat and let Ma know we'll be leaving for a spell."

Standing next to Snowflake, Maddy watched him leave, a deep, gnawing pain ripping through her at the love she felt for the handsome MacLaren. Blinking back tears, she steeled her resolve. Another man might be angry, unable to offer her a future. She reminded herself even if Fletcher never offered love, he'd keep her and their child safe.

Fletcher walked through the barn entrance, holding out her hat. "Here you are, lass. I'll help you into the saddle."

Settling the hat on her head, she lifted her skirt, placing a foot into his cupped hands. Her eyes widened at the effort it took to settle her added weight into the saddle, huffing out an excited breath as her hand closed around the reins.

"Are you ready, Maddy?"

So caught up in her excitement at being back atop Snowflake, she startled at his voice. "I'm ready." Her breath caught at the quick smile he shot her.

Nodding, Fletcher swung up onto Domino, then clucked to get him moving, reining north as they left the barn. He kept the pace slow, allowing Snowflake to catch up. Glancing over, his mood improved at the smile on Maddy's face. It had been a good decision to speak to his da and sister about the mare.

Kenzie had hesitated a moment at her brother's request, but in the end, neither objected to giving

Snowflake back to Maddy. His da and sister believed it to be the right decision. Seeing Maddy's excitement, Fletcher had no doubt it was.

Riding past the last house, he reined right, toward the river.

"Where are we going?"

Fletcher's mouth tilted into a grin. "To my favorite spot. It's where I go when I've the need to be alone."

"You won't be alone if I'm with you."

"Aye, lass. I've wanted to share this place with you for a long time."

Maddy's breath caught at his confession, brows knit in confusion. "You've thought of me?"

He considered lying, then changed his mind. Turning to look at her, he nodded. "I've thought of you many times, lass."

She tried not to let his answer give her hope. To her knowledge, Fletcher had never lied to her, and he'd been clear about his feelings. Allowing her to share his private spot didn't mean anything had changed.

Maddy didn't respond to his comment, her gaze focused on the trail ahead. "How much farther?"

Fletcher didn't let the way she ignored his comment hurt. What did he expect? She'd stay because it was her and the baby's best option. Maddy would do whatever she must, even exist in a marriage devoid of love, to secure their child's future. He knew she loved him, but doubted she'd ever express her love for him again. Not until he faced the truth and voiced it to her.

"The spot is around the bend up there."

When they made the turn, he reined Domino to the right and into an opening, stopping a few feet from the river.

"Oh..." Maddy reined next to him, eyes wide. She took in the tiny pasture, tall elms, and the sound of flowing water. "This is beautiful, Fletch."

Swinging to the ground, he tossed Domino's reins over a branch before lifting his arms to help her down. The instant his hands clasped her waist, Fletcher knew letting her go would be hard. Slowing his movements, he slid her down his chest, hearing a sharp intake of breath at the same time her hands gripped his shoulders.

After longer than needed, Fletcher allowed her to slide lower until her shoes touched the ground. He looked down at Maddy, waiting several moments for her to meet his gaze, noting she hadn't moved her hands from his shoulders.

When her eyes met his, a broad smile crossed his face at hearing her ragged breathing. The smile froze when she moistened her lips, squirming a little closer. His body responded even as his mind told him to let her go, move away before he did something more than just hold her.

"Are you planning to let me go, Fletch?" Maddy's low voice trembled enough to let him know she wasn't unaffected by his touch.

"Do you want me to, lass?"

Licking her lips again, she opened her mouth to speak, then shut it.

Lifting a brow, he moved his hands from Maddy's waist to her back. "Lass?"

Biting her lower lip, she forced herself to remember the type of marriage they would have after the ceremony on Saturday. The joy of his touch vanished, forcing her to face reality. Letting her hands drop to his chest, she pushed.

"Yes, it would be best."

Cocking his head to the side, he narrowed his eyes. "Best for who?"

"Both of us, Fletch." Pushing a little harder, she stepped away when his hands moved from her back to his sides. She ignored the quick flash of disappointment on his face, refusing to allow her true feelings to show.

Turning away, Maddy took determined steps, reaching the river in a few strides. Resting both hands on her stomach, she scrutinized the rushing water, feigning more interest than she felt.

She still trembled from the way Fletcher helped her off Snowflake. His touch elicited memories of what it had been like before he left for Settlers Valley, how she'd fallen so hard for the tall, attractive rancher.

Maddy remembered the rush of excitement when she spotted him walking into Buckie's each night, how much she missed Fletcher when he left her bed before dawn.

Staring at the rushing river, she also recalled how much it hurt to read his goodbye note. Even now she felt the pain, as if she'd been kicked by a mule. The message had been brief and unexpected. It had taken several hours to accept how little she meant to him.

Choking out a bitter laugh, she swiped a tear from her face at the thought she'd be marrying him in a few days. Over the last few days, she'd spent hours talking herself into going ahead with the union for the sake of their baby.

Standing alongside the riverbank, Maddy let out a resigned breath. She couldn't...no, wouldn't go through with it. She loved Fletcher too much to go through with the farce of a marriage.

Thinking through it, Maddy decided she had two solutions, neither good, but each better than participating in a marriage devoid of love. She could have the baby and ride away, leaving their child to the care of the MacLaren family. It would create the best future for the baby, but the worst possible option for her.

Or she could leave now. Fletcher would hate her for taking away his child, maybe try to find her. Eventually, though, he'd meet a woman he could love, marry, and build a life with. At some point, he'd realize Maddy's leaving had been the best for him.

"Maddy?"

She felt his arms wrap around her waist from behind, his hands resting over hers, which remained splayed across her stomach. An instant later, she felt his breath brush across her ear a moment before he pressed a kiss to her neck. Closing her eyes, Maddy allowed herself to enjoy the feel of his lips against her skin, wishing it meant as much to him as it did to her.

"Are you all right, lass?"

No, she wanted to shout. Instead, she said what he expected. "I'm fine. Your private spot is beautiful, Fletch. Thank you for sharing it with me."

Lifting his head, he pressed another kiss against her hair. "I'll be sharing everything with you, lass. Whatever it is you'll be needing is yours. What's mine will belong to you, Maddy." Tugging her closer to his chest, he looked beyond her, enjoying the same view as had captivated the woman in his arms.

"I wish..." Maddy's voice trailed off, stopping herself from revealing too much, exposing the love exploding within her.

"What do you wish, lass?"

Shaking her head, she turned in his arms, stepping away. "We should be getting back to the ranch. I need to help with the plans for Saturday."

Fletcher held out his hand, which she accepted. "We've time to sit for a few minutes before leaving." Tugging her a couple feet closer to the edge of the water, he helped her sit down before settling beside her. "This is where I sit when I've thinking to do." Reaching out, he plucked a few strands of grass, tossing them one at a time into the river.

Watching him, a measure of peace washed over her. "What do you think about?"

He shrugged. "The ranch, the future, and you, lass."

Eyes growing wide, she let out a surprised breath. "You thought about me?"

Glancing over at her, he frowned. "Aye."

"Because of the baby?"

Studying her face, he cocked his head. "You and the bairn. I've not been able to think about you without wondering how I'll do as a husband and a da." Looking back at the river, he rested his arms across bent knees. "I've been watching Brodie and Colin with their laddies, and I'm concerned I'll never be as good with our bairn."

Maddy's jaw dropped a little at his confession. She'd always thought of him as a confident, proud, and somewhat arrogant rancher, a man who could intimidate anyone with a look or make a fast friend with his charming smile. The man sitting next to her exuded insecurity, something she didn't quite know how to handle. She placed a hand on his arm.

"You'll make a wonderful father, Fletch. I believe you'll be even better than Brodie or Colin, and they're the best." Whatever else she planned to say stuck in her throat at the sound of gunfire.

Jumping to his feet, Fletcher held out his hand, helping her stand. "We need to be hurrying, lass." He led them to the horses, lifting her into the saddle. "The gunfire came from the north. We're riding south. We've got to warn the others."

They rode fast, her mind racing at the same pace as her mare. Her heart sank with the truth of what she had to do. Maddy would miss Fletcher. She'd miss the entire MacLaren family, but she couldn't stay. Sitting next to him, wishing for so much more than he could give was slowly killing her. A marriage wouldn't solve anything. Her decision wouldn't make sense to most people. It did to her.

Maddy would leave in the morning, and she knew exactly where she'd go.

Chapter Nineteen

Slowing in front of the barn, Fletcher jumped to the ground, helping Maddy off Snowflake before turning toward the house. Ewan rushed outside, Lew right behind him. Fletcher didn't miss the way Maddy's steps faltered at the sight of the second man.

"We've a problem, lad. This is Lew Quick. He's the man who brought Maddy to the ranch." Ewan glared at Lew. "He used to ride with Dob Colbert."

Fletcher pulled back the hand he'd intended to offer to Lew. "Colbert?" He shot a look at Lew, then at Maddy. "I'll be thanking you for bringing Maddy to me, but why are you here now?"

Ewan spoke first. "He's here to be warning us about Colbert and his plans."

Placing fisted hands on his hips, Fletcher glared at Lew. "What plans?"

Crossing his arms, Ewan nodded at Maddy. "Get the lass inside and we'll talk."

Fletcher hadn't noticed how she stood behind him until he felt her hand rest against his back. The touch said a great deal. She either feared or didn't like Lew, which bothered Fletcher a lot. Glancing down, he noticed her other hand on her stomach in a protective gesture.

"Come on, lass." Taking her hand, he led her into the house. Once inside, he turned her toward him. "You know the lad." It wasn't a question.

She winced, the color draining from her face. "Yes. He rode with the gang while my father was still alive."

Pulling Maddy down the hall, his eyes narrowed on her. "Why don't you like him?" His jaw clenched. He thought he knew the reason, but wanted to hear it from her.

Clasping her hands together, she shot a furtive glance toward the front door. The muscles in her face tightened. She didn't look at him.

Using his thumb and forefinger, he lifted her chin, forcing her to look into his eyes. "Maddy, what about the lad worries you?" Again, he waited, becoming impatient. "We'll not be leaving the hall until you tell me."

Closing her eyes, she sucked in a deep breath, swallowing the knot of shame. "He, um..." She bit her lower lip, shaking her head slightly. "Lew..." Her throat squeezed.

Lowering his voice, Fletcher stroked her cheek. "Is he the one?"

She didn't have to ask what he meant. Wincing, she nodded. "Yes."

The instant the word left her mouth, she regretted telling him. His face colored to an angry red, nostrils flaring, a muscle in his jaw pulsing. Fury building, he started to turn away, stopping when she gripped his arm.

"No. I need to explain. Please don't do anything until you hear what happened." Her panicked gaze met his angry one.

"Fletcher?" Ewan's voice broke the tension long enough for Fletcher to gain a measure of control.

"We'll be finishing this talk, lass."

Letting out a shuddering breath, she nodded. "Promise me you won't do anything until I explain, Fletch. Please."

"Ach. There you are, lad. Come into the study."

Fletcher waited until Ewan walked away before glaring down at Maddy. "I'll be waiting until we talk, lass. I'll be expecting the truth." Leaning down, he brushed a kiss across her lips before leaving for the study.

Watching him leave, she felt another wave of confusion. He claimed to not love her, but Fletcher's actions often said something else. Maddy closed her eyes, rubbing her temples. She hoped his meeting with Ewan and Lew lasted long enough for her to prepare what she'd tell Fletcher. After his reaction, she had to be careful what she said. It wouldn't do to have her baby's father arrested for murder. Especially when his older brother was the sheriff.

Fletcher took a seat across the desk from Ewan and next to Lew. He had a chance to study the man for a few moments when he entered the study, doing his best to contain his anger.

Lew wasn't bad looking. He appeared to be in his thirties, older than Fletcher expected. He had so many questions, but he'd stay quiet until Maddy explained, and he'd keep his temper under control.

"Lew came here to warn us about Colbert. He's working with another gang, rustling cattle and horses." Ewan narrowed his gaze on Fletcher. "He's also wanting Maddy."

A harsh curse left Fletcher's lips as he shot to his feet. "Why Maddy?"

"She's seen too much and can recognize everyone in the gang."

Lew's calm voice irritated Fletcher to the point he cursed again. Settling fisted hands on his hips, he walked to where Lew sat, glaring down at him.

"Why didn't you tell Da about Colbert when you brought Maddy here?"

Standing, Lew faced him, not intimidated by the anger rolling off Fletcher or the murderous look in his eyes. "I'm telling you now. Are you ready to hear all of it, or do you need time to settle down?"

Fletcher's jaw clenched. He wanted to grab the miscreant by the collar and slam him against the wall. Instead, he took a few slow breaths and crossed his arms. "Go ahead."

Lew gave a curt nod and sat down. "Not long ago, Dob rode with his brother, Byron—Maddy's father. They got along well enough, but Dob wanted to lead the gang without interference from his older brother. He forced

219

an argument, knowing Byron would fight him." Lew took a sip of the whiskey Ewan handed him. "Byron had Dob on his back, landing blows to his face. Not enough to leave real damage, but Dob didn't see it that way." His jaw worked as he thought about what to say next. "Byron was a better leader, but Dob had brought most of the men together. After a quick nod at one of his most loyal men, Byron fell away from two shots in the back. He died within seconds." Lew looked at Fletcher. "Maddy saw it all."

Scrubbing a hand over his face helped muffle a long string of curses. After a few moments, Fletcher's hard gaze bored into Lew. "What's the rest?"

"Byron's wife killed herself a week later, leaving Maddy alone. There's an older brother, but he took off a long time ago. He hasn't been heard from since. Dob made life miserable for Maddy, threatening her, forcing her to cook meals for all of us and wash our clothes. I did what I could to protect her, but..." Lew glanced away, unable to voice the worst of what happened to Maddy. "She rode off one night. We've been chasing her ever since."

"If the lass hasn't gone to the law yet, why keep chasing her?" Ewan asked.

"She knows all our faces, names, backgrounds, and what jobs we've pulled. Right now, there aren't any wanted posters out on us, and Dob means to keep it that way by killing anyone who can identify us."

Fletcher's brows drew together. "But everyone knows of the Colbert gang. I'm not understanding why there are no wanted posters."

"A man who served with Dob during the war thought he recognized us robbing a stagecoach he was on. He talked to a reporter who published the story. Other papers ran the story, too." He snorted. "It wasn't us. The men who did rob the stage were caught and hanged, but the story stuck. The law wouldn't put out wanted posters on men who hadn't committed the crime."

Fletcher rubbed a hand over his forehead. "How long has Colbert been chasing Maddy?"

Lew let out a long breath, shaking his head. "Going on two years. That gal's been through hell. Meeting you is the best thing that's ever happened to her. And I can tell you, if she says she was never with another man in the saloon, she wasn't. Maddy can't lie worth spit."

Fletcher wanted to say something else about her being with one other man, but promised Maddy he'd get the story from her first. Knowing the man was Lew, it took all his willpower to not haul him up by his neck and give him what he deserved.

"Rustling MacLaren cattle provides some bonus money for Colbert. As far as I know, he doesn't know Maddy's here. But I know Dob. He'll be scouting out this place for days before he joins with the other gang to take the herd. If he spots Maddy, he won't hesitate to take her. The fact she's pregnant won't matter, either. The man will shoot anyone, including women and children.

With Maddy, though, he'll draw out her death as long as possible. He enjoys seeing people suffer."

Fletcher leaned forward, resting his arms on his legs. "But the lass is his niece."

Lew barked out a mirthless laugh. "Dob doesn't care about them being related. Hell, he ordered the death of his own brother. Besides, he never took to Maddy or her mother."

The room went silent, each man considering what to do next. Fletcher knew what he wanted to do, doubting Maddy would agree to stay inside the house until they were certain Colbert had left the area or been killed. Fletcher hoped for the second.

"What do you want to do, Da?"

Ewan scratched his chin, his gaze wandering to stare out the window. "I should be talking to Ian, but the lad's in Sacramento to finalize another order."

"We can't be waiting on this, Da."

"Aye, we can't. Fletch, you'll be talking to Maddy. Make the lass understand she'll be needing to stay in the house for a while."

"She won't be liking it."

Ewan chuckled. "Nae, the lass won't. But she's carrying your bairn, living in the house, and she'll be doing what's needed to keep both of them safe."

Fletcher nodded. "Aye, Da. I'll be talking to her as soon as we're done."

"All right." Ewan stood, walking around his desk to lean against it. "This is what we'll be needing to do."

Maddy sat on the bed, hands clasped in her lap. Her few belongings either hung in the wardrobe or had been folded and placed in the dresser. The old, well-used hair brush lay on the vanity alongside the mirror her mother gave her when she turned sixteen. Everything she owned took up little space in this room, second only to Suzette's as the cleanest and nicest place she'd ever lived. After Saturday, she'd be moving all of it across the hall into Fletcher's room.

She stilled at the thought. Would she be here on Saturday or back in town at Suzette's? She'd planned to leave in the morning. The thought brought a sharp pain to her heart, causing enough agony to force Maddy to reconsider her decision to run. Then she thought of the visitor downstairs.

Why had Lew come to Circle M today? Whatever the reason, she knew it couldn't be good.

A soft knock preceded Fletcher joining her. "How are you feeling, lass?"

A little sore from the ride, exhausted, worried about the reason Lew rode out. "I'm fine. What did Lew have to say?"

Sitting next to her, he took Maddy's hand in his. "It's not something you're going to be liking."

She choked out a humorless laugh. "I didn't think he rode all this way to meet you, Fletcher."

He shook his head. "Nae, he didn't." Fletcher shifted to face her. "Dob Colbert is looking for you."

"Yes, I know."

His eyes widened a little before he continued. "Colbert is working with a gang of rustlers who've been raiding in this region. They already stole from us and are determined to do it again. Lew is certain Dob will be scouting our ranch, the houses, barns, and corrals, for several days before they strike." He watched as her features changed, understanding coming slowly. "You'll need to be staying in the house until we catch or kill him, lass."

She sucked in an unhurried breath, a slight frown pulling down the corners of her mouth. "What about the wedding?"

Fletcher massaged the back of his neck, lips pursed. "We'll have it inside. I'll not be putting it off any longer, lass. By Saturday evening, you'll be my wife."

His wife. It should've brought a jolt of excitement. Instead, a surge of disappointment wrapped around her, squeezing until her chest hurt. "All right, Fletch."

Something in her voice had him leaning forward to study her face, seeing a sadness he hadn't expected. "Maddy—"

She jumped up, pulling her hand from his. "I'd best go let your mother know." She moved to the door. "The wedding will need to be smaller." Gripping the knob, she pulled the door open. "Less food, less people..." Stepping into the hall, the bravado she worked so hard to keep in place faltered, her throat constricting. "I..." Swallowing, she shook her head before shutting the door, leaving Fletcher staring after her.

Fletcher started to say something, stopping when Maddy shut the door. Jaw dropping, he couldn't move. The woman whose spark, easy laugh, and challenging manner had captivated him from the first night they'd met had disappeared. Instead, those qualities had been replaced with a sullen sadness that cut straight through him.

Following her downstairs, he heard female voices and headed to the kitchen. Standing in the doorway, he waited until Maddy noticed him, his narrowed gaze locking with hers. He didn't look away when he spoke to his mother.

"Did Maddy tell you about the changes needed?"

Lorna took a step toward him. "Aye, and we'll be having the wedding in the house. There's no need to be worrying, lad. We've time to make changes."

Bending down, he kissed his mother's cheek before locking his gaze on Maddy once again. Walking to her, Fletcher gripped her hand.

"If you won't be needing Maddy for a while, I'd like to speak with her."

Lorna waved a hand in the air. "Go on with you. I'll send Kenzie to get Kyla, Audrey, and Gail," she answered, mentioning the other three aunts. "Maddy, did you and Emma write the list of what's needed in town?"

She pulled on Fletcher's hand, forcing him to stop walking out of the kitchen. Glaring up at him, she glanced back at Lorna. "Yes, ma'am. She'll be going to town in the morning."

"Ach, that doesn't give the lass much time to finish your dress, but it'll have to do." Lorna turned back to the stove.

"Come on, lass." Fletcher tugged on her hand, leading Maddy through the living room and down the hall to one of the guest rooms. Leaving the door open, he ushered her inside, pointing to a chair.

Crossing his arms, he stared down at her. "You need to tell me what's going on in your mind, lass."

"I don't know what you mean."

Pulling the other chair next to hers, he sat down. "You're not happy, lass. I'm wanting to know why." He didn't lean closer, didn't reach for her hand. "And don't be lying to me."

Maddy's heart pounded so hard, she felt certain Fletcher could hear it. She had a decision to make and no time to assure it would be a good one. Ignoring the regret clawing at her, she met his gaze. The time had come for her to say what haunted her heart.

"You don't love me, Fletch. Your offer to marry me is honorable, and I appreciate it. The truth is I'm not interested in a marriage without love." She gripped her hands together until the knuckles turned white. "I'm sorry, Fletch, but it's too hard being in love with you knowing you'll never feel the same."

Tilting his head back, he stared at the ceiling. Chest heaving, Fletcher tried to find a way to convince her marrying him wouldn't be as bad as she expected. But he'd spoken the same words several times, doing his best to change her mind. He'd succeeded for a few days. Now he understood the decision broke her heart.

"I need more time, lass." Fletcher wasn't sure where the words came from or why he spoke them.

Her sad eyes met his. "More time?"

This time, he reached over and took her hand in his. "You're important to me, lass. You and the bairn."

Squeezing his hand, she gave him a pleading look. "How would you feel if you did love me and I wasn't able to return your love?"

He didn't hesitate. "I'd not be liking it. I'd also not be liking you leaving. Give me time, lass. Time to figure out how I feel."

Desperation laced her features. "You've had enough time. Don't you see? We could have an amicable marriage, live in quiet acceptance, and never experience real love."

Fletcher's head began to spin. She'd said the same so many times, Fletcher started to believe she might be right.

"I also understand marrying a former saloon girl would be a significant blow to your pride."

His features hardened. "Pride?"

Closing her eyes for an instant, she let out a frustrated breath, pulling her hand from his. "You're a proud man, Fletcher. The MacLaren family is well-respected. Marrying me won't help your image."

He exploded. "My image means *nothing* to me. I'll not be letting you think less of yourself because you worked in a saloon." Standing, he paced a few feet away before turning back toward her.

Her mouth dropped open. "But—"

"Nae, lass. I'm no longer worried about what others think." He blew out a breath. "You're the only lass I want. Now and forever." Walking back to her, he knelt, taking both her hands in his. "Don't be leaving, Maddy."

Chapter Twenty

Maddy pulled the covers under her chin, staring at the ceiling. Her mind had been fighting sleep for hours, long enough for her body to ache and head to throb. No matter how hard she tried, Maddy couldn't get Fletcher's words out of her thoughts.

His beseeching look and sincerity in his voice melted her resistance. Something else also struck her. Fletcher did love her. He may not know it, fought to accept it, but Maddy heard it in his voice, saw it in his eyes. Leaving would destroy any chance he'd figure out how he felt, and Maddy couldn't think of anything she wanted more.

Before Fletcher left her yesterday to return to work in the corral, he'd asked Maddy to think about what he'd said. He also requested an answer the next day. She didn't need the time, but kept the knowledge to herself. Maddy had already made the easy decision not to leave Circle M—not when she knew in her heart Fletcher loved her. The idea made her feel giddy, the troubles of the past fading away, if only for a short time.

Maddy had also decided to shift her reason for staying to something else. She wouldn't tell Fletcher the truth. Instead, she'd blame Colbert. With him and his gang searching for her, moving back to Suzette's would put her friend in danger. Maddy refused to bring any harm to the lone friend she'd made since returning to Conviction. It wasn't a lie, but not the entire truth.

Huffing out a breath, Maddy glanced out the window, impatient for the sun to rise. She guessed at least two more hours remained before light filtered into her bedroom. Two long hours before she'd dress and head downstairs to help Lorna with breakfast. Unless...

Throwing off the covers, she hurried to slip into her clothes. Maddy knew Fletcher wouldn't approve of what she planned. In fact, he'd be furious, thinking she'd be putting herself in danger. Maddy knew better.

Almost nothing could get Colbert and his men out of their bedrolls before sunrise. If she rushed, Maddy could ride for an hour and get back before anyone would miss her, including Fletcher.

Grabbing her coat, she carefully opened the door, peeking into the hallway. Empty. Creeping down the stairs, she hurried out the front door. By the time Maddy reached the barn, her breath came in short pants. Pausing a moment, she continued to Snowflake's stall and winced. That was when she comprehended saddling the mare could be a real problem. Pursing her lips, Maddy squared her shoulders.

Refusing to let being six months pregnant prevent her from the ride she so desperately desired, Maddy removed the saddle and blanket from the rack. It took longer than usual, but with a great deal of effort, she completed the task.

It took three attempts before she settled into the saddle. Shoving aside the exhaustion already moving through her, Maddy guided the mare out of the barn and looked around. Seeing no one, she headed north, straight for Fletcher's special spot.

Dragging a hand down his face, Fletcher stood at his bedroom window, glad to see clear skies. He hadn't slept well, getting maybe three hours of sleep, and wondered if Maddy fared any better. A loud knock had him crossing his room to open the door, surprised to see Quinn in the hall.

"You've a problem, lad."

Fletcher's brows drew into a confused frown. "What problem?"

Shoving one hand into a pocket, Quinn pointed down the stairs with his other hand. "Maddy rode north a few minutes ago. I would've gone after her, but—"

Fletcher's roared curse interrupted him.

Quinn stayed in the hall, watching Fletcher slip into his pants and shirt, then pull on his boots. Grabbing his hat, he pushed past Quinn.

"Thane's saddling Domino for you."

Pausing at the top of the stairs, Fletcher glanced over his shoulder. "Thanks, lad." Bounding down the stairs, he heard Quinn right behind him.

"Thane's also saddling Warrior. I'll be coming with you, Fletch."

They didn't talk again before taking the reins and swinging into their saddles. Kicking the horses, they galloped north, Fletcher having a good idea of Maddy's destination.

"Where are we going, lad?"

Glancing at Quinn, his jaw clenched for a moment before he answered. "I've a spot along the river. I took Maddy there a few days ago."

"The lass liked it."

"Aye." What Fletcher didn't understand was why she rode off knowing Colbert and his men searched for her.

Neither slowed their pace, riding low in their saddles as Fletcher took the trail which ended at the river. He began to relax as they got closer. Spotting Snowflake through the trees, he let out a relieved breath.

Slowing, Quinn glanced at him. "I know you're angry, lad."

Fletcher gritted his teeth. "Aye."

"You'll need to be keeping it under control. At least until you hear why the lass rode out here alone."

Sucking in a deep breath, Fletcher did his best to heed Quinn's suggestion. It was hard. His heart still pounded, chest squeezing with the fear plaguing him during the ride. It had faded some, but the other emotions hung on, even if he couldn't quite define what they were.

Approaching the clearing, they saw Maddy sitting next to the river. Snowflake neighed as Domino and Warrior got closer, getting her attention.

Fletcher saw the instant she recognized them. Her eyes went wide, the color draining from her face.

Good, he thought as he reined his horse to a stop next to Snowflake.

"Keep your temper, lad," Quinn reminded him, deciding to stay with the horses.

Placing fisted hands on his hips, Fletcher drew in a deep breath to calm his irritation. "I'll be doing fine, Quinn."

Chuckling, he reached into his saddlebag, withdrawing a canteen and taking a sip. "Aye, but I'm still staying."

A wry grin crossed Fletcher's face. "Thanks, lad. I'll be making this quick."

"Do what's needed. You've plenty of time."

By the time Fletcher started for the river, Maddy had begun taking slow steps toward him. Her face was still pale, fear radiating from her eyes. He stopped, letting her come to him, allowing himself another minute to contain his waning anger.

"Lass."

She glanced at the ground before meeting his gaze. "Fletcher."

"Are you all right?"

Biting her lip, she nodded. "I'm fine."

Cupping her elbow, Fletcher guided Maddy away from Quinn. Turning her toward him, he rested his hands on her waist.

"You scared me, lass."

"I'm sorry. I just, well..."

"What, Maddy?"

The corners of her mouth slid up the slightest amount. "I couldn't sleep and decided to take a short ride. And before you yell at me, I did think about Dob and his men. I've never known them to rise before dawn."

"So riding out in the dark seemed safe to you, lass?"

The bravado she'd felt earlier disappeared under his intense glare. "You're right. After our talk last night, I needed to get away from everyone...even you."

A new wave of fear began in Fletcher's gut. Shoving aside the doubt tearing at him, he tightened his grip on her waist. "Did getting away help?"

She placed her hands on his arms, nodding. "If it's still all right, I'd like to stay."

He couldn't contain his relieved breath, or the broad smile breaking across his face. "Aye, it's more than all right." Fletcher moved his arms around her, drawing her close. "So you'll be marrying me, lass?"

Maddy laughed. "I love you and absolutely will marry you."

Dob, Ross, and another of his men watched from a safe distance away, a sneer on Colbert's face. His decision to scout Circle M in the early morning had been a good one. He hadn't expected to find Maddy, but couldn't have been more pleased.

Ross stared through his field glasses. "She's pregnant, boss."

Dob held out his hand, taking the glasses to confirm what Ross said. "It doesn't matter. We'll be going ahead with our plan. Nothing's changed."

"I don't know, boss. Murdering a woman is one thing. Killing a pregnant woman is something different. It just doesn't sit well with me."

Dob's narrowed gaze bored into Ross's. "You know what doesn't sit well with me?"

Ross shook his head.

"Leaving her alive to talk to the law. She knows our names, faces, and how we work. That knowledge is dangerous for us."

"Lew knows the same," Ross countered.

"And he'll be the next to fall. I don't intend to leave either of them alive when we ride out."

The third man, who'd stayed quiet until now, pointed toward the three riders. "They're heading back to the ranch, boss. Do you want to follow them?"

Dob rubbed his jaw, watching the three make their way along the trail. "No. We know Maddy's there. All I need to do now is keep watch on the place until most of the men are gone. That'll be our chance to take her."

Lorna, Ewan, and several others waited impatiently for Fletcher and Quinn to return with Maddy. News of her leaving had spread fast when the two rode out as if being chased by a raging bear. It had been all Ewan could do to keep Bram and Camden at the ranch when they heard about it.

"There they are." Bram kicked his horse, riding out to meet them. He spared a quick glance at Maddy before reining Bullet around to ride back with them. "Where'd you find the lass, Fletch?"

"By the river. Maddy needed time away."

"Did it help, lass?" Bram asked.

She flashed him a grin. "It did. Now I need to work with Emma on my dress. Saturday is only a couple days away."

Bram glanced at Quinn, raising a questioning brow at his older brother. "It's a shame about it being moved inside. Still, it'll be a grand wedding."

When they reached the row of houses, Bram and Quinn split off while Fletcher and Maddy continued to where Ewan and the others waited.

"Are you all right, lass?" Ewan walked up to Snowflake, raising his hands to help her down.

"Yes. I'm sorry if I caused any worry."

Lorna stomped up to her, arms folded across her chest. "Of course you were causing us worry, lass. Riding off while dark, not letting Fletch or anyone else know. It wasn't right of you."

"Ma." Fletcher slid to the ground.

Lorna stood her ground. "With Colbert searching, who knows what she would've been riding into."

When Fletcher started to respond, Maddy put a hand on his arm. "She's right. It was selfish of me to go without letting anyone know."

Ewan held up his hands. "It's over now and you're safe. We'll be going inside for breakfast, then we've a lot of work to do." He looked at his three youngest children. "Kenzie, Clint, Banner, take care of their horses."

Fletcher took her hand, stopping on the porch while the others continued inside. Grasping Maddy's shoulders, he lowered his voice. "After breakfast, you'll be telling me what happened between you and Lew. I'll be having no more stalling on this, lass."

Maddy knew he was right. Fletcher deserved the truth about what had happened with Lew to cause her to flee her home, living on the run for close to two years. It wouldn't be easy. Even thinking about it made her stomach churn. Regardless, it was time.

"All right, but you have to promise me you'll listen to all I have to say without interrupting. And you won't go after Lew when I'm finished."

Uncertainty flashed across his face. "I'll be doing my best, lass."

Jutting out her chin, she glared at him. "You'll promise me, Fletch, or I won't tell you anything."

Choking out a laugh, he nodded. "Aye. I'll be staying quiet until you're finished. I cannot promise anything after that."

Frowning, she nodded. "All right. I suppose it's the best you can do."

Smiling, he put an arm around her waist, leading her into the house. "Aye, lass. It is."

Conviction

Suzette cleared tables, keeping watch on the ones with diners. One of the servers sent word he wouldn't be coming in. He'd taken ill and wasn't sure when he'd return. His absence meant Suzette had no choice but to take his place.

Placing the dirty plates on a counter, she turned, stomach clenching when Bay and August walked in. She didn't want to deal with Bay, his snide remarks and condescending words. With only one other server, she didn't have a choice. If she wanted to keep her job, Suzette would continue the façade as best she could, forcing herself to smile, ignore his actions, and swallow her pride. She'd been doing it long enough, it should come easy. It didn't.

"Good morning, August, Bay. Would you like your regular table?"

August nodded. "That would be fine, Suzette. Seems you're short on help this morning."

"Unfortunately, one of the servers is ill. It isn't a problem, though. I'll be the one serving you." She held her breath, waiting for Bay to make one of his nasty comments, surprised when he stayed silent.

August took a seat, waving off her offer of a menu. "I'll have eggs, bacon, and toast. Oh, and coffee."

She looked at Bay.

"I'll have the same. Except add flapjacks to mine."

Turning away, she stopped at Bay's next words.

"Suzette, we need to talk."

Chapter Twenty-One

Circle M

Maddy chewed on her last bite of bacon, wishing there was more on her plate. Fletcher had already finished, signaling the time had come for her to explain what happened between her and Lew, the man sitting across from her. She glanced up at the scraping sound of chair legs on the wooden floor.

Lew fixed his gaze on Ewan. "If you'll excuse me, I'll be riding out to see if I can spot any sign of Dob and his men." He looked at Lorna. "Thank you for a wonderful breakfast, Mrs. MacLaren."

"You'll be joining us for supper, Mr. Quick."

Lew hesitated before answering. "I'll do my best."

Maddy watched as he left the house, wondering if she'd ever see him again. After what had happened, it surprised her how much she wanted to believe he'd be safe.

"Lass?"

She jerked her attention to Fletcher, who stood beside her, offering his hand. Taking it, she drew in a slow breath, steeling herself for the conversation to come.

"Thanks for breakfast, Ma. Maddy and I'll be on the porch."

Walking outside, he nodded to the porch swing, waiting until Maddy sat down before sitting beside her. They said nothing for several minutes, Fletcher not rushing her. When she began, her eyes took on a glassy look, her focus on the barn.

"Lew was the only member of the gang who was nice to me. He did his best to protect me from Dob, stepping between us on several occasions. Lew made sure I was safe after Dob murdered my father and my mother killed herself." She choked out the last, pursing her lips as she regained composure. "He made sure I ate and guarded my room while I slept. Lew was the only one I trusted. Dob eventually noticed the way he protected me and ordered him to stay away." She glanced over at Fletcher. "Lew refused, telling Dob they needed me safe, as I was the only one who cooked and washed their clothes. I was also the one who drove into town for supplies. Dob backed off for a while, until he and Lew got into an argument about the next stage robbery. Then the argument turned to me again, and this time, Dob refused to listen to anything Lew said."

Fletcher's anger rose, gut clenching as she continued, but he remained silent. Noticing her hands clasped tightly in her lap, he reached over, resting his hand over hers. Giving her an encouraging smile, Maddy continued.

"Dob had been drinking all night. At some point, he punched Lew in the jaw. No one interfered as they fought, rolling around in the dirt. I knew someone would die. Probably Lew because no one would dare go against Dob. I started screaming, begging them to stop. They were both bloody, their faces already swelling when Dob ordered a couple of the men to drag Lew off him." Her voice began to falter, face paling as she remembered what happened next. "Dob took several more swallows of whiskey before drawing his gun and pointing it at Lew's head. That's when he gave the order."

Maddy took several deep breaths, eyes watering.

Fletcher watched her struggle, hating to see her in so much pain. "You don't need to be saying more, lass." Leaning over, he brushed a kiss across her lips.

A haunted look crossed her face. "No. You need to know all of it. Afterward, I won't blame you if you decide to call off the wedding."

His eyes widened at this, but Fletcher shook his head. "I'll not be changing my mind, Maddy. Nothing you'll be saying will make me decide against marrying you." He watched her throat constrict and tightened his grip on her hands.

"Dob ordered two of the men to hold me down and pull up my dress. Then he ordered Lew to...to..."

Fletcher scooped her up, settling her on his lap. "Don't say any more, lass."

"I have to finish, Fletch. Please, I need to finish."

He drew in a breath, then nodded. "All right."

"Lew had no choice. Dob said he'd kill both of us if Lew didn't do as ordered." She swiped at the tears flowing down her cheeks. "Lew kept saying he was sorry as he did what Dob ordered. He told me to close my eyes and not open them until it was over. I did as he said. When it was over, he helped me up. I've never seen a man look more stricken. He held me for a while until Dob ordered him to take me to the cabin." She drew in another shaky breath. "Lew gave me money, told me to ride out that night, that he'd keep watch on the others as long as he could. He told me Dob would hunt me down, so to just keep riding. Lew promised to do what he could if they found me, but, well...we already knew what Dob would do if he caught me." She buried her face in Fletcher's shirt, heavy sobs bursting from her.

Tightening his hold, he rocked her, sick at the thought of what Dob had done to her. He'd ordered Lew to take her virginity in front of the entire gang, then chased her across country when she fled.

"I'm so sorry, Fletch. So very sorry."

Tears began to sting his own eyes, heart aching at her loss. "Ach, lass. It's not your fault. And it's not Lew's. All the blame is on Colbert." Kissing the top of her head, he worked to contain his growing anger at Dob and his men, vowing to find every one of them and make them pay.

He didn't know how long they stayed out there before her sobs stopped. "Lass, let me carry you inside. You'll be needing to rest now."

Maddy didn't protest, glad she didn't have to face anyone else after what she revealed to Fletcher. Laying her under the covers, he drew them up before sitting down next to her. He stroked her back until he heard the soft sounds of sleep. Bending down, he kissed her cheek.

"I *do* love you, lass," he whispered. Taking one last look, he left the room, halting in the hallway. He needed time to deal with what she'd said, to push aside his anger before he did something foolish. Leaning against the wall, he scrubbed both hands over his face.

Glancing at the closed door, he mumbled a string of curses. It had taken everything she had to open up to him and share what Dob did to her. Maddy was the strongest woman he'd ever known. Fletcher felt a surge of pride, knowing in a couple short days, she'd be his wife.

Thrusting away from the wall, he thought of the beautiful lass he'd come to love, vowing to do whatever he could to find justice for the woman who owned his heart.

Lew slid from his horse and crouched, watching Dob and the others huddled in the camp below. It wasn't noon and most of the men, including Dob, were already deep into whiskey.

He scanned the area around the camp, looking for a location where he could get close enough to hear their plans. It wouldn't happen given the location of their site. Although hidden in the trees, they'd be able to spot anyone who came close and wouldn't feel even a slight twinge of regret at shooting any intruders.

Leading his horse several feet away, he tossed the reins over a low branch. Pulling the rifle from its scabbard, he returned to rest against a tree and wait.

At the rate they were consuming whiskey, it wouldn't be long before most passed out, giving Lew a chance to sneak in and take their guns before running off the horses. If all went as planned, he'd have enough time to ride back to Circle M.

Resting his arms over bent knees, he settled in to watch the men, especially Dob. When he lost consciousness, the others would follow. All except one man. Dob always selected at least one of his men to guard the camp with strict instructions not to drink or fall asleep.

Lew began to count. If Dob hadn't added anyone, one man was missing, and Lew already knew who it was. Ross Sheehan.

Picking up the field glasses he'd taken from his saddlebags, Lew scanned the area. It shouldn't take long to locate the man he'd fought beside and ridden with on more robberies than Lew could count. The sound of a gun cocking told him Ross had found him first.

"Stand up, Lew."

He shifted enough to see the revolver pointed at his head, but didn't stand. "Good morning, Ross. How are you and the boys doing?"

"This isn't a social call," Ross snapped.

"No? And here I thought we were friends."

When Ross shot a look toward camp, Lew's hand slid to the handle of his gun. He stilled when Ross shifted back to him.

"I thought so, too, but you rode off."

Lew lifted a shoulder. "It happens when someone wants you dead and you don't know why."

Ross gave him an icy stare. "Dob's the boss. You accepted that when you decided to ride with him."

"That was before, Ross."

"Before what?"

"Before Dob went crazy, killing his brother and threatening anyone who disagreed with him. The man's volatile. One minute, all is fine. The next, he's got his gun pointed at you. It's your decision if you're comfortable with his behavior. I wasn't. I decided to get out before he killed me."

Shifting, Ross's brows knitted. "Dob's ordered you killed." He took another glance toward the camp, allowing Lew to slip the gun from its holster before Ross focused his attention back on him.

Shrugging, Lew forced himself to appear unconcerned. "Can't say I'm surprised. It's his way."

"What I don't understand is why you didn't ride out, get as far away from these parts as possible. You had to know staying would get you killed."

Tightening his grip on the gun, Lew moved enough to lift it quickly when the opportunity arose. Friendship meant little when Dob gave an order.

"Why don't you ride out with me, get away from Dob's irrational behavior."

Lew watched Ross's throat work. Unless he agreed to leave, the instant Ross looked at the camp again, Lew would make a move.

Frowning, Ross let out a stream of curses. "You know I can't leave."

Lew cocked a brow. "No, I don't know. Why the hell can't you leave?"

Ross shook his head in a way that implied he didn't know either. Riding with outlaws for a long time changed how you thought of yourself. Lew knew. He'd felt the same until he'd gotten out.

"You can start over, Ross. Find a peaceful life. You don't need Dob to make a living."

Giving a quick shake of his head, Ross growled a response. "Enough of this. What are you doing out here? Spying on us?"

"Hell no," Lew lied. "I rode north to see what's there, which wasn't much, then came back this way. I'm on my way to Sacramento."

Ross's gaze narrowed, a sick gleam in his eyes. "You *were* on your way to Sacramento." The statement indicated everything had changed, the same as it always did with Dob. Taking careful aim, he glared at Lew. "Sorry. It shouldn't have ended this way."

At the same time Ross pulled the trigger, another shot rang out, this one from Lew's revolver. He felt a searing pain in his arm, saw Ross stumble backward and fall. Rolling away, Lew aimed and fired again. Before he could reconsider, he glanced at the camp, bile rising in his throat at the sight of Dob and the men running to the horses.

Standing, he holstered the gun, pressed his hand to the wound, and ran to his horse. Pain ripped through him as he pulled himself into the saddle. Sagging forward, he kicked the horse, blinking a few times to ward off the dizziness threatening to topple him out of the saddle.

Shouts and gunfire had his horse moving into a run. He glanced behind him, thankful Dob reined up for a moment to look down at Ross's still form. Lew had no idea if his friend was alive or dead, and right now, he didn't care. All he wanted was to get to the trail heading south and live long enough to warn the MacLarens.

Circle M

"Rider!" Thane shouted, pointing north. Running toward the horse, he waved his arms, slowing the animal's progress. Grabbing the reins, he spoke softly, calming him until the gelding stopped. Hearing someone come up behind him, he nodded to the rider. "It's Lew Quick."

"Hold the horse, lad. I'll get Lew off and into the house." Camden lifted his arms.

"I can get myself off," Lew rasped out, blood soaking through his shirt, sweat thick on his forehead.

"I'm sure you can, lad, but I'm still helping you." A moment later, Camden had Lew on the ground, a strong arm securing him to his side.

"Colbert." Lew ground the word out, wincing with each step toward the house. "He's here." He choked, bending forward.

"Who is it, Cam?" Bram put his arm around Lew from the other side.

"Lew Quick. Shot in the arm."

"Colbert," Lew spat the outlaw's name out again.

"Bring the lad inside." Camden's mother, Kyla, held the door open, pointing down the hall toward one of the guest rooms. "Sarah, get hot water and rags." Colin's wife nodded, hurrying to the kitchen. "And whiskey," Kyla yelled after her.

Camden and Bram laid Lew on the bed, opening his shirt to check the wound. Camden glanced up at his ma. "The bullet went on through."

Kyla studied the wound from the other side of the bed. "Aye. The lad's passed out. It'll be making this easier."

"What else will you be needing, Ma?"

She shook her head. "Go find Ewan and Fletch. They'll be wanting to know what happened."

Bram caught Camden's shoulder, stopping him. "I'll go. You stay with Aunt Kyla."

Bram ran to Ewan's house and slammed the door open, coming to an abrupt stop. The women were seated or standing in the living room and dining room, working on the upcoming wedding.

Lorna walked toward him. "What's wrong, lad?"

"Lew Quick's been shot. He's at Aunt Kyla's house."

Maddy's head whipped around at Lew's name. Setting down the fabric, she walked toward them. "Is he all right?"

Bram studied her for a moment, then nodded. "It's a shoulder wound. The bullet went through, so the lad should be fine. Where's Fletch?"

Maddy opened her mouth to answer before realizing she didn't know where he was, glad Lorna had the answer.

"The lad's with Ewan, past the last corral. Ewan's been thinking of adding another one."

Bram nodded, already moving to the door. "Kyla wants them at the house."

"I'll come with you."

He gave Maddy a quick shake of his head. "Nae, lass. There's nothing for you to do, and you've a wedding tomorrow."

When she began to object, Lorna placed a hand on her shoulder. "Bram's right. Kyla and Sarah will take care of the lad."

"Cam's with them," Bram yelled over his shoulder before disappearing out the front door.

Catching her lower lip between her teeth, Maddy gave a reluctant nod. She knew Lew believed she hated him, his presence repulsing her. It wasn't true.

At first, she'd hated what happened, shocked to have the one person who'd been her protector take her virginity. The rational part of her mind knew he had no choice. They'd both be dead if Lew hadn't gone through with it. He'd been the one to carry her back to the cabin, provide money, and watched when she'd ridden off.

Over the months she'd been on the run, Maddy thought of him often, knew how much he hated what he'd done. Lew blamed himself, and for a short time, she blamed him, too. Telling Fletcher what happened helped her see how much Lew was a victim as much as her. The initial fear she felt at seeing him in Conviction transformed to empathy since she'd come to Circle M. A part of her wanted him to stay, work for the MacLarens. She doubted Fletcher would feel the same, deciding it best to leave the decision to the men.

Sitting down, she picked up her stitching, her mind still on Lew. He'd been the only other man to have her. Somehow, even knowing the circumstances, she sent up a prayer for the only man to stick by her during one of the worst periods of her life.

Chapter Twenty-Two

Conviction

Bay strummed his fingers on the desk, checking the time on the gilded walnut clock on the wall opposite him. Quarter to three. Suzette had agreed to stop by between two and three o'clock. She still hadn't appeared.

Running a hand through his hair, he stared at the papers in front of him. He'd prepared them within days of her arriving in Conviction, meaning to have her read and sign them soon after. Each time the opportunity arose, he'd slid them back into the safe, unable to go ahead with his plan. If she didn't arrive soon, his determination would falter, and once again, he'd secure them behind the metal door.

Hearing the sound of footsteps on the stairs, he braced himself. When the door opened, it wasn't Suzette who walked in, but Bram MacLaren.

Standing, he held out his hand. "Bram. What can I do for you?"

Shaking Bay's hand, Bram drew off his hat, wiping a sleeve across his forehead. "Brodie asked me to see if you'd be available to help us."

Raising a brow, he cocked his head in surprise at a request from the town's sheriff. "I'll do whatever I can for you and your family. What is it you need?"

Bending forward, Bram rested his hands on the desk. "You know Maddy?"

Bay's concern deepened. "Of course. She worked for us at the restaurant. Brodie told me she's marrying Fletch."

"Aye. They're to be marrying tomorrow."

He rubbed the back of his neck. "So the baby is Fletch's."

"Aye. There's no problem with that. It's her uncle. He's coming for her, vowing to kill her."

Bay walked around the desk, already reaching for his gunbelt. "Why?"

"The lass knows too much about him and his gang. She can identify each one of them and list all their crimes."

A chill sliced through Bay. "And who is her uncle?"

"Dob Colbert."

They met Brodie and Sam at the edge of town, taking off for the ranch at a brisk run. Each had heard of the Colbert gang, but only Bay had come up against them on his trip west. They'd held up a stagecoach. He'd been a passenger, along with an older gentleman and his niece, a young, vivacious woman.

During the robbery, the woman was shot. Bay killed two of the outlaws before the leader ordered them to ride off. He wouldn't have known who they were except one of them yelled Colbert's name. At the next town, Bay tried to convince the sheriff to put up wanted posters, but the man refused. The robbery took place in Kansas, Dob's home state, and few were willing to go up against him and his men.

Consequently, Colbert had never been formally linked to any specific crime, which in Bay's mind was a complete travesty. He welcomed any opportunity to do his part in taking the man out of this world.

At the fast pace, they reached the ranch in half the time it usually took. Reining to a stop, they hurried toward the men already congregated outside Ewan's house.

"Thank you for coming, Bay."

He shook Ewan's hand, nodding to the others. "What's your plan?"

"We've been talking about it." Ewan glanced around. "Lew Quick was shot earlier when he ran across Colbert's camp."

"Quick works for you?" Bay asked.

Ewan shot a quick look at Fletcher before nodding. "We've been discussing it. The lad has personal reasons for finding Colbert. With Fletch marrying Maddy, it's personal to us, also."

Bay pulled out a six-shooter, checking the cylinder. "How do you want to go after them?"

Brodie stepped next to them. "We'll be needing to split up into three groups."

"Aye, lad." Ewan gazed at Colin. "You'll be leading one group, Brodie another, and Quinn the third. Bay, you'll be going with Brodie. We'll be riding in an arc, moving toward the location of Colbert's last camp, flanking them. We've no room for error, lads."

"What if they've moved, Da?" Fletcher asked Ewan.

"Then we'll be needing to search until we find them. Colbert's wanting to kill Maddy, and we'll not be letting that happen."

Fletcher stuffed extra ammunition into his saddlebags, tying it before his gaze wandered to the porch. Maddy stood alone, hands resting on her belly, her features unreadable. They'd planned to marry tomorrow. Depending on the outcome of their search, it may be delayed, something neither of them wanted.

"Are you ready, lad?" Camden stood next to him, his voice as serious as the resolute expression on his face.

"Aye, but I'm needing to talk with Maddy before we go."

Giving him a knowing nod, Camden took the reins of Fletcher's horse. Camden would be riding with his older brother, Colin, Fletcher with Brodie, and Bram with his brother, Quinn. It seemed odd not riding together. Camden couldn't remember the last time they'd been separated. Fletcher's wedding would change their lives even more, as it had when the older brothers had married. Shaking off the thought, Camden started walking the horses toward the other riders.

"I'll be waiting for you with the others."

Lifting a hand in acknowledgment, Fletcher continued up the steps and put his arm around Maddy. "Are you all right, lass?"

Leaning into him, resting her head against his shoulder, she nodded. "I'm fine."

"Nae, you're not. I'm sorry, lass, but we've no choice but to go after Dob."

Pulling away, she looked up, studying his face as if committing it to memory. "I know. I'm just sorry you and your family are putting yourselves in danger because of me. If anything happens to you—" She stopped when he placed a finger over her lips.

"Shhh, lass. No one is blaming you."

"Including you, Fletcher?"

Leaning down, he kissed her lips. "Especially not me. I'll always be doing whatever is needed to keep you safe. Always." Tugging her closer, he kissed Maddy again. "You'll be safe at the ranch. Thane will be staying here, and the other lads and lasses know how to use a gun. I'd not be leaving if I thought you'd be in danger."

She pushed away from him, her bright blues eyes deepening in anger. "I don't care about me. I'm worried about *you*, Fletcher."

His anger flared to match Maddy's, his voice harsher than intended. "I'll not be having you say such things. You and the bairn are more important to me than anyone, lass." He cupped her face with both hands, forcing her to look at him. "You'll not be riding out or doing anything to put yourself or our bairn in danger.

Promise me, lass." On the last, he noticed the tears in her eyes, moisture on her face, and whispered a quiet curse. He used his thumb to brush the tears from her cheeks. "Ah, lass."

Bending down, he crushed his mouth to hers, deepening the kiss at her soft moan. Letting his hands wander down her back to rest on her hips, he groaned. He hadn't been with her in months, yet it felt as if no time at all had passed since they'd made love. *Love.* Had he always felt this way about her, not knowing what it was?

Raising his mouth, Fletcher gazed into eyes glassy with passion. Groaning once more, he placed another kiss on her swollen lips before stepping away.

"Stay inside, lass." Swallowing the odd lump in his throat, he bounded down the steps, not turning until he heard Maddy's voice.

"I love you, Fletcher."

Conviction

Austin DeBell left the sheriff's office. Swinging into the saddle, he reined east toward Circle M. After leaving Carson City months before, the bounty hunter rode to Sacramento, moving on to Oakland, San Francisco, and numerous smaller towns. Too many for him to recall. Following Colbert hadn't been easy.

One brave sheriff in Kansas had finally issued a wanted poster on Colbert, Ross Sheehan, and Lew

Quick, three of the men in the tintype he kept with him. The image and angry complaints from stagecoach drivers had been what prompted the sheriff to print and send the posters to lawmen in the Midwest.

Austin hadn't seen a single one in Nevada or California, believing the posters had never made it this far west. He doubted Dob knew anything about them, which pleased him. Before leaving the sheriff's office in Conviction, he learned Brodie MacLaren and one of his deputies had ridden to the MacLaren ranch, hoping to capture a group of men threatening one of their women—Dob Colbert and his men.

Picking up his pace, Austin felt the beginnings of excitement course through him. He'd never gotten this close to the gang. Capturing them would mean he'd have enough money for the ranch he wanted to start, the only dream he had left.

From their hiding place yards behind one of the barns, Dob and two of his men watched the MacLarens leave the ranch. A feral smile crossed his face when the last group disappeared down the trail. They were riding in a direct path where Lew had last seen the gang. His plan had worked better than he'd anticipated.

"They left a bunch of children to guard the women. This ought to be easy, boss." Arnold White lowered his field glasses.

Dob considered what his man said. He'd seen the boys and girls carrying weapons, waving to the men who rode off. He also knew mistakes were made when making assumptions.

"Don't underestimate any of the MacLarens. Young or older, I'm betting any of them can fire a gun better than most." Dob rubbed his stubbled jaw. "From what we've heard about the family, we can't misjudge a single one."

"Do you think Lew is holed up in one of the houses?" Erv Champ, one of the older members of the gang asked, his gaze moving over each building.

"I'm certain of it. Maddy's in there, too." Dob had overheard a woman talking to a man in Conviction, unaware anyone else listened. She mentioned Maddy, how she'd left to stay at Circle M. The woman hadn't spoken of Lew, but Dob felt certain he'd been the one to take her to the MacLarens. The timing and Lew's refusal to discuss his absence had been all he'd needed to convict his longtime friend of a dangerous betrayal.

Arnold stared through the field glasses again. "How do you want to do this?"

"We wait and watch, make certain the men don't return. Then we go after Maddy and Lew."

Fletcher rode alongside Brodie, Sam taking a spot behind them. He had a hard time focusing on the reason for the trip, his mind filled with images of Maddy, her last words haunting him.

I love you, Fletcher.

What bothered him weren't the words themselves. The fact he hadn't returned the sentiment gnawed at him. She deserved to know what he'd already accepted. He loved her. If anything happened and he didn't return from the search for Colbert, she'd go through life not knowing. Regret filled him. Fletcher's mouth twisted as he considered the only solution. He glanced at his older brother.

"Brodie?"

"Aye?"

"I've a favor to ask." Fletcher shifted in the saddle. "If I don't make it back, I'm needing you to give Maddy a message."

Brodie slowed, narrowing his eyes at Fletcher. "Don't make it back, lad? Of course you'll be making it back."

Fletcher blew out a breath. "But if I don't, will you give Maddy a message?"

"Aye, but you *will* be going back. What do you want me to tell the lass?"

For an instant, Fletcher wanted to take the request back, knowing it was too late. "Tell Maddy I love her."

Brodie choked out a strangled laugh. "You've never told the lass you love her?"

Shaking his head, Fletcher felt heat flush his face. "Nae. I wasn't sure of my feelings until a few days ago."

Unable to hide his surprise, Brodie stared at him. "Fletch, you've been in love with the lass since you laid eyes on her."

Brows furrowing, his jaw clenched. "How would you be knowing that?"

"Everyone knows it, lad. One look at the two of you together and how you feel about each other is obvious." Brodie shook his head. "Ach, lad. If I'd known you'd been this blind, I'd have said something sooner."

Fletcher winced at the subtle rebuke, surprised at what Brodie said. How could everyone else know his feelings when he wasn't sure? Had he always loved Maddy, not allowing himself to accept it out of misplaced pride?

He admitted believing his family wouldn't approve of his feelings for a saloon girl. His father had said as much when discouraging him from seeing her again. But as Fletcher thought back on their talk before he volunteered to assist Blaine, he realized Ewan hadn't discouraged him as much as insisted he get his head back on ranch work. There'd been no condemnation in his father's voice, only a request to spend less time at Buckie's.

An amused grin tipped up the corners of Brodie's mouth. "Fletch, don't worry about Maddy. The lass knows you love her. And you're going to make it home. Now, no more eejit talk about it."

Fletcher's mouth drew into a thin line. Brodie had made two important points. First, everyone, including Maddy, already believed he loved her. Second, his brother would make sure she knew it if he didn't return. Both thoughts gave him a measure of gratification. Still, he'd make it his first priority to make sure Maddy had no doubt about his feelings for her. She'd been honest with him. The time had come for him to be honest, as well.

"Up ahead." Sam caught up with Brodie and Fletcher, pointing to a spot a couple hundred yards away. "Looks like a camp."

They slowed their pace, moving into the cover of large boulders and wide trees before dismounting. Pulling out their field glasses, being careful to stay hidden, they crept to the edge of the large rocks.

Brodie raised the glasses and peered around the boulders. Sam did the same on the opposite end while Fletcher dropped to his stomach and crawled forward. Brodie spoke first.

"I'm counting eight men, eight horses. One of the men is on the ground."

Fletcher lowered his glasses. "Does the lad look to be alive to you?"

Brodie looked again, giving his head a quick shake. "I can't tell from here."

"Could be the lad Lew shot," Fletcher said as he studied the camp.

Moving back behind the boulder, Brodie knelt next to Fletcher. "I thought Lew told you he killed one of them."

"The lad wasn't sure." Fletcher shifted the glasses beyond the camp. "Colin's group is riding up on the east side."

"Can you see Quinn?" Brodie asked.

"He's taken a position on the north." Sam walked closer to them. "They've got more cover than Colin. If there's a guard, he's sure to spot them."

Brodie hurried to his horse. "Get saddled. I'll signal Colin and Quinn. It's time to ride in."

Chapter Twenty-Three

Brodie watched the camp another few minutes, making a final decision. He, Colin, and Quinn had agreed their groups would surround the camp so Brodie and Sam could arrest them. If the outlaws resisted and fired, the MacLarens wouldn't hesitate to shoot back.

He glanced at Fletcher and Sam. "All the lads are in place."

Raising his rifle, Brodie pointed it into the air and fired. A split second later, the three groups charged toward the camp, surrounding the men within a couple short minutes.

Brodie didn't know what he expected, but the quick capitulation of the outlaws surprised him. Not one drew a weapon. All raised their hands, backing into a tight circle.

"Where's Colbert?" Fletcher shouted, his gun trained on one of the men.

A tall, wiry man with a long, gray beard took a step forward. "He's not here."

"Where is he?" Colin yelled.

Several shrugged, looking away.

Fletcher pointed his gun on the man with the beard. "Where is Colbert?"

He shook his head. "Dob didn't tell us. He just said to stay here until they got back."

Brodie nudged his horse closer. "They?"

"Dob took Arnold and Erv with him."

Fletcher's chest tightened, afraid of where they'd gone. "What direction did they go?"

The man lifted one shoulder, turning toward the trail Colbert took. "South."

"Well, what do we have here?" Dob stared through the glasses, a savage smile lifting the corner of his mouth. Maddy stood on the porch, shaking out a small rug, her gaze focused to the north. "She's in the second house. I'm guessing Lew's in the same one."

Arnold lifted his glasses. "I've only seen a young girl and a couple boys come outside. If that's all the protection she has, this is going to be quick."

Dob glanced at the waning sun before he pulled his gun from its holster, checked the cylinder, then shoved it back into place. He indicated for Arnold and Erv to do the same.

"We'll wait for her to go inside, then ride around to the back of the house. Arnold, you'll take the side closest to us. Erv, you'll take the other. I'll enter the kitchen from the back. When you hear me enter, you two come in from the front. Don't let anyone leave. We'll get everyone in the kitchen. Erv, you'll move through the house to make sure we haven't missed anyone."

Arnold shifted in the saddle. "You don't intend to shoot the women and children, do you, boss?"

"We'll tie up everyone except Maddy. If any of the others draw a weapon, shoot them."

Erv and Arnold shot a look at each other but didn't respond. Hurting women and children had never bothered Dob. On the contrary. He seemed to enjoy inflicting pain on those weaker and smaller than him.

"What about Lew?" Erv asked.

Dob's face sobered. "I'll take care of him."

The other men understood what Dob meant. Lew wouldn't be alive when they left the house with Maddy.

"Do whatever is needed to keep Maddy quiet while I take care of Lew. We'll go out the back. She rides with me."

Arnold frowned. "Back to the camp?"

Dob shook his head, a feral gleam in his eyes. "We ride south toward Sacramento."

Austin could see the rooftops as he rode closer to Circle M. Reining to a stop, he lifted the canteen from his saddlebag, taking a long, slow swallow. Slipping it away, he pulled the wanted poster from his pocket.

Three faces stared back at him—Dob, Lew, and Ross, the leader and his two closest associates. He intended to collect the bounty on each one, dead or alive. He didn't care which.

Folding the paper, he tucked it into his pocket, picking up the reins. The sun had begun to plunge behind the western hills. Austin started forward, his horse moving at a moderate pace.

Rounding a bend in the trail, he halted. Three riders were skirting the outside edges of the ranch, moving in a wide arc. His awareness rose, excitement building within him. Even in the approaching darkness, he knew the identity of one of the three men. Dob Colbert. The others might be Lew and Ross, but he couldn't be certain from this distance.

Absently touching the handle of his gun, he followed, careful to stay far enough away they wouldn't notice. Austin perused the area. The quiet bothered him.

From talking to the deputy in town, he knew the MacLarens were a large clan. Four families, each with their own house and barn, most with at least five children, a few of the older ones married with children of their own. With so many people, he'd expect more activity, children running around outside, women keeping watch on them.

The entire place was quiet, no one outside, and few horses in the corrals. An uneasy feeling crept through him. Keeping watch on the men, Austin continued to take quick glances at the houses and barns, waiting for someone to emerge. No one did.

Forcing his attention back to the riders, he noticed they'd turned left, heading toward the back of the second house. Understanding hit him.

Dob planned to go after anyone left inside the house, and from the look of the ranch, there wasn't anybody to protect them. When Dob and the others disappeared behind the house, Austin kicked his horse, heading to the front.

Dismounting before coming to a stop, he drew his gun, bending low as he took the steps to the porch. Glancing around, still not seeing any activity, Austin gripped the doorknob, a relieved breath escaping when it turned.

Sneaking inside, he closed the door an instant before hearing the sound of boots on the porch. Austin moved to a window and looked out. One man knelt a few feet away, gun drawn, a determined expression on his face.

"Drop your gun, mister."

Holding his hands out, Austin turned away from the window. A girl of maybe twelve or thirteen stood a few feet away, a rifle pointed at his chest. He decided to take a chance.

"Do you know who Dob Colbert is?"

Kenzie's features hardened, the rifle shaking enough for Austin to notice. "Are you riding with him?"

He glanced behind her toward the kitchen, knowing they didn't have much time. "No, but Dob is here, probably at your back door right now. Two of his men are ready to come in the front. You need to warn anyone else in the house. If I'm wrong, you can shoot me."

Eyes widening, Kenzie bit her lip, hesitating.

Austin shifted, heart pounding. "We're running out of time."

"Kenzie, what are you doing..." Lorna's voice trailed off at the sight of Austin.

"I found him in the house, Ma."

He held up his hands. "There's no more time. Dob is here and I won't let him do whatever he has planned." Austin moved forward with a speed unlike anyone they'd seen, ripping the rifle from Kenzie's hand. "Grab any other guns. You're going to need them."

The words had barely left his lips when the front door crashed open. Spinning, Austin drew his gun, aimed, and fired. "Get down!" he shouted just before another man appeared. Firing again, he spun around at the sound of someone kicking open the back door.

Thrusting Kenzie and Lorna out of the way, Austin held the gun in front of him, peering into the kitchen. Dob Colbert had entered from the back, his arm around a pregnant woman, a gun pointed at her head.

"I don't know who you are, but here's what's going to happen. Maddy and me are going out the door behind me. You and everyone else will stay inside until we're out of sight. If anyone comes outside, I'll shoot her."

Maddy squirmed in his grasp. "No. Please, Dob. Don't do this."

A bitter laugh burst from his lungs. "Hell, girl, you know I don't care a bit about you." Stomping on his boot only made him laugh again, his grip tightening. "Don't fight me, Maddy." Dob looked at Austin. "You stay where you are."

Dragging her out the door and down the steps, he kept his gaze fixed on the back door. Dob edged toward the far side of his horse. "Get up there. If you try anything, I *will* shoot you." Letting her go, he kept the gun aimed at her. This time, he pointed the six-shooter at her stomach.

Heart thundering, Maddy put a foot into the stirrup, gripping the saddlehorn. Using all her strength, she bounced a little on her other foot, and with a great deal of effort, swung atop the horse. Looking down, she winced at the gun still pointed at her stomach.

"Move forward." His weapon on Maddy, Dob looked over the horse's back at the door to the kitchen. Seeing no one, he quickly mounted, grabbed the reins, and kicked the horse.

Austin watched from inside, aiming the rifle at Dob, cursing when the outlaw kept Maddy between him and the house.

Handing the rifle back to Kenzie, he ran out the front door, swinging into the saddle in one smooth movement and kicking the horse. Cautious to keep a decent distance between them, Austin followed. He refused to let Dob get away with the pregnant woman he called Maddy.

It had taken longer to get the captured outlaws ready to ride than Fletcher expected. They'd tied their hands and helped them onto horses before starting south.

"Fletch, take Bram, Cam, and Bay and head back."

Surprised, he shot a look at Brodie. "You won't be needing us?"

"Nae. We'll be fine, and you need to make sure Maddy is safe. I've spoken with Quinn and Colin." He waved an impatient hand at Fletcher. "Get the lads and go."

He'd wanted to ride ahead, relieve his fear Colbert hadn't gone after Maddy. "Thanks, Brodie." Reining around, he saw Bram, Camden, and Bay waiting a few feet away. A moment later, the four raced toward home, aware of the urgency and possible danger ahead.

It didn't take long for the ranch houses to come into view. Slowing, Fletcher felt beads of sweat on his face, the hair on his neck bristling. Something wasn't right.

Thane rode toward them, his face set in a deep scowl. "Colbert took Maddy. Come on." He took off before they could ask questions. "He rode south," Thane shouted as they passed the last house. "A bounty hunter rode after them."

Fletcher's brows drew together. "A bounty hunter?"

"Aye. That's what Kenzie said." Thane took the trail toward Sacramento, following the route Kenzie and Lorna swore the bounty hunter took.

With each mile, Fletcher's determination rose. He wouldn't give up. He would find Maddy if it took days or weeks.

Thane stopped where the trail split. Going right would take them east into Nevada, the other south to Sacramento.

Bay slid to the ground. Of the five men, he had the most tracking experience, had been a hired gun before coming to Conviction to join August in the law practice, and knew more about outlaws than any of them.

271

Kneeling, Bay studied the tracks, looking in both directions before standing. "If I was Colbert, I'd head to Sacramento where few people will ask questions. He still has Maddy with him, Fletch."

A brow rose. "How can you tell?"

"The horse is carrying two riders. The extra weight digs deeper into the ground. That's how I'm certain they're riding south. If the tracks change, the weight gone, well..." Bay didn't have to finish. They all knew what that meant.

Dread gripped Fletcher, bands of fear tightening around his chest, making it hard to breathe. Not waiting a moment longer, he kicked Domino, ignoring the shouts of those behind him. His mind wrapped in worry over Maddy, he didn't notice Bay ride up alongside him.

"Slow up, Fletch. We may miss something if we're moving too fast."

Ruled by fear, he paid no attention to Bay's warning, keeping up the hard pace.

"Fletch!" Bay leaned toward him and grabbed the reins, unfazed by his friend's loud curses. Pulling, he slowed Domino, preparing for the fight he suspected would result from his action. "Stop. We need to talk about the best way to find Colbert and Maddy."

Fletcher knew Bay was right. If only he could convince his heart of it. Forcing himself to calm down, he nodded. The two men didn't speak as they waited for the others to join them. When they did, Bay rubbed his chin, staring at the trail ahead.

"Our first priority is making sure Maddy is safe. I'm thinking Colbert isn't going to do anything to her until he's sure we're no longer following. He sees her as a hostage, leverage for getting away. We have to be smart or he'll panic. If that happens, Maddy will be the one to suffer."

Massaging the back of his neck, Fletcher tried to get himself under control. "What are you suggesting, Bay?"

"I'm convinced Colbert is going to hole up in Sacramento and figure out what he'll do next. We'll follow the trail as long as possible, but we're going to lose it when we reach the town. Two riders on one horse and Maddy being pregnant should draw attention. We'll need to move fast, but stay together. Getting separated will weaken our ability to confront him and free Maddy." Bay looked at Fletcher. "We will find her, but we've got to be smart about how we do it. Agreed?"

Lips drawing into a slim line, he nodded. "Aye."

Bay studied him for a moment before tilting his head toward Sacramento. "Let's go."

Fletcher's heart rate quickened as they rode down the crowded main street. Bram and Camden were on either side of him, Thane and Bay behind them. The boardwalk was packed to such a degree, he wondered if they'd ever be able to pick out Colbert. A moment later, Bay spoke.

"Slow up. He's up ahead on the right, standing by the hotel entrance. Maddy's beside him. Fletch, you and

Cam stop here. Bram and Thane ride on past about twenty feet. Wait for my signal. Try not to let Maddy see you. She might do something foolish if she recognizes anyone and we don't want Colbert to run."

"What about you, Bay?" Fletcher asked.

"I'm going to walk down the boardwalk toward them. It's been a long time. I doubt Colbert will recognize me."

Fletcher's brows shot up, eyes wide. "You know him?"

"Yes. The world will be a lot better off without him."

Bay didn't wait for Fletcher to ask more questions before riding on and reining to a stop outside the general store. Keeping his attention on Colbert, he pulled out his revolver, checking the cylinder. Shoving it back into place, he tossed the reins over a rail.

He took a quick look behind him, seeing Fletcher and Camden standing on the boardwalk, their gazes fixed on Colbert. Bay saw Fletcher's hand resting on the handle of his gun. Ahead, Bram and Thane slid to the ground, stepping onto the boardwalk to await his signal.

Settling his hat lower on his forehead, he almost ran forward at the sound of Maddy's angry cry. Bay sent a warning look at Fletcher, certain he'd also heard it. Seeing Fletcher's body tense, he stopped him from moving toward her with a quick shake of his head.

Taking a deep breath, Bay settled himself as he had done so many times in the past. Flexing his hands, he touched the handles of the pair of six-shooters strapped around his hips. Ready, he took several steps before he stopped, his eyes narrowing on a man he suspected was the bounty hunter moving toward Colbert.

Bay didn't have a chance to signal the others before striding ahead, determined to get between the stranger stalking Colbert and Maddy. Too late, he saw the bounty hunter draw his gun, keeping it concealed at his side. An instant later, the man lifted his hand, aimed, and fired.

Bay and the four MacLarens ran, each meaning to grab Maddy and push her to safety. Their attempt didn't come in time. An ear-piercing scream wrenched from Maddy's lips, her head whipping from side to side, panicked eyes searching.

As Colbert slumped to the ground, a strong hand wrapped around her arm, dragging her away from the body.

"It's all right, lass. You're safe." Fletcher's voice shook, his body trembling at what could've happened.

The familiar voice broke through the haze, her eyes darting up to see who held her. "Fletcher..." Maddy didn't say more before strong arms pulled her close. The sobs came within seconds.

Stroking her back, he rested his chin on the top of her head. "Ah, lass. I've got you."

"Is she all right?" Camden stood next to them, studying Maddy's features. Bram and Thane joined them a moment later.

She swiped tears from her eyes. "I'm fine, Cam." Looking up at Fletcher, she kissed his chin. "He didn't hurt me."

Loud voices drew their attention.

"What you did was stupid, DeBell. You could've shot Maddy."

"I did what I thought was right, Donahue. You'd have done the same."

Bay moved to within a few inches of Austin, features unyielding. "Not with a pregnant woman so close."

"He had a gun on her, Bay. I couldn't take a chance he'd shoot her if he spotted any of us." Austin glanced down at the body slumped against the building. "It doesn't matter now. Colbert isn't going to hurt anyone else again." A satisfied gleam showed in his eyes.

Fletcher watched the two argue, figuring they'd obviously known each other before today. Shouts caught his attention. A man of average height with a rotund belly pushed his way through the crowd. Seeing the badge pinned to his shirt, Fletcher led Maddy away.

Continuing down the boardwalk, he led her into a small restaurant. Sitting next to her at a table near the front, he settled an arm over her shoulders. "Are you hungry?"

"A little."

"Pie and coffee?"

A tentative smile tilted up the corners of her mouth. "That would be perfect."

After placing the order, he turned toward her. "I'm so sorry, lass."

Confusion drew her brows together, her hand reaching up to cup his cheek. "It wasn't your fault."

He shook his head. "I never should've left you."

"You didn't know what he planned. You did what you thought best."

The knot in his stomach tightened. "I could've lost you."

Her blue eyes twinkled. "You'll never lose me, Fletch. You're stuck with me."

Closing his eyes a moment, he shoved aside the images of her with Colbert, the fear deep in his gut at the thought he'd never be with her again. "Aye, and you'll be stuck with me, lass. You deserve better."

Maddy shook her head. "I'm the lucky one. You're who I want. Who I've wanted since the first night I saw you. I love you, Fletch."

Unable to hold back his feelings any longer, he stroked a hand down her face. "I love you, too, lass. I'll always love you." Ignoring the surprise on her face, he leaned down, brushing a kiss across her lips. "Always."

Epilogue

One week later...

Fletcher's arm settled over Maddy's shoulders, drawing her close. Since rescuing her from Colbert, he'd been unable to let her out of his sight. He also hadn't been able to stop telling her how much he loved her. Sometimes when they were alone, other times in front of family. Fletcher didn't care. He wanted everyone to know how he felt.

"Congratulations, Fletch." Brodie kissed Maddy's cheek, handing each a glass of punch. "Welcome to the family, lass."

Face heating, Maddy leaned into her husband. "Thank you, Brodie."

Kissing the top of her head, Fletcher tightened his hold. "I'm wondering who will be next."

Brodie tilted his head. "Next?"

A contented smile played at the corners of his mouth. "Aye. Bram or Cam."

Brodie looked across the room to see the two laughing. "Ach, those lads aren't ready to take care of a lass. I'm thinking it may be someone else."

Maddy glanced around the room at those old enough to marry and still single. If Sean weren't in Scotland at veterinary school, he'd be a good choice. Her gaze landed on Sean's sister, Bridget. At nineteen, she knew the young woman wanted a family, the same as her older cousins. Coral, another who wanted to marry, stood next to her. Maddy had heard Deke Arrington, the owner of the local saddlery, held an interest in her, and Coral felt the same. Then she spotted someone else.

"Perhaps it won't be any of the MacLarens."

Fletcher kissed her again. "Who do you mean, Maddy?"

"What about Austin DeBell?"

Brodie's eyes flashed. "The bounty hunter who shot Colbert?"

"Why not? Bay said he might stay in Conviction for a while. He's handsome with a devastating smile, and—" Fletcher's low growl and mouth covering hers stopped the list of Austin's qualities.

Laughing, Brodie tilted his glass against his mouth, finishing the last of his punch. "Well, we know the lad can shoot."

Fletcher nodded. "Aye, he can."

Brodie thought a moment. "Maybe I'll be talking to him about becoming a deputy." He looked at his empty glass. "I'm going to join Colin and Bay. First, I'll be needing more punch." Eyes twinkling, he started across the room, knowing Fletcher and Maddy understood he meant punch with a liberal dose of whiskey.

When he got far enough away, and before anyone else could join them, Fletcher dropped another kiss on her mouth. "I love you, Mrs. MacLaren."

Her blinding smile sent his pulse racing. "And I love you, Mr. MacLaren."

Shifting when Quinn and Emma approached, Fletcher's gaze landed on Colin and Bay standing in a corner of the dining room. They'd been talking for a while, their serious expressions piquing his curiosity. And something else. Bay's attention kept straying to Suzette.

Bay hadn't been able to keep his eyes off Suzette. Not today, not years ago when they'd first met. She'd been the only woman to keep his interest, fire his passion. The one woman he wanted beyond all others, the reason there'd been no others for longer than he could remember. His chest squeezed with desire each time his gaze landed on her.

"I'm not understanding why you don't court her, Bay." Colin handed him a glass of punch. Both knew it had already been spiked with whiskey. Bay downed it in one swallow, causing Colin's brow to rise. "I'll be getting you another if it will fortify you enough to speak with the lass."

The knot in Bay's stomach tightened. "No, thanks."

Colin studied him. "She's a bonny one. I'm confused as to why you don't at least speak with her."

Bay didn't look over at Colin. "I have my reasons."

"They must be good ones if you're able to ignore her." Colin lifted his glass to his mouth, taking a sip, then choking at Bay's reply.

"They are. Suzette is my wife."

Thank you for taking the time to read Fletcher's Pride. If you enjoyed it, please consider telling your friends or posting a short review. Word of mouth is an author's best friend and much appreciated.

Watch for book nine in the MacLaren's of Boundary Mountain series, Bay's Desire

Please join my reader's group to be notified of my New Releases at:
https://www.shirleendavies.com/contact-me.html

I care about quality, so if you find something in error, please contact me via email at
shirleen@shirleendavies.com

About the Author

Shirleen Davies writes romance—historical and contemporary western romance with a touch of suspense. She is the best-selling author of the MacLarens of Fire Mountain Series, the MacLarens of Boundary Mountain Series, and the Redemption Mountain Series. Shirleen grew up in Southern California, attended Oregon State University, and has degrees from San Diego State University and the University of Maryland. Her passion is writing emotionally charged stories of flawed people who find redemption through love and acceptance. She lives with her husband in a beautiful town in northern Arizona. Between them, they have five adult sons who are their greatest achievements.

I love to hear from my readers!

Send me an Email
Visit my Website
Sign up to be notified of New Releases
Check out all my Books
Comment on my Blog

Other ways to connect with me:

Facebook Fan Page
Twitter
Pinterest
Google+
Instagram

Books by Shirleen Davies
Historical Western Romance Series
MacLarens of Fire Mountain

Tougher than the Rest, Book One
Faster than the Rest, Book Two
Harder than the Rest, Book Three
Stronger than the Rest, Book Four
Deadlier than the Rest, Book Five
Wilder than the Rest, Book Six

Redemption Mountain

Redemption's Edge, Book One
Wildfire Creek, Book Two
Sunrise Ridge, Book Three
Dixie Moon, Book Four
Survivor Pass, Book Five
Promise Trail, Book Six
Deep River, Book Seven
Courage Canyon, Book Eight
Forsaken Falls, Book Nine
Solitude Gorge, Book Ten
Rogue Rapids, Book Eleven, Coming next in the series!

MacLarens of Boundary Mountain

Colin's Quest, Book One,
Brodie's Gamble, Book Two

Quinn's Honor, Book Three
Sam's Legacy, Book Four
Heather's Choice, Book Five
Nate's Destiny, Book Six
Blaine's Wager, Book Seven
Fletcher's Pride, Book Eight, Coming next in the series!

Contemporary Romance Series

MacLarens of Fire Mountain

Second Summer, Book One
Hard Landing, Book Two
One More Day, Book Three
All Your Nights, Book Four
Always Love You, Book Five
Hearts Don't Lie, Book Six
No Getting Over You, Book Seven
'Til the Sun Comes Up, Book Eight
Foolish Heart, Book Nine
Forever Love, Book Ten, Coming next in the series!

Peregrine Bay

Reclaiming Love, Book One, A Novella
Our Kind of Love, Book Two

Burnt River

Shane's Burden, Book One by Peggy Henderson
Thorn's Journey, Book Two by Shirleen Davies

Aqua's Achilles, Book Three by Kate Cambridge
Ashley's Hope, Book Four by Amelia Adams
Harpur's Secret, Book Five by Kay P. Dawson
Mason's Rescue, Book Six by Peggy L. Henderson
Del's Choice, Book Seven by Shirleen Davies
Ivy's Search, Book Eight by Kate Cambridge
Phoebe's Fate, Book Nine by Amelia Adams
Brody's Shelter, Book Ten by Kay P. Dawson
Boone's Surrender, Book Eleven by Shirleen Davies
Watch for more books in the series!

The best way to stay in touch is to subscribe to my newsletter. Go to www.shirleendavies.com and subscribe in the box at the top of the right column that asks for your email. You'll be notified of new books before they are released, have chances to win great prizes, and receive other subscriber-only specials.

For permission requests, contact the publisher.

Avalanche Ranch Press, LLC
PO Box 12618
Prescott, AZ 86304

Made in the USA
Coppell, TX
17 August 2020

33524247R00164